HEARTBREAKER

The Unbreakable Series

HEARTBREAKER

The Unbreakable Series

Kat Bastion
with Stone Bastion

Cover Design by ©Sarah Hansen, Okay Creations
Image provided by Love N. Books
Photographer: Scott Hoover
Model: Hollis W. Chambers
Interior Book Design by:

emtippettsbookdesigns.com

First Printing, March 2016
ISBN-13: 978-0996418157
ISBN-10: 0996418156

Kiki Michaelson wants one wild night to forget her starving-artist worries. Simple.

Only instead of Darren Cole becoming her one-night stand, he taunts her with a challenge. Then while she's trying to best him at his own game, he turns out to be the last thing she's prepared for: someone she wants to keep.

Which means all he can ever be…is a friend.

Darren Cole never allows a girl to get close—not close enough to matter.

Then storms in Kiki Michaelson, a beautiful, fearless temptation that rocks his world off-balance. But he fights their attraction, unwilling to gamble something physical with their close ties. Until the passionate sculptor exposes her heart and breaks his wide open.

In that moment it becomes clear: she could never be *just* a friend.

Sometimes what you run from…is exactly what you need.

emotion in every situation they encounter. It has been a long time since a story has made me feel that way let alone an entire series!"

~ *Under the Covers Book Blog*

"The story of Cade & Hannah's relationship is realistic, heart-warming, and filled with real-world connections that shook me in a way that few titles I've read this year have managed...I have loved every minute of the No Weddings series."

~ *That's What I'm Talking About*

OTHER BOOKS BY

Kat Bastion
with Stone Bastion

Standalone Novel
The Espionage Effect

No Weddings Series
No Weddings
One Funeral
Two Bar Mitzvahs
Three Christmases
For Valentine's
(a steamy nightcap novella)

BOOKS BY

Kat Bastion

Highland Legends Series
Forged in Dreams and Magick
Bound by Wish and Mistletoe
Born of Mist and Legend
(future release)
Found in Flame and Moonlight
(future release)

Romantic Poetry for Charity
Utterly Loved
Foreword by Sylvain Reynard

In memory of our beloved brother.
Jim, you are missed.

1
THE TARGET

Kiki...

For a blessed few hours, I forgot.

Loading Zone did that to me. The nightclub's Industrial Grunge feel, which I'd helped design with its exposed brick and rusted steel, wrapped itself around me like a comfortable blanket. Heavy bass thumped, vibrating into my bones. My thighs burned from dancing back-to-back songs. Three lemon drop martinis in the last two hours hummed warmth through my veins.

"C'mon," my sister Kendall shouted above the loud music as she grasped my hand, then tugged me forward. "My toes are numb."

Out of breath, I nodded and we headed toward the corner booth the eight of us had crammed into earlier. I dance-walked in the narrow path through the crowd behind her, each step a hip shake and head toss to the pulsing rhythm.

The moment we reached the table, our oldest sister, Kristen, pulled her husband from the booth. "Time for us to go. Jason has an early flight tomorrow."

Cade, our brother and silent partner of Loading Zone, guided his new wife, Hannah, out right after them. "Last dance, Mrs. Michaelson?"

Which left Cade's two best friends: the scruffy prodigy surfer Mase, his former roommate; and clean-cut businessman Ben, the other owner of Loading Zone. I slid over the black distressed leather before landing in the center of the wide, shallow booth to face the dance floor while Mase abandoned his spot on the opposite side to anchor the end next to me.

I grasped the stem of my martini glass, sipped the last bit of the tart lemon drop, then let out a happy-buzz sigh. Being around these three—including rising-star architect Kendall—all of them with their shit together, lent some grounding *yin* to my artistic *yang*.

"Sex on a stick, twelve o'clock," Kendall announced.

My heart suddenly slammed into my ribs. But I exhaled slowly, trying to hide my reaction.

I'd been excited about tonight for several reasons: banish my secret problems from my head, surround myself with my favorite peeps, and *Darren Cole.*

Ben snorted out laughter while Mase dropped me a deadpan look. "'Sex on a *stick*'?"

I shot Mase a sidelong glare and elbowed him in the ribs.

He grunted and nudged my arm away.

By the time I glanced up, corded forearms shot over the outer edge of the table. Large hands planted with a hard smack on the brushed metal tabletop. A familiar folded strip of paper skittered out from his fingers, sliding in a wide arc toward Ben.

My breath caught as I stared into Darren's dark green eyes. A lock of his shaggy black hair fell over his forehead as he tilted his face downward. He set his jaw, expression hardening, as a scuffle between four guys unfolded right behind him, the apparent cause of his sudden hand-plant. He gave me a piercing look. "Twenty minutes."

Then he turned and grasped the nearest offender by the scruff of his shirt. Security arrived an instant later and manhandled the others into submission.

As Darren flexed his left arm while leading his guy toward the exit of the club, the tapered point of a tribal tattoo peeked out from the back collar of Darren's black T-shirt. My imagination began to paint what lay hidden from view: thick black ink arcing across sculpted back muscles, a woven design that twisted downward toward his tight…

"What's that?" Kendall leaned over the table.

I tore my gaze away from Darren and reached for the note, but Kendall snatched up the slip of paper first. She unfolded it and read its message aloud, "'*Gimme a* ride? *K.*'"

"Oh, sure." Mase took a long pull from his beer, then swallowed. "Kendall gets to innuendo the fuck out of this, but I don't?"

Ben arched a brow. "Twenty minutes. That's one helluva ride."

"Shut up. Both of you. Guys objectify women. We can do the same. And it's a ride home, smartass." I tried to shoot Ben an annoyed glare, but the corners of my mouth twitched into a smile and ruined the whole thing.

"*Suuure*…a ride home." Mase winked at me, then glanced over to where Darren strode along the edge of the room as he headed back toward his DJ booth. "I suppose he qualifies."

"Worthy of objectifying? Darren more than qualifies." I pinched the message *meant for Darren's eyes only* and ripped it from Kendall's grasp. "He doesn't say much," I continued. "Leaves the club with different women. Built like the perfect male specimen…"

Ben choked on his beer. "And what are we? Male rejects?"

"Ewww." Kendall scowled. "That's incestuous."

"You're like our brothers. Can't even…" I scrunched my nose and blanked out my mind, willing myself not to visualize it.

"Not looking for love?" Ben asked, tone softening.

At that, all of our gazes drifted toward the dance floor. One of the last songs of the night streamed a fast tempo from the speakers, but in the center of a thinning crowd, Cade and Hannah stood oblivious. Wrapped together, they swayed to a slow rhythm only they seemed to hear. The look of adoration on their faces as they stared deep into each other's eyes spoke volumes.

"No," I said with absolute conviction. "Heartache lies down that road."

Mase laid a gentle hand on mine. "As your pseudo-brother, I'm warning you: Be careful."

I had no idea whether he meant Darren specifically or men in general. It didn't really matter. I'd learned my love lesson early. And I'd never trusted a guy enough to let one hurt me since.

Darren? The only kind of guy I was willing to play with. A beautiful man I refused to form any attachment to—easy to leave.

The quintessential heartbreaker.

In Darren's truck. Again. A vast awkward distance between us. *Again.*

The drive took only about ten minutes. But the ride home from Loading Zone in Philly's Old City Arts District to the outskirts of sleepy Glenhaven—the third since last summer—stretched eternal.

Why? A hookup shouldn't be this difficult.

My gaze shifted toward him. Powerful hands gripped the steering wheel, thumbs knocking some unheard drumbeat into the silence of the cab. Sculpted forearms stretched up toward cut biceps that vanished under the thin black fabric of the T-shirt that hugged them. His expression was serious, but relaxed. As if he didn't feel the weight of the moment like I did.

Now or never, Kiki.

I took a deep breath and ran a flattened hand over the gauzy material of my skirt, trying to calm myself. Then I inched closer to him, needing some sort of validation that whatever tenuous thing we had between us was moving toward something…fun…instead of away from it.

Tonight didn't have to be a big deal. He either wanted me or didn't. Two other platonic drop-offs didn't mean anything significant. Maybe he was shy. Or a gentleman.

As we drove, yellow pools of light from wrought iron lampposts marked the passing time in a visual cadence. *Light…dark. Light…dark.* The streetlights soon began to feel like a countdown, as if they mocked me for just sitting passively in their spotlights.

Yet how to breach the uncomfortable silence? My mind tumbled over the possibilities: *How did your sound board glide tonight? Wow, how 'bout the heavy bass on that last song?*

He cleared his throat, beating me to it. "Sooo…talk to me. How's the art going?"

"Good." *Good? Really?* I winced at my pathetic attempt at conversation.

We made the second-to-last turn, my time running out, as he gave a single nod in reply.

Buck up, Kiki. You either want him or you don't. Stop being a pussy. "Actually, it's a smaller sculpture. A single orchid sprouting from a rocky riverbed."

He glanced my way. "You work with metal, right?"

"Yeah." I leaned back, staring out the windshield, finally calming a bit as I thought about my art. "This piece is bronze. The lone color is the violet on the flower."

"Sounds cool." His voice lowered. He cleared his throat again.

Had he moved closer?

Impossible. He was driving. Behind the steering wheel, as always.

Yet our legs nearly touched. The rough denim, tight over his thigh, had slid over the tan leather seat to within an inch of my bared knee; he'd spread his legs wider.

The man already consumed most of the space in the truck with his commanding presence. But instead of moving away, I automatically drew closer. My thundering pulse throbbed heavier, warmer…lower.

I swallowed hard, attempting to find my way back to the conversation. "How did your night go?" Maybe his sound board was a medium for his art, like metal was for me.

"Good." The corner of his mouth twitched into a barely perceptible grin, then relaxed.

He dropped his right hand from the steering wheel and floated it in the infinitesimal space between us. Gentle pressure rubbed through the flimsy fabric that covered my upper thigh.

My gaze lowered from the dashboard at the exact moment the knuckle of his index finger trailed in slow motion up the skin under my hem.

I held my breath.

I haven't been imagining things.

But then his hand suddenly lifted and fisted. His expression hardened as he stared straight ahead. We made the final turn onto my street, and he eased off the gas, letting us coast. The ride I'd been waiting all night for—six long months and two failed attempts for—appeared to be over.

We rolled to a stop in front of the white picket fence that

surrounded the darling butter-yellow Victorian. Then he shifted the truck into park, letting it idle.

Refusing to give up, especially when I sensed him struggling with an attraction we both knew was real, I made a final direct attempt. "You don't have to drive right off. You could come in for a drink."

"No, I can't."

"Why not?" The two words tripped out flippant in my pitiful effort to sound nonchalant.

"You're Cade's little sister."

"No, I'm n—" I blinked.

The pad of his finger pressed to my lips. Warm. Firm. Suddenly, I thought of nothing else. My whole world became our tantalizing first contact.

He didn't move. Simply stared at me.

I closed my eyes. My head eased back against the headrest, but the contact remained as my lips pursed into the gentlest kiss against his fingertip. I wanted to flick my tongue out, taste him. But then he pulled away.

I blinked my eyes open.

He'd half-twisted on the seat toward me. "You deserve better than a one-night fuck, Kiki."

"What I deserve," I muttered, then snorted.

Damn right, I deserve better than that.

But one night was all I could handle.

"Doesn't matter." What I continued to tell myself. "What I want right now is you." There, I'd said it. Out in the open. Bold and direct.

"What you deserve *does* matter. Don't ever forget it." His

voice hardened with every word. His dark brows furrowed to the point a deep crease marred the tanned skin between them.

Without thinking, I reached up and pressed my thumb along that vertical line, massaging until his face began to relax.

He stared at me with renewed intensity. "What are you doing?"

"Trying to get you to chill out." I let my thumb slide a fraction to the right until I found a pressure point, then I spread the rest of my fingertips across the line of his eyebrow. "Is it working?"

"No." The corners of his mouth twitched again.

"Liar."

"Okay. A little."

"Seriously, though," I continued as if I hadn't been distracted by his impressive scowl. "I'm an excellent one-night fuck."

He jerked his head away, then lapsed into a coughing fit.

I arched a brow. "What? Don't think so?"

He shook his head. "No." His mouth fell open. "I mean, I'm sure you are." He blew out a heavy sigh, cheeks puffing from the effort. "You just…"

"Unnerve you?"

"*Yes.*" He thrust a splayed hand into the open air between us with the curt word. "Are you trying to kill me?"

A smile began to curve my lips. "No, I'm just trying to—"

"Don't say it."

The word hung on the tip of my tongue. "You know I'm thinking it."

"Stop thinking it." He took a measured breath, his chest gradually rising, then falling.

Enjoying the loaded tension between us, I remained still, waiting.

When he turned toward me again, I leaned closer and deeply inhaled his earthy scent. "Look. This doesn't have to be complicated just because I'm Cade's sister. You're an adult. I'm an adult. Aren't you attracted to me?"

Every telltale sign he'd shown suggested that he wanted me. But I'd never encountered so much resistance in a guy before. Then again, I'd never had one in my sights so long before either. I ignored the implications in that.

"Of course I am." He draped an arm along the top of the seatback.

His warmth lured me in, and I edged even closer until my entire side crushed against his. He made no move to stop me and didn't flinch away, but his lengthy pause indicated that he resisted committing to anything.

"All it has to be is one night," I whispered, my lips nearly touching the warm skin of his neck.

Another heavy sigh ruffled the hair above my ear, shooting chill bumps down my side. "You gotta know, if I could...I would. It *is* complicated. I can't explain. But no matter how badly either of us want to, this can't happen."

I blinked, confused and lost in uncharted territory. Never had a guy not taken the bait I'd offered. And he was being so nice about it. My mind couldn't process what was happening. "You want me."

"Fuck, yes. I mean, no." He growled in frustration.

"Goddammit, Kiki. Just get out of the truck. Please."

I pulled away from him and straightened in my seat, almost laughing at the desperation in his tone. Then I dared a glance at him. His expression grew tortured. A tiny part of me felt bad for putting him in a position I didn't understand. The rest of me beamed that I wasn't the only sexually frustrated one in the vehicle.

Not yet willing to admit defeat, I gave him a smile and grasped the cold metal door handle. "Thanks for the ride, Darren."

I wouldn't ask for one again. But I didn't need to. The seeds had been planted. My work was done. Either he wanted me enough to get past whatever obstacle was cock-blocking his way, or he didn't.

Meanwhile, I'd go back to the life I'd been trying to forget, once my mind-numbing buzz wore off.

I wanted to glance over my shoulder as I unfastened the painted wooden gate, double-check to see if he was still watching, but I fought the urge.

The low hum of his idling truck engine remained unchanged. But had his mind?

This lonely girl can only hope.

2
THE GIRL

Darren…

The truck door slammed shut. I stopped breathing.

Idiotic.

Responsible…but fucking idiotic.

I watched a great girl, one I could get into—*really* get into—walk away.

Because I told her to.

I stared out the passenger window at an expanse of toned legs that stretched up under Kiki's fluttering skirt before she stepped behind the white picket gate and fastened it.

She shivered as she walked up the brick path, then rubbed her hands up her bare arms. She didn't look back once. Why would she?

Yet after she climbed the two steps to her front stoop, fumbled with a handful of keys until she stabbed one into the lock, then tucked her slim purse under her arm, she turned and waved at me with a warm smile.

Or was it a smug smile?

Or a wave off?

While she stood under the porch light, a breeze blew the ends of her dark hair across her face, plastered her tiny dress to her generous curves.

The universe punished me at every turn.

Do the right thing. Don't do the right thing.

My life had been crammed with disappointments and challenges. Because of them, I'd walked the narrow path of responsibility for two long years.

But now I was being tested. Kiki was a temptation I hadn't expected. I didn't know how or why: With only a few random conversations at the club and three awkward rides home she'd burrowed under my skin.

Which was exactly why I couldn't see her again.

No way in hell could I follow through on her invitation.

"Fuck."

I'd never been so turned on and pissed the fuck off all at the same time. But wanting and not being able to have—story of my life.

I sucked in a sharp breath. "Get a grip, D."

Her scent filled my nostrils. Vanilla and something a little spicy. Like a damned mouthwatering cookie.

The air in the cab sweltered. I cranked the AC up. Then I finally put the truck in gear and pulled away from her house. When I reached the end of her street, I hooked a left and headed toward Downtown Philly.

Her scent got stronger with every breath, like her essence still lingered where she'd sat. Which was ridiculous. I glanced toward where she'd been seat-belted in, trusting me to get her home safely—where she had straightened with confidence, asking me to stay the night.

What a night it would have been. Unforgettable. *Unforgivable.*

Dark fabric caught my attention. I reached over and tugged on a mass of silky material, but it was caught on something. With a frown, I pulled over to the curb, then turned the cab light on and leaned over. Not wanting to rip the delicate fabric, I followed its length with my fingers, then untangled its corner from around the plastic molded base of the passenger seatbelt where it was secured into the floorboard by the door.

I stretched the find out between my hands. It was a tiny jacket of some kind. If jackets were made of see-through material—almost all sleeves, no buttons or zippers.

Unable to stop myself, I lifted it toward my face. And inhaled.

Kiki.

"No wonder you rubbed your arms," I grumbled. "You were freezing your ass off. Not that *this* thing would even help."

I turned the truck around, then headed back toward her house.

"Some plan of staying away from her." Hadn't even made it back to the city. But the sudden backtrack was only to return her jacket-thing. All it was.

Her yellow house still had its porch lights on. But all the windows were dark. Not even a light glowed upstairs. Maybe she'd passed out on a couch.

I parked on the opposite side of the street, then got out, her soft jacket bunched in my fist.

A flash of movement in the narrow alley beside her house caught my attention. The alleyway led behind the house. Widely spaced streetlights along its edge disappeared into near darkness halfway down. Two large figures strode down the middle, arms spread wide as if corralling an animal.

A smaller silhouette walked beyond them with a familiar sway of the hips, flutter of a skirt.

Kiki.

I couldn't make out her face in the dark, but I knew her shape, how she moved.

My heart thundered as I marched toward them.

One of the guys called down the alley. "Come on, girl. We won't hurt you."

"She's with me," I growled.

Startled, the guys spun around. Young. Not much older than me. Shadows marred their expressions, made them appear more menacing. Didn't matter. I would beat the shit out of them.

One stepped closer, eyes narrowing. "Don't look like she's with you."

I tucked her jacket into one of my back belt loops.

The guy on the left pulled something from his pocket. Metal gleamed in the lamplight.

"She is." I tilted my face down, glared at the punks from under drawn brows. "Right, babe?"

"Right." Kiki stopped within my peripheral vision. Nervous, she shifted her weight from one foot to another.

Problem was, we were in a bad situation: Kiki on one side, me on the other, danger between us. *What the hell was she doing out here?* Had they broken into her house? Chased her down the alley?

Best-case scenario? Them leaving at my end of the alley, without incident.

Didn't even want to give thought to a worst-case.

With slow steps, I arced away from them, moving flush with Kiki's higher backyard fence. It gave them a wide exit path. As I advanced, they took the hint and moved opposite me. They circled around, mad dogging me the entire time. I stared back. And I never took my attention from their hands, nor the way they shifted their bodyweight.

"She's not worth it," the farthest one bit out before spitting on the pavement between us.

Not for you, she isn't.

After another few steps, they turned and vanished around the corner.

I waited a full two breaths before turning to find Kiki standing right beside me.

"Thanks," she said. Her tone was casual, like I'd just held open a door for her.

"What the fuck?" I put a protective arm around her shoulders, needing to touch her. "Are you okay?"

She leaned further into my side. "Yeah. They wouldn't have hurt me."

"Don't be naïve. They sure as fuck would have."

"I can take care of myself." She whipped out her keys and brandished a five-inch black metal *kubotan* that dangled from the keyring.

"No you can't." I knocked it from her grip to prove it. The keys arced through the air, clattered onto the ground, then skipped across the concrete until they crashed into a heap against the base of a wrought iron lamppost.

"Hey!" She shoved out of my hold. "You don't have to be mean about it."

"I'm not being mean. *They*" —I pointed toward the end of the alley— "would have been mean."

When she huffed away to retrieve her keyring, I rushed alongside her, then scooped it up before she had a chance. I shook out the jumbled keys, rubbed them over my jeans to dust them off, and handed them back.

With a fierce glare, she swiped them from me. Then she stormed ahead, back toward the street. I followed. But after two steps, she whirled around.

She propped her hands on her hips. "Why did you come back, anyway?"

Adorable didn't begin to describe how she looked: dark hair tousled, pale skin flushed, full lips drawn down into the sexiest pout.

I walked closer.

She held her ground.

By the time I stood within reach, she'd half-turned toward her house. A nearby streetlight bathed her face in a golden glow. Her eyes narrowed. "Why did you come back?" she repeated, her voice just above a whisper.

Hope washed across her face a split second before those delectable lips twisted into a smirk.

I tugged her jacket free from my belt loop, then held it up. "You forgot this."

Her hopeful expression fell. Then she snatched the fabric from my hand and stomped backward.

I strode toward her.

She paused, letting me.

A foot. Half a foot. Two inches. As I closed the distance, her head tilted back, gaze locked with mine.

"What are you doing?" Her voice went breathless.

"Don't know." Mine grew ragged.

Something unnamable drew me to her. Seconds later, the reason hit me. Being near her quieted all the racket in my head. Until I didn't even hear the never-ending rhythm. And all I saw was her.

My world narrowed to the pulse at the hollow of her neck, her throat as she swallowed.

Her gaze lowered to my mouth. Those luscious lips parted.

Then she stared into my eyes, lashes fluttering. "When will you know?"

Good question. And as I stood there, seconds ticking by as we both breathed harder and harder, no answer came.

Her eyes began to widen, like the electric thing buzzing between us surprised her too.

Frustrated and tired, I grabbed her hand and led her back to her front porch.

"You're going inside your house. Safe and sound. I'm going home."

She didn't resist. Or say another word.

Maybe we didn't have to. Too much had already been exposed in what hadn't been said.

In the twenty minutes it took to drive home, I'd cleared my head. Mostly. Windows down, cold air whipped through the cab while I'd lectured myself on all the reasons taking Kiki up on her offer was the last thing I needed.

Once I pulled into my short driveway, put the truck in park, and cut the engine, I'd wiped all thoughts from my brain about what I couldn't have. Easy to do. Been doing it long enough.

A stereo blasted from inside as I stuck my key into the dead bolt.

I stepped in, slammed the door, and threw the bolt. Then I slid the chain across.

No change in the haunting alternative rock that vibrated our plaster ceiling.

The only light in the room was the one I'd left on above the stove. I dropped my keys onto the counter, crossed to the foot of the stairs, and stared up toward the dark second-floor hall.

"Lo?" I shouted loud enough to wake the neighbors… across the street.

The only response? The music turned up a couple more decibels.

I dropped my gaze, stared at the worn edge of the bottom

step. The caring half of me wanted to pound on her door, check on her. The smart half knew better.

With a headshake and a heavy sigh, I retreated to the safety of the kitchen. I popped open the fridge, grabbed a beer, then went to the living room and dropped onto our threadbare couch. Tired to the bone, I closed my eyes. Then I guzzled down the bottle, absorbing the chill of the liquid along with the soulful music.

I accepted my situation. The girl upstairs? What I'd signed up for.

She was the reason I couldn't take Kiki up on her offer, wouldn't take something for myself.

Because apparently I didn't get to have happiness.

A part of me wondered if I had any left to give.

As I sank into sleep, thoughts of Kiki flowed in: the confident girl in the alley hell-bent on proving she could take care of herself, that glint of hope in her eye.

3
THE LIGHT OF DAY

Kiki…

A scratching sound permeated my brain.

"Wha—" The word strangled in my dry throat, then died.

My eyelids were glued shut. I blinked down hard, twice, before they opened.

Bright white assaulted my eyes. *Lots and lots* of white…

Disoriented, I pushed upright. On a white slipcovered couch.

"Oh." I'd never made it past the living room.

Fuzzy memories sharpened by small degrees as my gaze wandered over the pristine snowy rug, then up pale maple shelves to linger on a stack of books with pastel-colored spines. Yet despite the innocence of my surroundings, my mind gravitated toward the debauched thoughts I'd had last night.

I smiled when it landed on the subject of said thoughts. *Darren.*

He'd followed me halfway down the darkened alley. Then he'd "rescued" me from two guys I definitely could've handled, or at least my self-defense instructor and I bravely thought so.

The scratching sound resumed, followed by a pitiful high-pitched cry. I groaned and shoved up off the couch. When my bare feet left plush carpeting, they met cold porcelain tiles in—of course—another shade of white. White marble covered the countertops. A white apron-style country sink sat below a window draped with white sheer linens.

I opened the back door and let the little guy in. "Hey, munchkin."

In trotted a teenaged calico kitten as if he owned the place. While he prowled the inside perimeter, I opened the fridge, grabbed a carton of milk, and poured it into a saucer. The little devil launched onto the counter, nudged his head in, and began lapping away before I had a chance to put the saucer down on the floor.

Laughing, I ran my fingers down his silky short coat. "At least one guy wants what I'm offering." Strong purrs vibrated under my fingertips. I stroked him twice more before I put the carton back into the fridge. Then I hunted human liquid fuel. The caffeinated kind.

After a few shakes, a pour, and a switch flipped, the coffeemaker began brewing a strong dose of morning medicine. Drips and sizzles filled the silence while I stared over the counter, back into the living room.

The muted color, or absence thereof, did have a calming effect. Cleared my head, in a way. Helped me begin to analyze the bewildering crash-and-burn that had happened last night.

It didn't matter a great deal that Darren had rejected me outright. Just threw me a little. I'd never had to offer myself up on a platter like that.

But in those last moments, a spark *was* there. At least I'd thought so.

Maybe it said something that I'd strayed outside of my usual type. Sure, he was drop-dead gorgeous, but even with the pretty face, he was different: a little edgier and much quieter. And yeah, his body drew my eye, but the lines were lean and muscular, not bulked out from too much weightlifting for sports.

Music suddenly streamed from inside my purse on the edge of the counter, playing Ariana Grande's "Focus"—Kendall's ringtone. I leaned over, grabbed my phone from my clutch, then hit the control button. "Yyyello."

"So how was the *ride*?" she teased.

"Wouldn't you like to know?" Redirection sounded better than "nonexistent."

"Well, duh. That's why I'm calling."

I snorted. "When have you *ever* known me to kiss and tell?"

"Never. In fact, this is the first time I've ever seen you into a guy. I was beginning to wonder if you played for the other team."

With all the luck I'd had last night—with all that I'd ever had—maybe I should've begun to wonder myself. "Well, don't get used to it. There's a reason my love life is classified."

My family was under the impression my *very private* personal life had to do with the traditional Michaelson gauntlet that suitors had to survive before being stamped as "acceptable" by our clan. That was part of it—even though most of their scrutiny was really playful teasing. But no one knew the real reason I'd kept my personal life under wraps. And I planned to keep it that way.

A heavy sigh sounded out over the phone, seconds before a low grunt. She'd probably plopped herself onto her overstuffed couch. The crinkling of plastic told me she had a bag of chips. A loud crunch followed.

"Nothing? Can't even feed your girl a breadcrumb?"

"Damn." I whistled low, intent on diversion. "We cannot let this appalling info leak out. The Michaelson girls are sounding really hard up."

"We are," she groaned.

"Sad." But apparently true. The coffee maker chirped. I opened a cabinet, pulled out a mug, and poured myself a cup as I considered her request.

"Okay." *She wants a breadcrumb?* "The instant he touched me" —my mind flashed to his finger on my lips— "my body burst into flames."

"Ugh!" I heard a slap and imagined her palm smacking her forehead. "Cheap tease!"

I grinned. Then I blew out a measured breath through pursed lips, remembering how my first intimate contact with

Darren actually felt—more like a slow-burning fuse that crackled and popped along my nerve endings.

Damn. Why couldn't he be a good, typical, hormonal guy like all the others? Take the bait. Lay the girl. Be happy when she nudges you out the door before morning and doesn't ask for your phone number.

"You asked." I felt zero remorse.

"Fine. But one of us *must* get laid sometime this century or people will start talking."

"About us *not* having sex?"

"Sure: *Those Michaelson girls are such nonsluts.*"

Suppressing a smile, I blew on my coffee. "Mmm-hmmm. The country club membership committee? *They no longer represent our standards, simply not hussy enough for us.*"

Her voice developed a throaty high pitch, lilting with a foreign accent. "*The antithesis of promiscuous.*"

"Our critics are now British?"

"Sure." Another crunch sounded. "Mary Poppins. Pygmalion." She mumbled around food in her mouth.

"Henry Higgins would be so proud."

"Iiieeey…" Her vowels twisted on a whine. "Eeey's Professor Iggins ta yew, eeey is."

I nearly choked on my coffee, laughing at her London street-urchin imitation. "Goodbye, Kendall."

Hilarious subject closed, I clicked off the phone.

In the sober quiet that followed, her underlying point echoed loud and clear. One of us needed to get laid. I definitely did. My withering lady bits could only handle a sexual vacuum for so long.

But as I stared into the overwhelming white of the room, its starkness glared back at me. All the same things no longer seemed to be working. My optimistic self was taking a beating, no matter how deserved.

Maybe a change was long overdue.

I shooed the furry munchkin off the counter, washed his bowl, grabbed my purse and coffee, then stepped outside behind the little guy, locking up. And all the while, I couldn't stop thinking about Darren. Something more lay hidden behind that sexy broody exterior. Maybe it was the unspoken challenge he presented.

Frustrated at everything *that wasn't* going according to plan, I growled at the injustice of it all as I walked toward the alley again, back on the course I'd intended last night. Back to the only thing that soothed my soul regardless of the unfairness in life.

As I closed the front gate behind me, cat darting out at the last minute, my phone played Adele's "Hello." *Kristen's turn.*

I pulled it from my purse and swiped it on, lowering my voice. "Grand Central Station."

"That busy?"

"Yep. Just missed Kendall the Inquisitive."

"Ah." As usual, Kristen didn't pry. "I forgot to send you the dimensions you needed for the party." She referred to our next event for Invitation Only, the party-planning business I'd help create with my brother and sisters. "The client loves Loading Zone's design so much, she wanted your flare with more than the finishing touches. She insisted on using your

'Industrial Grunge' nickname for the event. Hope that's okay."

I paused halfway down the short sidewalk, something nagging at my sluggish brain. "Sure. I don't own the trademark."

"And she keeps saying, 'Make sure Kiki casts her welding magic.' To which I keep replying, 'You know this is Kiki, right'?"

My heart tripped, beginning to race even though I stood stock-still, planted to the cement.

"I just emailed you the measurements for the DJ equipment. Two sound boards, also a front panel for the bar and…"

My brain froze. DJ equipment. *Darren.*

When Kristen paused, I finally sucked in a lungful of oxygen. "Gotta go." I muttered absently. "I'll look for the email."

In trying to forget my problems at Loading Zone last night, then while in hot pursuit of my next conquest, I'd completely forgotten about the project I'd been tasked with.

Having to do with said conquest.

"Idiot," I grumbled. Darren had become too entwined in the periphery of my life to have kept him in the running for casual sex play. When he'd first caught my eye, he'd been Loading Zone's new DJ. But then Cade had hired him on for a couple of Invitation Only parties. Which had eventually become nearly every one. The moment he'd attended the first, I should have discounted him.

With a resigned sigh and enormous willpower, I forced him from my thoughts.

After a few measured breaths, I began to feel close to normal and resumed my routine path. I rounded the corner of the white picket fence and began my ninety-seven usual steps toward my destination, kitten trotting alongside me in perfect feline balance on the cement curbing. At step number thirty-nine, my stride slowed. Before I hit forty-three, I stopped altogether.

My breath caught. My heart began to race as memories flooded in.

Two feet away from where I stood, hundreds of minutes ago but what seemed like the blink of an eye, Darren had stepped into my space—gotten too close.

In that early morning hour, where temps had dipped into the low fifties, he'd towered over me, radiating blast-furnace heat. The spiky black ends of his hair had softened, those deep emerald eyes had darkened, and that broad chest had huffed in ragged breaths.

But out of all that, I was struck by one instant. Suspended in the space between one hard pulse-beat at his throat and the next, through the impenetrable shield he'd erected to keep me and the rest of the world out, he'd been vulnerable.

Breath held, I closed my eyes, reliving the split-second moment: *His intoxicating scent coiled around me, sweet with a touch of salty spice. Recognition flashed in his eyes as he gazed down at me.*

Of what?

I sucked in a fast breath. My eyes snapped open and I stared at the spot where we'd been.

In the bright light of day, a glaring revelation hit me: I'd chased after someone *too* like me.

With a hard headshake, panicked about what that meant, I hurried down the alley. Running from the implications made me feel like I had some power in my out-of-control world.

But nothing eradicated the truth: Drastic change had already begun.

4
SPARKS FLYING

Darren…

The following afternoon, I returned to Loading Zone. As usual on Mondays, I laid soundtracks for the upcoming weekend.

But it was the first time I'd been back in the club since…

I shoved the thought from my mind.

I refused to think about Kiki.

"I need you to stop by Kiki's." Cade glanced up from where he stood behind the bar.

Fuck.

"What for?"

"The Industrial Grunge party this weekend. She needs to secure the metalwork she's made to your equipment."

Right. My brain pinged back to the email I'd gotten from him Friday about the latest party Invitation Only had hired me for. I'd fired off a reply with measurements. Then I'd totally spaced it.

He tore off the bottom edge of a paper pinned to his clipboard, scribbled something on it, then handed it to me.

I scanned the paper. "I've been there. Gave her a ride home a few times."

"Only transportation?" Doubt weighed his tone.

"Yeah."

Cade planted his hands on the bar top, then dropped me a hard stare. "Tread lightly there."

"Can't tread any lighter."

"I mean it. She's…" Cade lowered his gaze, then glanced up. "There are things she keeps inside. She seems tough. But more is there than meets the eye."

"I know, man." I gave him a hard nod. "Nothing to worry about. We're just friends."

He snorted. "Good luck with that."

Why? Because Cade hadn't been able to be "just friends" with Hannah? Night and day comparison: He'd been available then, I was nowhere close.

"Nah, I'm good."

I drove the usual route from the bar to Kiki's, but something nagged at me. When I turned down her street, I dug into my front jeans pocket, then pulled out the paper Cade had given me. The last number in the address was different. Same street. But instead of *2115* it was *2117*.

I slowed in front of the picket-fenced house: *not* the address. Cruising past, I checked out the house numbers of the neighboring property. Too high.

How could her address be in between?

I stared down the alley—the one she'd been standing in thirty-six hours ago. Then I turned into it, following the fence line until white wood pickets ended and chain link began.

A large warehouse with corrugated sides and high glass windows towered in the back of a property littered with scrap metal. Walls made of mangled items stood four to five feet high in an undulating maze through about a quarter of an acre: a rusty oxygen tank here, a weathered motorcycle fender there.

Mounted into a post made of dozens of welded metal parts that now resembled a gnarled tree snag was a mailbox, camouflaged as a dark knot in the trunk. Out of the side jutted a four-inch iron "broken branch" with a red cardinal that pivoted up to indicate outgoing mail.

I glanced at the address Cade had given me. The numbers on the mailbox matched.

Confused, I pulled up beside a light blue Prius, then parked in a space just beyond it. "Kiki, what the hell?" I muttered aloud to the industrial area no girl should be hanging out in.

A glass-and-wrought-iron security door stood propped open a few inches by a good-sized rock. I rapped on the doorframe, then waited. After a couple of minutes with no reply, I let myself in.

A blower-like noise echoed off the walls as the door banged against the rock behind me. A second later, the sound stopped.

"Chip Monkey? Is that you?" Kiki's voice echoed from somewhere ahead.

Before I had a chance to respond, the low-pitched blowing noise resumed.

I followed the odd sound, weaving through metal sculptures spaced a few feet apart that stretched from one wall of the warehouse to the other. After a dozen yards, all the metalwork disappeared. I stepped into an open area lit by several large skylights that were in the metal roof some thirty feet up.

To the left, a couple of worn couches faced each other, one green, the other yellow. Both had throw pillows covered in bright flowers in each of their corners. Clothes had been tossed haphazardly over the back cushions. A low metal table sat between them, fashion magazines scattered over its surface. Dead ahead was an enormous wooden worktable, rusted clamps and vices fastened to various edges, some gripped pieces of metal, others were screwed open, ready to be used. To one side sat two stacked piles of envelopes, a coffee mug, a plate with a half-eaten sandwich with sprouts spilling out between two pieces of grainy bread, and an unopened green banana.

Beyond the table, in a wide-open space surrounded by large pieces of equipment, the source of the sound became apparent: A bright white light glowed from a torch in Kiki's hand.

I froze, not wanting to startle her.

And to just watch her.

Her face was hidden by a metal welder's mask with a viewing slot, but wild pieces of black hair poked out from under the back strap, curling off in every direction. She leaned forward in steady concentration, applying a now-orange flame to the joint between a curving section of rebar and some kind of woven-metal latticework.

Sparks arced in all directions from the contact point. I winced, averting my eyes after I caught myself staring at the blinding core of the flame.

Seconds later, she turned her torch off again.

I cleared my throat.

She jumped slightly, rested the torch tip on the cement floor with a soft clang, then lifted her mask.

"Darren." An instant smile curved her lips as she pulled off a pair of leather gloves.

And damn, if that bright smile didn't warm a spot in the center of my chest.

Not for you, D.

I blew out a quick breath. "Cade wanted me to bring the sound equipment for the party..."

"Yes!" She stood and pulled the mask from her head before tossing it onto the worktable. Her hair tumbled down around her shoulders.

Charcoal smudges marred her face, one dotting the tip of her nose, another streaking just below her cheekbone. A pink flush crept up her olive-colored skin from her collarbone to her cheeks. Under thick dark lashes, her eyes turned electric blue in a shaft of sunlight that angled down from a high window.

She blinked heavily, smile widening a fraction.

I blinked too. I tried to remember why I'd come, needed to think of something to say to fill the growing silence.

Instead, my gaze lowered. Used to seeing her in nightclub outfits, earlier a skirt, sometimes jeans and a sparkling top, the casual clothes were something new—better, in my opinion.

Beneath a tan leather welding apron with three pockets riveted into the bottom, she wore two tank tops; a purple one peeked from under a green one, the straps of both twisted chaotically together on one side. Black yoga pants hugged her hips.

Suddenly she moved—breaking my dumbfounded trance—and crossed to the table. She lifted her mug, then paused with it halfway to her mouth. "Want some coffee?"

"Nah, I'm good." Was I? Something needed to jolt me out of my sudden Kiki-stupor. "On second thought, coffee would be great. Black."

With a satisfied nod, she turned and went to a narrower table running along the wall, lifted a half-full pot from her coffeemaker, and poured steaming dark liquid into a red mug with white lettering. When she handed it to me, I read the saying aloud, "'Eat, Drink, and Be Merry'?"

She gave a one-shoulder shrug while gulping from her mug. "If only life were so simple." Her tone was laced with cynicism. Which surprised me.

Then I realized her place looked lived in. Like *lived* in. "So you work here?"

Her gaze darted to the clothes thrown over the couches.

Mine wandered to other signs that she spent a lot of time in her workspace: two small pizza boxes stacked on a plastic trash can in the far corner, those stacked envelopes on the table looking a lot like unopened mail—to her, with her same address on it.

She let out a low sigh as her shoulders slumped. "And live here."

"Why the big production with the dolled-up house in front?" She'd lied to me. Or at least stretched the truth.

Slowly her shoulders shrugged up to her ears along with her eyebrows. The hint of a smile curved her lips. "I didn't want you to judge me?"

"For where you live?" I shook my head. "My house is no palace."

Her hands dropped to her hips and she leveled a piercing look at me. "I was after sex. This?" She gestured around us with a wide sweep of her outstretched arms. "Only provokes questions."

"Like where you sleep?"

Her soft laugh broke the tension. "Yeah. Up there, by the way." She pointed above our heads to a large room built into the rafters. In the center front wall of that room stretched two floor-to-ceiling glass windows. Soft light glowed on a finished ceiling beyond them.

"This place is cool. Why wouldn't I like it? It's like a giant man-cave."

"For a girl." Her tone was off, but I couldn't place why. She seemed…nervous.

I glanced around at all the heavy tools and rust. "Not much girly in here."

"True." She unfastened and pulled off her welding apron, then dropped it over her stacks of mail. "Where's your sound equipment?"

"Back of the truck." I took a sip of coffee, then winced. For a girl who created awesome art, she made nasty coffee. I put the mug safely on the table.

"Want to fasten it together out there?" She gave a nod toward her front door.

"Would that work?"

"Might need to pull it down, but no sense in dragging it all the way in here. C'mon. Help me with the panels."

She pulled a screwdriver off a workbench, tucked it into the back of her pants and grabbed her gloves. She put them on as she led me through her work area. We entered a back corner loaded with large stacked items. Industrial shelving units lined the walls and held open boxes of sorted smaller pieces.

"So whose house is up front?"

"Landlord's." She moved aside what appeared to be a metal coatrack in progress.

"And you have a key to his place?"

"*Her* place." She nodded toward a stack of six metal sheets. "And yeah. She owns five parcels: three houses up front, two industrial properties behind. The prior owner collected and worked on motorcycles. She rented the warehouse and scrapyard parcels to me when she couldn't sell them."

"What's that got to do with you having a key to her house?"

"I watch over it when she travels on business trips. She's gone most of this month."

"But…I'm seeing where you live now. How did you expect to give me the panels?"

She pegged me with an exasperated look. "We were supposed to have one night of wild sex. End of. But we didn't. Then Kristen emailed me with the specs. On Sunday. Day *after* said wild sex was supposed to happen."

Ah. Her attempt to set boundaries. Play. Work.

"Technically, same day. I dropped you off at 2:30 a.m. On Sunday. And how did you make them so quickly?"

Her nostrils flared.

Yeah, I was giving her shit—couldn't help it. Also couldn't help noticing how sexy she looked when annoyed.

Her cheeks grew a deeper shade of pink. "I accomplish amazing work when channeling sexual frustration."

Ah, got it. I scanned her warehouse filled with art. "You must be frustrated a lot."

Gaze locked to mine, she exhaled slowly. Then she squatted beside the stack of panels. When she glanced down and wrapped her hands around the edge of one, a lock of her dark hair fell over her face.

With a stout puff, she blew the curl away from her eyes and stared up at me. "We swapping life stories…or are you helping me?"

I didn't answer. Because learning about where she lived and what aggravated her only made me want to know more—what made the fascinating girl in front of me tick: what made her scowl, what made her laugh.

So I bent down, gripped my side, then lifted.

The metal panels she'd created were incredible. Rusted foundations supported fluid patterns of countless smaller welded pieces: a slice of gleaming hubcap, rows of oxidized chain, curling strips of tarnished steel, a field of uniform scales.

"These are amazing, Kiki."

Her eyes lit up. "Thanks."

And then she smiled. At first, it was tentative, a gentle curve of her lips while she scanned over her work. Then she glanced at me, and I got the full effect. Genuine. Heartfelt.

Damn. I suddenly wanted to learn more of how to make *that* happen.

Not for you, D. If I repeated it in my head enough, maybe I'd believe it.

The panels were heavy. It took us three trips to transport them to my truck, two stacked panels per run. The edges of each sheet were curved inward, so even though she wore gloves, I gripped them with no problem. Once we laid the last pair outside, I pulled my sound board stands down from the truck bed and set them on the ground.

She pointed to the nearest panel. "That's an end. Lift it and hold it in front of the right side."

When we moved it into place, she inched it forward. "There. Can you lean that against the frame? Good."

We followed with the longer front piece, angling it up until the seam lined up flush with the first.

"Can you hold them steady like that?" She examined the edge where the pieces fit together.

I nodded, then lowered into a comfortable squat, keeping a firm hold on each panel.

The ends had hinged brackets bolted onto the outside. She reached behind her, pulled out the screwdriver from where she'd tucked it into her waistband, then began screwing them into place.

She hovered close, near enough for her vanilla scent to waft around me. A slight breeze caught strands of her hair, brushing them over my arm. When she tilted her head and turned, her upper body leaned into my side. She fit perfectly there.

My brain fogged. "Plenty of places for sex."

Her twisting hand paused, midturn. "What?" she croaked.

"At your *real* place, the warehouse. No questions. Plenty of places."

Her chest expanded, then the screwdrivering resumed. "Thought we weren't having sex."

"We aren't."

"Then why are you talking about it?"

"I'm not."

"Uhhh…" Her soft laughter puffed warm air over my forearm. "You are."

With a flex of her wrist, she tightened one last turn before crouching lower, breaking our intense side-to-side contact. My brain cleared in that fraction of a second.

Change the subject, Einstein.

I ignored logic. "Only pointing out facts. Guys don't ask questions. When sex is on the table, it's *on the table*, the floor, couch end, sturdy piece of art…"

Another pause in her twisting lasted only a second. Then she picked up the pace, screwing furiously. "Well, if we aren't having sex—"

"We aren't," I reiterated.

"—then maybe we shouldn't be talking about where we'd *do* this imaginary sex."

"I didn't say 'we.'"

"Uh-huh." Her tone held doubt.

I grinned, loving every moment of frazzling her. Had no idea why I'd started, but I couldn't seem to stop.

"There." She suddenly burst up, then backed away from me.

I stood from my crouch, stretching my legs.

She eyed me warily. From a good four-foot distance.

"So, no sex." She pointed the screwdriver at me.

"No sex." Decision made. But the ban on sex didn't mean I couldn't tease. I enjoyed the hell out of riling her.

As she stood there glaring at me with suspicion, my gaze traveled down her body. Couldn't stop myself. All five-foot-five of her—hair wild, dark smudges on her face, hands now propped on her hips—grew more adorable when provoked.

You do not *want her.*

My body didn't listen; arousal lingered behind the fly of my jeans.

"Stop staring at me." One of her brows arched provocatively. "*No* sex."

She crossed her arms, which pushed her breasts together—*not helping*. But then she leaned onto one hip and propped her other foot out.

I stared at her exposed shoe. I blinked hard, surprised. "What *is* that?"

"What?" She followed my line of sight, glancing downward.

"Your shoe." I nodded toward it.

"They're Vibram FiveFingers."

"Specialized footwear." I knew what they were. Just shocked as hell she wore them. Her mellow artist type didn't match the purpose of those shoes.

"For running." She nodded, pivoting her foot on her big toe to expose the side of the black-on-black shoe.

I cleared my throat. "They have…toes." Had to give her shit about them. Anything to veer my mind from the sexual path it had been charging down.

"Yup." She tapped the ground between us, pointing them at me. "Sexy, right?"

Incredibly. But the shoes had nothing to do with it.

"You run." The skeptical question came out flat. Couldn't wrap my mind around it. Was she in great shape? Absolutely. But running seemed so…off…for her.

"'Bout to. Stumbled across an article about the shoes. A lot of people are challenging themselves to do a Couch to 5K, or something like that. I've been wearing them around the warehouse for a couple of months, getting used to them."

"Ever run?"

"Nope."

"Why now?"

"I want to get in better shape and need something different. Separate from art. Out of doors. Something just for me."

"And a 5K is your idea of 'out of doors'?" My mind flashed to a disturbing picture of her running between tall buildings…down dark narrow alleys.

She shrugged. "It's not cooped up in the warehouse with sculptures and a comedic kitten."

"Kitten?" I suddenly remembered what she'd called out when I'd arrived. "Chip Monkey?"

"No, not 'Chip Monkey' with two words. He's part chipmunk and monkey blended together. Chipmunky." She gave a hard nod, as if that explained everything.

Then she turned and cupped her hands around her mouth. "C'mere, Chipmunkeeey. Here kitty, kittyyy."

A few seconds later, in bounded a fuzzy blur of color. He had a reddish-brown body and duplicate thin black-and-white stripes of color that ran down either side of his back. His tail vibrated. I smiled at the comical little guy. "He does look like a chipmunk."

"Wait for it…" She reached into a small pocket stitched into the bottom of her tank top.

Tail still twitching, he raised up on his hindquarters. His front paws swiped at the empty air in front of him. She tossed him a green fish-shaped treat.

The kitten watched it bounce once on the ground before it landed right in front of him. Using both paws, he plucked it from the dirt, reached his muzzle forward, and chomped the treat into his mouth before crunching it twice then swallowing it down.

"See? Chipmunky."

Simple as that. Her world was colored with the unusual that made perfect sense.

Except the idea of her running down a city street didn't make sense to me at all.

Without thinking, I blurted, "Want a personal trainer?"

She blinked.

So did I.

When in my chaotic life would I have time to train her?

But the thought of leaving with my sound boards in a few minutes then *maybe* catching a glimpse of her—at one of Invitation Only's parties while she and I both worked, or once every few months at Loading Zone where I worked and she danced—didn't sit well with me.

I would *not* to do anything physical with her. We couldn't have a relationship. But maybe we could still see each other under the pretense of something she wanted.

Her slender brows furrowed in slow motion. "For running a 5K?"

Not exactly... "For training to be *able* to."

"And we would be..."

"Friends." My tone was firm. Maybe I tried to convince not only her, but myself. All I could handle right now. But I had plenty of friends, most were guys.

None of them were anything like spirited Kiki.

When she didn't reply, I repeated. "Just friends. No sex. Think you can handle that?"

Her eyes narrowed at the challenge. Like she didn't like the idea. As if the word "friends" had four letters not six.

After a couple of beats, her lips curved into a smile. She gave a nod. "Just friends."

Good. All it could ever be.

But then her stance widened. Her chin raised. A glimmer flashed in her eyes as if she'd thrown the challenge back at me.

Do not look at the sexy girl standing in front of you.

Do not notice the vulnerability in her gaze behind all that bravado.

I let out a slow breath, mind focused on the only thing I could do to have her in my life, the only way it would ever work. "9:00 a.m. tomorrow good for you?"

She gave me a nod, eyes narrowing a fraction again. "Yeah, I could do that."

"Good. Meet me at 2450 North Lexington."

Challenge accepted.

5
THE MUSCULAR FORM

Kiki...

Nine hours had passed since Darren had rattled me; the last thing I needed was a guy friend I was physically attracted to—a guy I wanted, even if only for one sordid night. But when he'd baited me with a way to spend more time together under the pretense of training, I hadn't been able to resist.

And my body warmed the instant he texted late that night.

You got regular shoes?

Amused at the blunt question, I replied.

REGULAR shoes? And don't FRIENDS get a hello first?

A blue bubble appeared as he typed.

NOT shoes with TOES. Tennis shoes… Cross-trainers…

Mmm-hmm…

Not answering until you say it.

A good ninety seconds ticked by before his reply.

HELLo

I pressed my lips together, fighting a smile.

Cute. Swearing AND a greeting, rolled into one.

After a few more seconds, another text flashed up.

I'm talented like that. Well?

Tired eyes drooping shut at the midnight hour, I replied before I passed out.

Yes. I have regular shoes.

I fell asleep during the unlit silence that followed.

In the morning, I'd found his last text.

Good. Wear em.

No "please" or explanation had come with it. Only an order barked through in text form.

Fine. Two could play at his game. He wanted to be bossy? He wanted to pound the point of being "just friends" home? I would be the best friend he'd ever had.

Of course, while I demonstrated my stellar friendliness, no harm in highlighting my best qualities: flirtatiousness, adorableness—sexiness.

"Wait. Can I be both adorable and sexy?" I questioned aloud while driving in my empty car.

After I turned onto Lexington Avenue, I straightened in my seat. A quick glance in the rearview mirror made me smile. Hair in a fluffy ponytail, cheeks lightly pinked, a swipe of mascara on my lashes, and a dab of lip gloss? Check for adorable.

A smile tugged at my lips as I thought about what I'd worn: tropical-flowered sports bra, low-cut T-shirt, and hip-hugging yoga capris. Nothing else but plenty of skin? Check for sexiness.

After I swung right to curve along a roundabout, then pulled into a small parking lot, I blew out an anxious breath. *Why so nervous?* I shook my head.

"Rely on your instincts, Kiki. You got this." Flirtatiousness? I had down cold. Pretty much had since birth.

Confident with all the stealthy weapons in my arsenal, I turned off my car. I twisted toward the back seat and grabbed my bag and water bottle.

Yet when I opened my door and put my *tennis-shoe'd* foot onto the asphalt, I frowned. Then I double-checked the address. "2450." The numbers, plain as day, were in big bronze letters above commercial double doors on a massive brick building.

Right address. Wrong assumption.

For some reason, I had thought I'd be meeting him at his place.

Even with my sunglasses, I raised a shielding hand over my brow to block the glare of the morning sun. I stared for a confused few seconds at the nondescript building. Then my gaze panned to sprawling grounds off toward the right.

The neighboring property resembled an abandoned school—with no school buildings. Instead, brick structures appeared to have been converted into quaint apartment homes. Pretty awnings covered large windows. Colorful spring flowers lined sidewalks that led to brightly painted front doors. Playground areas were filled with a collection of toddlers, moms, and strollers rather than older school-aged kids.

But I'd parked next to Darren's black F150, so I'd apparently found the right place. I adjusted my bag onto my other shoulder, shut my car door, and walked toward the entrance.

After tugging open one of the heavy metal doors, I propped my sunglasses on top of my head as I followed the distant sounds of low grunting down a dimly lit tiled corridor; half of the dozen overhead florescent lights had burned out. Around the corner, the stark hallway ended in a set of gray double doors, the right one had been propped open by a weight bench.

Four guys occupied what appeared to be a converted basketball gym: one skipped rope, one lay on a bench while lifting a barbell below his spotter, the last was separated off in a far corner. Although the large space felt comfortably cooled, three oscillating fans hummed along the perimeter, sweeping back and forth in out-of-sync cadences.

Since logic told me the fourth guy had to be Darren, I gravitated toward him. And as I approached, I watched his prone body lower, then lift.

Lower.

Lift.

My breath caught and my stride slowed as I drew closer. My mouth gradually fell open. My eyes widened.

Shirtless, baseball hat spun backward, hands sunk into silver metal pails of sand, he performed the most unique pushups I'd ever seen. His skin glistened with a sheen of perspiration under the section's brighter lights. Taut muscles along his back, shoulders, and arms flexed under the strain of every measured drop and rise.

The world around me seemed to stop—except for him. Art in motion. Beauty in action. Every woman's fantasy-come-to-life coalesced into one surreal moment where my mind fabricated my body beneath that incredible male form, under all that raw muscle and energy.

On the next downstroke, he paused. Then he glanced up. His gaze locked with mine.

Busted.

Yet powerless to stop myself, I studied the rigid contours of muscle as he held that position. The artist in me flared to life, imagining those lines sketched in charcoal. *His tattoo.* My gaze lingered on three thick curving tribal-style crescents. The largest began at the base of his neck, where its tip fanned into multiple points. Two smaller crescents overlapped tips with the first, each arcing a different direction, one toward his back, the other curving beneath his arm.

My skin began to heat under the spotlight of his attention, and I burned the image into my memory for when I had a quiet moment, later.

My mouth had gone dry.

I swallowed hard.

Then I found my voice as my brain cells finally began to fire again. "Really? You invite me here and do that" —I gestured toward him with a wild wave of my fingers— "and I'm supposed to think only *friendly* thoughts?"

His lips twisted into a smirk. "Try."

I forced my attention back to his face and held his stare. "All I see is sex on a stick."

Oh, shit. I blurted that out loud.

His knees lowered to the floor, then he pulled his hands from the sand. "Try *harder.*"

Nice. Flirtatiousness? How about smoothness? I sighed heavily. "Not helping with your word choice."

He ignored my quip, stood, then grabbed the buckets

by their handles before lining them up against the wall. All business. Like he hadn't noticed my skimpy outfit. Or my sexiness. Or maybe he had—but I'd been too gobsmacked by his erotic pushups.

"What's with the sand?" I followed him.

He grabbed a white towel, then wiped it down his neck and over his chest. "I straighten my fingers, then sink my hands and curl them in a partial fist to anchor myself. Builds hand strength for drumming."

"You're a drummer?" I paused midstep with a heavy blink.

"Since I was five."

"I had no idea."

He regarded me for a moment. "You never asked."

True. But then, I hadn't needed to know much about a guy who was supposed to be a one-night stand. Now that we'd sidetracked into friend territory, the rules had apparently changed.

I nodded toward the buckets. "I wanna try."

His brows lifted as he followed my gaze. "The sand?"

"Yeah. Why not?"

"No. You'll hurt yourself. And too coarse on your skin." He walked to a shelf, then grabbed two black metal handles on circular bases. "Try these."

I dropped my bag beside his, then watched as he placed the handles on the floor about my shoulder width apart. Dropping to my knees, I eyed the handles. Then I grasped their rubber-covered handholds with a solid grip and positioned myself into a plank above them.

Under his scrutiny, I tightened my body from head to toe, then lowered until my nose was a couple of inches from the floor. I held my breath as fire ignited deep within my muscles.

On a steady hard exhale, arms trembling, I pushed back up again. "Okay. I'm good." I dropped my knees then stood.

His deep chuckle rankled me.

"Fine," I grumbled. "Obviously I need to do more of this." I circled a finger around the gym floor.

He shot me an amused look. "Why don't we start with running?"

From a small refrigerator beside the shelving unit, he grabbed two bottles of blue Gatorade, then headed toward a far door. I followed, skipping my steps faster to keep up with his long casual stride.

"So what makes you such a great personal trainer?" I wondered if he'd offered because he wanted to be around me more...or if he'd done the same for others. "You a jock?"

"Ran track in high school."

"Ah." In other words, no big deal to show some girl how to run around a track.

Outside, the sun glared from a clear blue sky. I pulled my shades back on as a slight chill in the morning air danced over my skin. I surveyed the clay-colored rubberized track and the aluminum stadium bleachers that lined both sides.

"What is this place?"

He lifted his baseball hat and spun it forward before pinching the bill and tugging it down his forehead, shadowing his eyes. "Old private college. Town converted it to a community center a few years back." He tilted his head to the side, assessing me for a moment, then stared through the opening in the chain link fence. "We'll start with a nice-and-easy jog around the track for a warmup."

Sounded simple enough.

Once our shoes hit the track, he set that nice-and-easy pace—also known as brisk—which I matched, determined to keep up. Around the first turn, I grew seriously winded, uncertain I could keep up a conversation. Good thing Darren wasn't talkative while running.

Midway down the next straightaway, my lungs began to burn. My focus attuned to the individual elements of my body: long breaths gulping in and out, brain forcing tired legs to keep the tempo, arms pumping opposite every stride.

My pulse pounded my eardrums.

My lungs scorched with every breath.

My legs just…stopped…at the beginning of the second turn.

I doubled over, hands on knees, gasping for air. Dots appeared at the edges of my vision.

"Easy there, Flash. Stand straight. Hands behind your head with your chin up; you'll breathe easier." He clamped a strong grip on my forearms then lifted them.

Suddenly we were in each other's space. Him lifting my arms up above my head. "Breathe," he commanded in a low tone.

Close. Too close.

Sweat glistened on his face, a single drip falling from his hairline to his brow.

Right, "*You'll breathe easier.*"

My gasping breaths sucked in his controlled exhalations, mingling our air. Our lips hovered mere inches apart as he stared down at me for the briefest second.

Like we could throw caution to the wind and bridge the gap.

Like it didn't matter what he'd challenged, and I'd promised.

An instant later, the moment vanished as he released his hold on my arms. He lifted his hands above his head and locked his fingers of the right hand on his opposite wrist. Then he nodded forward and resumed our course in a casual stroll. "Keep that chin up, opens the lungs. Walk it off."

Unable to catch my breath, a sharp stitch stabbing my side, I mimicked his posture and pace, a few steps behind this time. I had no idea where my competitive streak had come from—easygoing and free-flowing more my style—but the limits of my body had overridden all else.

Along the curve of the track, we walked. When we reached our initial starting point at the end of the curve, he stopped. "Ready?"

No. "Yes."

And there it was, my newfound competitive streak, back with a vengeance. Maybe it wasn't running itself, but Darren that kept provoking it from me.

Or maybe it was frustration that my plan to flirt kept falling by the wayside. Every time I got close to him, he threw me off-balance.

On our resumed run, his pace slowed. And this time it was a bit easier to keep up with him.

One additional lap. No collapse.

Another: winded but hanging.

After the third nonstop lap, fourth if the lame first one was included, we slowed and eased up to two shaded metal benches where he'd left the Gatorades. Slight condensation beaded the surface of the bottles. Arms up again, we paced along the short length of the benches. Then he uncapped one of the bottles and handed it to me before opening his own and chugging.

After a slow inhale, I tipped my head back to let the sweet chilled liquid splash over my tongue and, with greedy swallows, coat my parched throat.

"Not bad." He wiped the back of his arm across his mouth.

His tone had lowered a timbre, almost as if he'd weighted the statement into a double entendre. But with his face tilted slightly downward and his eyes hidden under the shadowy bill of his hat, I couldn't decipher his expression.

I shrugged, acting nonchalant. "I'll get better." Just being out of the warehouse—away from the pressures of real life— boosted my spirits, made the abuse of my muscles worth it.

"Give me about ten while you cool off." He began jogging away.

"Where you going?" I screwed my cap back on, placing my half-full bottle beside his empty.

"Stadium runs." He paused and pointed up an incline of metal bleachers.

I eyed the bleachers that glinted in the bright sun. Before he had a chance to run off again, I smiled and raced to catch up with him. "Are you training me, or what?" I gave a light shove to his chest, then charged in front of him.

The last image in my mind was the corners of his lips twitching.

But soon, all thoughts of him vanished as the wisdom of my cockiness reared its painful head. Regardless, I forced myself upward, step after step—muscles screaming, me ignoring.

When I slowed a half dozen steps from the top, he caught up beside me. "You okay?"

"Yeah." All I could get out.

"You sure? Your face is turning red."

"No." Everything hurt. But I powered on.

When we reached the top row, he stopped. "No shame in taking it easy your first try, Flash. Better to pace yourself so you don't get injured and have to *stop* training."

My eyes narrowed. "Why are you calling me 'Flash'?"

He grinned. "Better than slow poke."

I punched his shoulder. "Kiki. The name is *Kiki*." I tore down the metal steps, legs shaking. "And I'm done." I shouted over my shoulder.

Rapid clanking followed until he was right behind me, voicing, "I've gotta shower then head to class anyway."

Second to the last step.

Last step.

Bottom.

And I hadn't fallen on my face: major accomplishment.

"What are you studying?" I didn't picture him in college. Yet another tidbit of info I hadn't bothered to ferret out of him.

"Sound engineering and music theory."

"Music theory?"

"We analyze how the great composers create. We learn the language behind the music. Sound engineering because musicians don't always make it. But there's usually a need for technicians in music, movies, and gaming."

"Wow. Sounds…technical." *Brilliant.* Clearly, my thumping heart had cut off my brain's ability to formulate educated responses; it had siphoned all the oxygen to my screaming muscles.

"So what do you think? Ready for something different next time?" He held the gym door open.

I brushed past him, doing my best to ignore the enticing heat from his body and his sexy-as-hell masculine scent. "I don't know. What constitutes different?"

"It's a surprise." He leveled a serious look at me, then waited a beat. "In or out?"

Both. My nerve cells pinged to life as my thoughts guttered. He looked incredible, all hot and sweaty and shirtless.

What the hell was I doing? Losing control. I kept guys at a safe distance. Man candy. Fun. That's all I'd ever felt comfortable enough after…

I swallowed hard, refusing to go there.

Alarm bells that should've been clanging my eardrums deaf seemed to muffle. Self-preservation instincts had gone nonexistent. Everything about the man standing before me tempted me to get closer, find out more, take whatever he had to offer…no matter the risk.

I took a deep breath, then blew it out, daring to face the unknown—enticed by it.

"In."

Most definitely in.

6
IN THEORY

Darren...

Quick shower. Race across campus.

I'd barely made it. I jogged faster, then shot my hand into the two-inch gap of the door slamming shut.

Everyone else in my class, all seventeen of them, had already settled into their seats.

As usual, I veered left, toward the back.

Trey gave me a chin up, then lifted a Starbucks cup. I grabbed it as I took a seat.

"Wasn't sure you'd show," he rasped right as the professor entered our tiered room from the opposing corner front door.

"Wasn't sure either."

Turned out, I hadn't been in a hurry to leave Kiki. I'd walked her to her car. Asked her what she'd be doing for the rest of the day. Got caught up in her description of a new sunflower sculpture she'd begun working on. Shocked the hell out of me when I'd realized the time—or that I'd lost track of it wanting to spend more of it with her.

Trey slouched in his chair until his shaggy blond head rested against the brick wall. He tilted his face toward me. "Got you the audition."

I blew out a relieved breath. "Thanks, man."

In the following seconds, as the professor droned on about the focus of transformational theory, excitement rocketed through me so hard my legs started to bounce.

It was a longshot: studio drummer for trumpeter Dino Mathis, a rising jazz phenomenon. The once-in-a-lifetime opportunity didn't typically come to working-class college kids like me. But Trey's dad owned a record label in New York. And I wasn't above using his connections.

Yeah, it wasn't exactly what I'd dreamed about as a kid. Wasn't my own gig in a band. Wouldn't be on stage in front of thousands of screaming fans.

But my dreams had changed in the last couple of years. Food on the table, stable home life, and everyone tucked into bed at night and waking up in the morning were my primary goals. Working multiple jobs, finishing my degree, and exercising like a machine—holding me on the better side of sanity—helped keep those goals in check.

No time for anything I wanted for myself. Not yet.

Time with Kiki fell into forbidden territory. Something that made me feel a little more alive. *Something for myself.* But the only way it worked? Keeping things neutral. And sliding it into already-scheduled workouts seemed like the perfect way to have it and not lose control of anything else.

Trey leaned his head toward me. "Audition's Friday at 9:00 a.m."

"Damn. That's early. And at rush hour." *In Manhattan.* A two-hour drive *not* in rush hour.

"Sorry, dude. I only put the good word in. Pops calls the shots. Still want to jam at Nick's?"

Nick's was on Thursday, right before I'd agreed to meet Kiki for her second training session. The audition was a whole day later. But Trey knew how crunched for time my schedule was. In order to blow a whole day for an audition, other things had to give. I'd miss two Friday morning classes and a monthly staff meeting at Loading Zone. But things were on autopilot at the bar, and I was set for the Invitation Only party on Saturday.

"Yeah, I'm good." In order to move up, make more money, and get more secure in life, sacrifices had to be made.

A studio drummer's salary could be more than quadruple what I made as a DJ. Maybe allow me to quit Loading Zone. Ease up on my time-crunch. Spend more nights at home.

The reminder of home warred with thoughts of Kiki. Guilt pinged through me. How did clearing room in my schedule for training Kiki mesh with the commitment I'd made to the one thing most important to me, the only person I'd promised to care for, make safe…love?

I blew out a hard breath, angry at myself for burying my head in work and exercise and school. I stewed about it for a solid ten minutes, staring at the clock over the chalkboard, not hearing a word of the professor's lecture. Then something fundamental shifted deep in my gut. The justification of keeping a shallow existence in order to avoid another disaster no longer sat well with me.

Why all of a sudden?

Kiki.

Damn.

The bright sculptor with an easy laugh and strong determination, a girl who strived for more in her life, made me want more for mine…and for everyone in it.

The girl I hadn't seen coming tugged at my heart—even though it couldn't belong to her.

7
SCALING MOUNTAINS

Kiki…

Thursday afternoon, I pulled up to the address Darren had texted me, ten minutes early.

Nervous excitement hammered my pulse, and I blew out a hard breath to calm myself.

I gripped the steering wheel, staring out the windshield at an empty street. Then I glanced in my rearview. "Flirtatiousness, adorableness, and sexiness." The words had been a fortifying mantra last time I'd met him.

And venturing into the uncharted territory of friends—*that I wanted to fuck*—at least I hadn't fallen flat on my face. Running or otherwise.

But it didn't soothe my nerves this time.

Friends. No sexual qualifier after. *Just* friends. My heartbeat began to gradually slow. After another few seconds of easier breathing, I stepped out of my car.

Older houses lined the well-maintained street on both sides. A handful of cars were parked along the curbs. A couple sat on driveways. Most were older vehicles.

A captivating bass rhythm caught my attention. It streamed from the house straight ahead and drew me halfway up a flower-lined walkway before I realized I hadn't shut my car door.

Yet I remained rooted in place. Something soulful about the sound penetrated deep into my bones. The effect was mesmerizing.

An errant breeze skittered a small brown paper bag down the sidewalk. Its crinkling racket continued until it lodged behind my back right tire. I returned to my car and shoved my door shut. Then I picked up the paper bag, crumpled it, and slipped it under the lid of a metal trash can set along the curb.

Seconds later, the incredible music stopped. The hum of a motor began as the two-car garage door slowly lifted, revealing the occupants inside. Five people stood in the empty space. Two college-aged guys held guitars. Haunting deep tones began to stream from the bass guitar, played by a girl, while a lanky guy draped a thin cover over a keyboard.

The fifth stepped out from behind a set of drums.

Darren.

He glanced my way for a split second before turning back toward his bandmates. One of the guys ducked his head under his shoulder strap, removing his guitar. The remaining guitarist stepped near the girl with the bass. They played a short rock riff, then stopped and laughed when she hit a wrong note.

Uncomfortable about intruding, since I *had* shown up early, I leaned a hip on the back corner of my car, waiting.

Darren secured his drumsticks into a case hanging on one of his larger drums, then walked over to the girl. She nodded, then glanced my way.

Did her charcoaled eyes narrow?

I narrowed my own, assessing her anew. She was young, maybe just out of high school. Her dark shoulder-length hair had a thick bright pink streak on one side. She wore frayed faded jeans, a dark gray henley that clung to a shapely figure, and a black newsboy cap that sat askew, dipping low over her right brow.

My view was suddenly blocked by Darren's body. He embraced her—as well as one could with a bass guitar between them—then stood there for a moment, head angled down. Seconds later, he turned my way and began striding down the driveway.

"Hey, Flash." He grinned.

I scowled at the nickname I'd inherited. "You ready?"

"Yep. Want to follow me or go in my truck?"

Hesitating, I glanced down the quiet street again. "It's okay to leave my car at your house?"

"Not my place. It's Nick's. But yeah, it's cool."

About to clarify which one Nick was—the girl or one of the guys—my jaw dropped open, mind blanking as I stared at his feet.

"Vibrams!" I pointed to his gray-and-orange shoes in accusation.

He shrugged and opened the passenger door for me. "Yeah, so?"

"But…you harassed me about mine."

He leaned in my open window, grin twisting sly. "Had to give you shit about something, *friend*."

"When did you get them?" Much as I loved mine, his wearing them blew my mind.

"While ago." He rounded the front of the truck, got in, started the engine, and pulled away before continuing, "You're right. They are the best shoe for your feet. But, in my opinion, it depends on where you run."

"Like where?"

"You'll see." At the end of the street, he paused, then turned toward the highway.

He said nothing further as he merged into traffic. We passed an exit, then another. A comfortable silence settled between us and I closed my eyes, wondering at the anomaly. What happened to the anxious girl needing her mantra?

Even so, without opening my eyes, I felt a subtle exhilarating tension between us.

I slowly exhaled, thrilling in the sensation. My breaths shallowed within seconds. My body began to warm.

I suddenly blinked my eyes open, off-balance yet again. Then I quickly focused on mundane things: green road signs, stripes on the pavement.

After another mile, once I'd gotten a handle on my libido again, I glanced at him. "So how was class?" He'd mentioned at the community center when he'd walked me to my car that he had two midday classes on Tuesdays and Thursdays.

"Good. Typical."

I snorted. "What? The class? Or your short *stereo*typical guy-speak?"

"Ha ha." He dropped a put-out look at me. "The professor's great. He plays alto saxophone and clarinet. Toured with Wynton Marsalis for a few years. Then performed with his Jazz at the Lincoln Center Orchestra for over a decade before deciding to teach."

"Sounds like a wonderful teacher."

He gave a short nod. "You can tell he loves it. Just hearing his stories gets my blood pumping."

"What kind of music were you playing back there?"

"That last was one of our original songs. Rock with a heavy drag rhythm. Did you like it?"

"Yeah. A lot. It was…different. Almost primal."

An easy smile curved his lips. "Why I like it too. Seeps into your pores."

I nodded. It had. "The band sounds really great. Do you have a lot of original songs?"

He shrugged. "Half a dozen or so. We noodled around after playing covers for about a year. Created our own sound during a drunken jam session late one night."

He leaned over, picked up his phone from the floor, then cast a quick glance at it. He took the next exit, slowing to a four-way stop.

We sat at the intersection, idling. "Okay. Decision time. Left or right? Easy or hard?"

"Easy sounds boring."

"Can be."

Vague. And interesting. "I choose the opposite of boring. Think I can handle hard?"

"I dunno. Can you?" His tone thickened with innuendo as he turned the truck right.

Okaaay. I'd actually meant running. My leashed libido snapped to life again.

"Not fair." I glared at him. "You want me to keep my mind out of the gutter, you have to help."

He let out a deep unapologetic chuckle. "I can't help where *your* mind goes. Challenge yourself. Show some discipline."

"Grrr…" I growled, pulling a laugh from him. Then I sighed, resigned to the task. "Fine. I'm up for it. Why not? I've been celibate this long."

"How long?"

"Whoa." I arched a brow at him. "Is this proper friend talk?"

"Sure." He fought a smile. "Friends can console friends on sexual frustration."

"Uh-huh." I didn't buy it. I had a hard enough time being in the same truck cab with him. At least today he wore a shirt. So I didn't have to keep picturing him naked.

Great. Now I'm picturing him naked.

"See." He interrupted, saving me from my dirty thoughts. "I'll go first: I've been celibate two months."

"Bullshit," I coughed out. I'd been at Loading Zone often enough. Had seen him leave with other girls. But maybe it hadn't been recent. The months seemed to blur together.

The roadside scenery thickened with pine, an occasional

sycamore or walnut breaking through. He slowed and downshifted as our gently winding road began to climb in elevation. "Well, I haven't been marking a calendar, but I'm pretty sure it was after Valentine's Day."

"Not before?" I smirked. "Afraid of the hearts-and-flowers holiday?"

"Not afraid. Just smart enough to avoid it." He gave a sharp nod, like it emphasized his wisdom. "Your turn."

For some reason, the laidback nature of our conversation lulled me into wanting to be truthful with him. A part of me wanted what he offered. Other than Cade, Ben, and Mase—all essentially brothers to me—I'd never had a platonic guy friend. After the disaster in high school, I'd avoided getting close to anyone, preventing any kind of emotion for the opposite sex.

However, in the spirit of keeping aboveboard with our experiment in friendship, I reflected back to the last time I'd had a hookup.

"*Waiting...*" He drummed both thumbs on the steering wheel.

"*Thinking...*" I crossed my arms over my chest, staring out the windshield at the dense forest on either side of the road as I searched my memory. The further back my mind went, the more it seemed hopeless to even give a date to it. Not since last summer. Not in the spring. Not after the New Year's Eve party where Cade had gotten some—and none of the rest of us had. "Damn."

"That bad?"

"Ancient."

"We talking months?"

"Over a year." I sighed. "Under two."

"Why so long?"

"Seriously?" I choked out a laugh. "Would've been a few days ago if you'd cooperated."

He cast me a penetrating look. He waited a silent beat. Then he glanced ahead again before changing lanes and turning into a gravel parking lot.

Once we parked, he twisted toward me, expression growing serious. "There *have* to be other guys that fit the bill."

"Sure. Athletes, mostly. My first stretch was football players. Then a couple of baseball players. One guy played hockey."

"Nothing serious?"

"Nope."

"Not even close?"

Yeah, *so* not going there. Apparently I had limits with the whole disclosure thing. "Not even a 'boyfriend' tag," I hedged, not fully answering the question. Fidgeting under his sudden scrutiny, I volleyed the topic back. "What about you? What's up with 'Mr. Complicated'?"

His expression hardened. "We don't have enough hours to cover that ground."

"Hmmm…interesting." I wasn't the only one who buckled under romance pressure.

He nodded his chin toward the dashboard. "Ready to tackle a mountain?"

I leaned forward and glanced up through the windshield. "Mountain?" I paused, swallowing hard. "You're kidding, right?"

"No. Don't be scared, Flash. It's just like the track. Only vertical."

"I'm not scared," I huffed, shoving open my door.

"Never thought it for a moment."

"Jerk," I muttered.

The corners of his lips twitched.

I shook my head with a soft snort, then tore off toward the trailhead, not waiting for him. He shouted something, but I couldn't hear him over the pounding of my feet and blood rushing past my eardrums. Of course, I slowed after about a minute. I'd learned my lesson the first time on the track. *Run at my own pace.*

Seconds after I slowed, he caught up to me. "Remember the instructions that came with the Vibrams?"

I gave a nod, slowing a bit more so I could talk. "Shorter strides. Forward and center of the foot instead of heel-striking."

"Right." He fell in behind me. "And for our first trail run, here's a few tips: Walk the downhills, sprint the uphills, and chart your path ahead of time—avoid rocks and sapling tree stumps."

"Why walk the downhills?" We approached a downslope, and I slowed to a brisk walk, picking my way down the dirt-lined sections.

"Until you're used to running on uneven terrain and downhill, it's safest. No point in risking a knee blowout or broken ankle."

"Or worse." We rounded a narrow bend in the trail, and I leaned toward the outside edge, peering over. "Damn. That's one hell of a drop." Not straight down, but a good seventy-percent grade, at least. Nothing I wanted to tumble down.

"Right. So stick to the inside edge of the trail. Especially with oncoming."

"Oncoming?" Through the dense trees, I could only make out the trail a few dozen yards ahead.

"Bikers, hikers, other trail runners."

"Sure. Because if running uphill with a sheer drop-off isn't enough, an out-of-control mountain biker at twenty miles an hour ought to scare some caution into you."

"It'll be fine." He shifted behind me as the trail narrowed.

"Wildlife?" Unfamiliar forest surrounded us.

"Will there be any, you mean?"

I paused at a tricky hairpin bend, brows raised. "Lions, tigers…bears?"

"Mountain lions, no tigers…black bears."

"Great." I turned back around picking my way along the rocky path, staring hard into the denser sections of foliage, suddenly feeling eyes staring back.

"Haven't you ever been out in the wilderness before?"

The slope leveled out, and I resumed my steady running pace. "Does the park count?"

"No."

I couldn't readily explain why I'd never been out in a forest. For some reason, I'd stayed indoors most of my life. Art had become my conduit to nature, something I created—a world I had control of.

"Uphill!" I tore off, concentrating on the trail. I charted my path around rocks and exposed roots, found softer earthen sections to land footfalls on, and willed all wild predators and oncoming mountain bikers to stay the hell back.

And the runner's euphoria I'd often heard about hit three-quarters of the way up the steep winding section of path. Gone were all my troubles. Sexual frustration? Obliterated.

In its place flooded a sense of rightness in the moment, in the beautiful expanse of nature around me—all with a guy who'd started out as a one-night stand candidate.

I could hardly believe what had begun to happen between us. Wasn't sure I even trusted it. When I'd stopped paying attention, Darren had transformed from just a guy I just wanted to get physical with…into something remotely, possibly, vaguely resembling a friend.

As the realization hit, a solid dose of fear shuddered through me.

The challenge hadn't been real. It had only been a guise for me to be around him more—lure him into that one-night stand status I knew I could handle.

Friends? I didn't know how to handle at all. Wasn't sure I could.

To cope with the sudden spike of anxiety, I ran faster, pushed harder. And I did what I seemed to be a master at lately: I put on a brave face and forced myself to ignore the threat.

8
FALLING OFF COURSE

Darren…

With a sudden burst of energy, Kiki raced ahead. "How's my running form look?"

Fucking spectacular. "Great."

I almost tripped. Her ass looked incredible in those tight yoga pants.

Get your shit together, D.

I shook my head to clear it. Needed to be on the program I'd made Kiki abide by. She was just a friend. All she could ever be.

At a level section a few yards ahead, she turned. Cheeks pinked from her sprint. Black hair pulled up in a swaying ponytail. Only her hair wasn't quite black; sunlight brightened the top of her head, glinting a flash of dark brown. Her breasts lifted and fell as she tried to catch her breath.

Eyes up, idiot. Yeah. The whole "friends" thing? Harder than I'd thought.

Happiness radiated from her eyes, bright blue in the angled afternoon light.

As soon as I got within ten feet of her, she tore off up the trail again at an even faster pace.

"Easy, Flash," I shouted, picking up speed. "I'm not scraping you off the ground."

Truth…I quickly closed the gap between us; I'd be sure to cushion her fall. Not in any other way than a friend. Protector. The role I'd assumed, because it fit me like a second glove.

My thoughts bled dark, painfully reminding me that I hadn't always succeeded. I'd failed one person. One time. In the worst way possible.

The memory served as both punishment and motivator. Helped me strengthen my resolve to never let another soul fall on my watch. And why I couldn't be more than a friend to Kiki. Because another someone who I'd vowed to protect above all others had to come first.

But on the trail ahead, Kiki was my charge. And— "*Dammit*," I growled under my breath as she raced out of my sight around a bend for the second time in as many minutes.

By the time I finally paced a few strides behind her again, we'd almost reached the summit. Not a great distance, but the perfect challenging beginner's trail run: thickly forested, a mix of undulating straightaways coupled with several steady climbs.

"WhooHooo!" She held her arms up in a V above her head at the summit viewpoint area and sucked in big gulps of air. Then she broke into a broad smile.

I grinned. Couldn't help it.

"C'mon, join me!" She relaxed her arms halfway, then shot them straight up into a V again. "Be the tree!"

I snorted out a short laugh, then pressed my lips together. I forced my tone comically flat. "Be the tree." I slowly raised my arms to join her.

"Yep. Be the tree. In the moment. One with nature. *Be. The. Tree.*" Her eyes widened as she punctuated each word. "I'm gonna make T-shirts."

Before I had a chance to weigh in, she was on the move again, energy in motion.

"Damn, Flash." I walked closer to where she paced a wide circle in the dirt of the flattened overlook. "Endorphins are your brand of drug."

"I feel amazing!" She burst her arms upward again.

"Thought you might like this better than a pavement run. You and nature."

"My art." Her smile softened.

"Exactly." Although it surprised me she hadn't made that leap before. I'd have thought nature would've been her second home.

"I never want to leave here," she announced with a hard nod. "That's it. Screw a 5K. I'm trail running."

Had no idea why her statement filled me with pride, but it did. Maybe because she'd found her element in a sport she'd been lured in by. And I'd guided her the rest of the way there.

In a sudden rush of energy, she charged toward the edge, angling toward a small flattened boulder. She coiled down as she approached, then sprang up, leaping onto it.

"*WhooHooo…Hooo…Hooo…*" Her excitement echoed through the canyon.

A squeak pierced out. Then she jumped straight up right as the boulder rattled, then gave way.

I lunged forward, but the distance was too great.

"Darren!" She clutched a pine branch, facing outward. About two feet beyond the edge.

Fuck.

Panic surged through me. "Hold tight, Kiki."

"Not going anywhere." Her tone turned somber.

Fuck. Fuck. Fuck.

"Can you turn around?" Adrenaline fired into my veins, sharpening what I needed to focus on.

Instead of answering, she tightened her grip. A couple of seconds later, she released her left handhold, and, in one quick motion, twisted her arm, crossed her wrists, then released her other hand and spun around.

Her eyes were wide with terror.

"You're okay, Kiki. Just look at me. You're almost there. Trust me."

She replied with a curt nod, then took a deep breath.

"Can you swing toward me?"

She frowned. "Not sure. The branch is bending. I feel like I'm dropping."

I'd noticed. Hadn't wanted to mention it. The newer wood hadn't gained enough tensile strength to bear her weight for long.

"Focus on me. Give me a hard swing. Then a second one. On the third, let go." I inched as close to the edge as I dared with the unstable soil.

She immediately flexed her upper arms, then swung halfway toward me. On the backswing, her eyes widened and she sucked in a panicked breath, legs dangling over greater open air. When she swung forward the second time, a loud crack happened from the force; the branch began to break.

Shit!

"Let go!" I shouted. Instinct had me dart toward the right at the last second so I could launch at her from the side. As I planted a foot, I crouched, sprang forward, and aimed for her legs. I wrapped an arm behind her knees and jerked forcefully toward solid ground.

We tumbled sideways in a tangle of arms and legs before landing in a heap on the dirt.

"*Fuck.*" I huffed out a relieved breath. "That was close."

The only thing that saved us—saved her—was a split-second reaction. A blink of time later and…I didn't even want to think about it.

Her body covered mine, hands clinging tightly to my shoulders, legs clamped to my hips. Her chest pressed against mine, amplifying how hard our hearts pounded.

With every lengthening breath, she began to ease her death grip on me.

Then her body began to tremble.

"Hey, it's okay." I murmured. "You're okay." I rubbed her back with an unpinned arm.

"Thank you." She spoke in the barest whisper. The louder-than-life girl who'd been shouting from a mountaintop seconds ago had been humbled by nature.

"No worries. Just another day running."

She didn't laugh at my dry humor. Made no move to get off me.

Adrenaline began to seep from my veins with the danger gone.

Then blood flooded elsewhere.

Her hold on my shoulders tightened. She pushed her body up enough to look me in the eye. "Ummm…are you growing hard for me?"

"Yes." No point denying it. The evidence emerged right there between us. "Can't help it. You *are* laying on top of me."

Her first smile since we'd landed on the ground slowly appeared. "You put me here." Teasing edged her voice.

Didn't bother disputing it. Better to have her safe and deal with a raging hard-on.

My gaze fell to her full lips; the lower one was red. I remembered her biting it while she'd hung from that tree limb. Frustration suddenly fired into me—that I'd let her endanger herself in the first place.

I blew out a heavy sigh, trying to expel the growing anger at myself.

Her smile faltered.

Then she pushed off me and rolled onto the dirt, arms flinging wide. The back of one hand thumped onto my chest.

She stared up at the sky, smile widening once again. "WhooHooo!" She shouted louder than before.

I shook my head, chuckling. Humor worked. Better than the wrong *near-deadly* turn we'd almost taken. *And the sexual path we'd stumbled toward…*

With a grunt, I ignored a flash of pain that fired through

my head from smacking it on the ground and shoved upright. Then I offered her a hand up.

She took it and we dusted ourselves off. Then we methodically bent our arms and legs checking for injuries.

I ran my hands over my arms and legs, then glanced at her. "Any holes?"

Her brow wrinkled, then the corners of her mouth twitched. "I wasn't shot; we fell." She patted herself down anyway then gave me a nod. "I'm good."

With a slow exhale, she plopped her hands onto her hips. Then she narrowed her eyes at the trail from the direction we'd come from before glancing toward where it continued. "Which way, Coach?"

I nodded back down the trail. "A one-and-a-half mile walk downhill back to the car. Another three if we continue on."

She arched her brows. "Running?"

"Running."

"Better keep up, then. No way in hell am I letting a little stumble get the better of me."

Without warning, she charged off around the next curve.

I raced after her, scared as fuck that her kamikaze attitude would throw her into another dangerous situation. There were plenty of other drop-offs and blind curves.

Around the following bend, I caught up, then jogged beside her. "As often as you can, scan ahead to anticipate anyone barreling toward you. Remember those adrenaline-junky mountain bikers take downhills at idiotic speeds."

She pressed our pace faster. As if testing me. Or our

ability to speak while running. "And your suggestion? If I find myself squaring off with a reckless biker?"

"Jump toward the mountain. Even if you have to throw yourself on it. Forces any oncoming to take the outside. Makes 'em slow the fuck down."

"Got it. Throw myself on the mountain." Her breaths came in shorter huffs between her words, yet she kept the challenging pace. "Any other tips?"

"Yeah. Watch for deceiving angles in curves. Logic tells you the grade would slope into a curve. Yet sometimes it does the opposite: slants toward the outside edge. Loose dirt and rocks are like ball bearings. Your foot slides if you lean too much toward the inside on an outward angle like that. The trail does what it wants and is merciless if you aren't on board with it."

Now I'd grown out of breath. So had she. And she hadn't been talking. Still we pressed on, pace gradually easing as the incline leveled off then angled into a gentle downhill.

As soon as a level straightaway appeared, she sprinted ahead. When she'd gained a dozen yards, she glanced over her shoulder. "Race ya!"

I tore off, picking up speed. Not trying to beat her, but hell-bent on keeping up.

The girl who'd wanted to "get in shape" had all kinds of surprises up her sleeve, including a natural running ability. And boundless energy. And no fear of mountains—or their drop-offs.

In my world of hustling from one thing to the next,

barely holding it all together, Kiki Michaelson was a breath of fresh air.

And I suddenly found myself wanting…more.

9
RACE AGAINST TIME

Kiki…

"Wait. Darren, there's a race for this?"

Slowing to a jog, I plucked the sheet from the trailhead's memo board, then paced in a wide circle. My breaths came in short bursts from sprinting the straightaway that had stretched from the end of the trail to the gravel parking lot.

"Sure. Diehards, mostly."

"This." I slapped the paper against his chest. "*This* is the race I want to run."

"You almost bit it at the top. Now you want to jump into it with a hundred other crazies?"

"Did you just call me crazy?"

"Yes." He raised his hand and palmed the top of my head,

rubbing his fingers over my scalp. "Sure you didn't hit your head?"

I shoved his arm away. "Positive."

I had no idea why I suddenly wanted to run a trail race, but I did.

Endorphins from running? Yeah. I had that going on. But all the nature, the trees, maybe all the oxygen from them, had me on a high. Something energized me from the trail—different than the track.

He plucked the race flier from my hand, then studied it. "Shortens the time window. Only five weeks away. Sure you'll be up for it?"

"I will if you train me." There, I'd said it—admitted that I wanted him to be a part of it.

I wasn't sure what had happened on that mountain. Although we hadn't consciously crossed any line regarding our agreement, something *had* happened. The constant attraction between us remained, but more had ignited in those tense seconds where life and death had collided. A bond had formed.

Then once everything had calmed, he'd gotten turned on.

By me.

On top of him.

And my body had instantly responded.

Maybe it'd been the adrenaline racing through my veins. The potent thrill of danger followed by the hard cage of his muscles surrounding me, protecting me, had to have supercharged my nerve endings.

So why is the same thing happening now?

My body warmed. Began to throb in all the delicious places we had touched. And I stood a good three feet away from him.

The threat I faced had nothing to do with high cliffs and deadly gravity. It stood before me, a six-foot-two male packed with lean muscle and a dry sense of humor. Yet no matter the danger, my common sense had apparently gone on vacation. Because something deep down made me want to push the issue—be near him any way I could.

Just friends.

I'd initially started our training adventure with an ulterior motive. I figured time together would convince him that he wanted us to have sex.

Now I began to wonder if being purely platonic was for the best.

Safer.

I exhaled a slow breath, watching his profile. He hadn't replied. I wasn't sure if he'd heard me, since he continued to read a page that had only two short paragraphs. "So will you? Train me?"

"Won't be easy." He cast a hard look at me.

"Easy equals boring. Thought we established that back in the truck."

"You sure you're up for it? My way? My methods?"

How hard could it be? More stadium runs? Sand-bucket pushups?

I didn't clarify, just nodded my head. "I can handle it."

He glanced at the ground for a brief moment, then looked up at me. "Yeah, okay. I don't have any more time in my schedule. But if you trained on your own in between, and we found a few more safe trails to run, we could get you ready."

"Ones without loose boulders?"

He shot me an unamused look.

"I suppose I don't have to go jumping on them. At least not without you around."

His lips twitched as he fought a smile.

Then his eyes smoldered a bit, and I knew I had him, knew his thoughts had gone where mine had, right back to the moment we'd shared. Not the *Oh my God I'm going to die* one but the *Holy shit! We're lying together on the ground and don't want to get up* one.

He gave a sharp nod. "We'll save boulder-hopping for group runs."

"Got it." I walked back to the larger trailhead map that was mounted under plexiglass. "What other trails are nearby?"

He pinned the trail race flier back to the memo board beside me, then pulled a folded map from a slender wooden compartment with a hinged top marked *day-pass.*

I plucked a small envelope from the holder, then scanned the information it requested: date, time, name, license plate number, and a note regarding a five dollar fee. There was a locked slot over a box beside the map-and-day-pass filled compartment. "Were we supposed to do one of these?"

After a pause, he glanced up. "*We* did. When you tore off the instant the truck hit park, *I* scrawled out our info. Might think about a season pass if we come here often. Save money that way."

"How much?"

He didn't look up from the map he was reading. Instead, he lifted the lid, handed me a fresh map, then tapped the bottom back corner of it.

Seventy bucks. I let out a low whistle. Not cheap. But more than once a month in a year would pay for itself. And I needed to train a few times a week, at least.

Finally he grabbed the pen at the top of the box, then circled a marked trail on the right side of the map. "This is the one closest to your house. Can you run before 7:00 a.m.?"

"Uhhh…" I usually slept well past 10:00 a.m. "I can set the alarm and see what happens."

"Good. A lot of executives from the city use these trails off-hours, more of them in the morning. If you come early enough, you'll have plenty of company for safety."

Because on those days, I'd have to run by myself. "You can't run then?"

His brows furrowed and he shook his head. But offered no explanation.

Right. *It's complicated.*

"Here's another nearby trail. Longer, but it's got steady inclines and easy elevation drops. Great for building your endurance."

On he went: explaining where I could safely go, how far each trailhead was from my house, what distance I'd need to run per day in order be ready for the race.

I squinted at the map, memorizing the few he'd indicated. "How many can you make?"

"What?"

"Runs. You promised to train me. How many runs will you be on?"

"I can train you Tuesday mornings. And Thursday and Saturday afternoons."

I grinned. "I'll take it."

Not thinking twice about it, I threw my body against him, wrapped my hands around his neck, and kissed his cheek. His entire body stiffened in surprise. But then he relaxed and curved his arms around my back into a gentle hug.

We both inhaled deeply while we held each other for those brief seconds, as if savoring another stolen moment. One where we didn't have an agreement to be just friends. One that didn't have my fears and his complications. One that ignored the fact that we'd already begun to blur the lines between what we couldn't have and what we wanted.

Hours later, I sat at my worktable in the quiet of the warehouse like I did so many nights—staring at the envelope.

Unopened, it almost appeared harmless. But starched ivory, inked letters, and two postage stamps with *Love* scripted in pastel colors on its outside surface didn't change the contents behind the sealed flap.

Underneath the stationery camouflage lay a grenade.

And I wasn't about to pull the pin.

Instead, I warily stared at it like I had the handful of other times since the postman had come to my door. Front side up, partially concealed by a stack of mail, its green perforated strips hidden on the backside were evidence that I'd acknowledged receipt.

"Open it. Don't open it," I grumbled. Then I took a sip of coffee, glaring at the damned thing, willing its contents and all they represented to poof into thin air.

But as usual, nothing happened.

And I wasn't kidding myself that anything would.

Common sense screamed the explosion would happen anyway.

But still, the nightly exercise, futile as it was, helped soothe my version of reality: that nothing would change. As long as I didn't open the envelope.

The longer it sat there, the more hazardous it felt, though. Like it was merely a grenade if I eventually took control and pulled the pin. If I didn't? Then it morphed back into what it had been all along: a ticking bomb.

10
RIDING THE EDGE

Darren…

Fucking *traffic.* Sucked that I'd left so early—only to be late.

I glared at the right lane, willing a spot to open.

Score. When a Jaguar inched forward, I gassed it, yanking the wheel hard to steal the opening. A horn blared from a white sedan I'd cutoff.

My lips curled into a smug smile. "You text, you lose. Idiot."

Not that I should talk. Multitasking had overrun my life.

As I barreled down the highway exit, I glanced at the time. Five minutes late, clock still ticking. I threw out the desperate hope that late happened all the time in the music industry. And that everyone else I'd be meeting had gotten snagged by traffic too.

A disembodied girly whine wailed through my truck speakers, dragging me back to the phone conversation. "Darren, are you listening?"

"Yeah, Logan. I heard you."

"You'll be there?" Her tone wavered with doubt.

I sighed, pissed at myself for getting distracted. She counted on me being present with her. Even when I had a million other things on my mind. "Of course. You know I wouldn't miss it."

"Awesome. It's at seven on the first."

"I'll be there."

"And Darren?"

I took a wrong turn onto 41st Street instead of 42nd. "*Fuck*," I bit out under my breath. Then I exhaled, calming down a bit. For her. For us. "Yeah, Lo?"

"Thanks. This means a lot."

My heart melted. All the crunch, all the multitasking, all the sacrifice was for her. Too often, lost in the chaos of it all, I forgot that.

"Love you," she said quietly.

"Love you too." I did. To my bones.

Yet sometimes love trapped you into a life you hadn't been planning—along with the worst possible events.

But I dealt the best way I knew how.

At nineteen, I'd been served my unexpected future like a prison term with no parole in sight. My only task? Make sure it wasn't a death sentence for her.

But day after day, week after week, two years and three months after our lives had been changed forever, a light had appeared at the end of my dark tunnel.

Kiki.

A girl I hadn't counted on. One I never thought I'd deserved. One I definitely didn't think could fit into my and Logan's unorthodox and unforgiving world.

In fact, I still wasn't sure. Could my crazy life—barely held together—handle Kiki? Would I be betraying Logan?

That was the kicker. Logan came first, over all else. I owed it to her. I'd promised.

And if dealt the same cards, I'd promise all over again, even knowing the difficult times I'd be committing the both of us to. Because for better or for worse, she was family.

Just because life seemed worse most of the time, didn't mean you abandoned your loved ones. It only meant you had to work that much harder to find hope in the middle of it all. That some days would be better.

Allowing Kiki into my life risked that hope. Threatened to upset the balance I'd tried so hard to maintain.

And yet, I couldn't stop myself.

She was like a drug—quieted the noise in my head.

In just a few short days, she'd become my escape. And a part of me didn't want to deny myself the best feeling I'd had in years.

Maybe I could have both…if I was careful.

Maybe.

Just…maybe.

11
SUGARCOATING MAN CANDY

"**O**h. My. God. My calves."

Upside down on Kristen's couch, feet planted on the wall while I surveyed the fresh coat of lilac toenail polish, my muscles seized. I sucked in a breath and dropped down with a sideways spin. Then I grabbed my big toes and flexed my feet upward, pulling them toward my shins.

I exhaled in relief.

Pain took my mind off of *other* things. But I could only handle so much.

Kendall stared at me from the other end of the couch, brows drawn low. "What did you do?"

"Ran up a mountain yesterday. In Vibrams."

"What 'ems?"

"Vibrams. Shoes specially designed to run as if you're barefoot."

"Why would you want to do that?" Kristen sat between us in the center of the couch, concentrating as she brushed a second coat of hot-pink polish on her toes.

The blender began to whir loudly in the kitchen.

I shrugged. "Something different. An activity to get me outside and in shape."

"By yourself?" Kendall plucked two polish colors from the rainbow lineup she'd been examining on the coffee table. "Blushing Harlot or Tourmaline Sky?"

Kristen snorted. "Since when does a harlot blush?"

"Well, damn. That's my color." Kendall replaced the bright blue into the cosmetics tray, then shook the frosty pink bottle she'd chosen. "I'm nothing if not a bundle of contradictions."

Blushing Harlot. Nonsex. Kendall's gaze shot to mine the instant our hilarious conversation about nonsluts and wannabe hussies slammed into my brain. We both inhaled deeply, lips pressing into firm lines as we fought laughter that threatened to bubble up.

When I narrowed my eyes a fraction, she gave me a nearly imperceptible nod. I shot her one back. Yep. Our twisted sexual sense of humor belonged just between the two of us.

"And I didn't run by myself."

Hannah emerged from the kitchen, cradling four strawberry daiquiris in her arms.

I grabbed one of the glasses from her. "I went with Darren."

Annnd…there goes my mind to other *things.*

"Sex on a stick!" Hannah and Kendall shouted in unison.

"Jinx!" They pointed at each other.

"Double Jinx!" Kendall and Hannah froze, watching their red drinks slosh in their glasses with their animated excitement. Then everyone burst out laughing.

"What is 'sex on a stick,' anyway?" Kristen swept a final brushstroke over her pinky toenail, then leaned back, arching her brows. "How can it be an actual guy? Isn't sex… on a stick?"

Hannah nearly choked on her daiquiri, coughing out more laughter.

I had no idea why I'd ever called him that; I'd first voiced it to Hannah months ago at Loading Zone. Probably because the description had sounded delicious at the time. And Darren? Definitely delicious—delectable…decadent. Darren got all the best D words.

And now, because I was with my girls—I played along for fun. "You know, all the best things are on a stick."

Kendall nodded. "Fudgsicles."

"Deep-fried Twinkies," I added.

Kristen gave a slight tilt of her head left then right, in the way she usually did when considering something, then her expression brightened. "Cake pops!"

"That's so wrong." Hannah dropped onto the opposite wingchair with an offended expression and planted her daiquiri glass down onto Kristen's end table with an echoing clang. Hannah used to own a bakery, Sweet Dreams, until she sold it to her two star employees. Now she made designer cakes for Invitation Only's parties, in addition to spending her time starting up a riverside restaurant with Cade.

Hannah sighed, shaking her head. "*Cake* is not meant to be a single bite, like a donut hole or a chocolate truffle. And some genius made cake pops round. Real imaginative."

"No." I maneuvered an aching calf onto my opposite knee, then dug my kneecap into the tight muscle with a groan. "Darren isn't a boring single bite. He's like an enormous lollypop. Your mouth waters and you can't wait to try and tackle it. Even though you aren't sure how to. Do you take long licks? Or do you suck?"

"Suck. Definitely suck." Kendall got this dreamy faraway look.

I landed a soft punch on her shoulder. "Hey. No fantasizing about my man candy."

She held her hands up in surrender, one still clinging to the stem of her glass. "I'm speaking in generalities."

On a long sigh, I dropped my head back onto the couch cushion, then stared at the ceiling. "Well, Darren is no longer sex on a stick."

"Why not?" Kendall glanced my way when I didn't immediately answer.

Tell the truth?

Why not? Who else was I supposed to bounce my problems off of?

I took a deep breath. "Because according to Darren, I 'deserve better than a one-night fuck.'"

"You do." Hannah gave me a serious look.

My chest felt heavy. None of them knew my story:

why I kept guys at arm's length, the reason I'd quarantined them strictly into sexy-heartbreaker-but-one-night-stand territory.

But our fun girls' night didn't need to be bogged down with my issues. So I veered far away from the serious therapy talk. "Yeah, well *sometimes* a girl wants only a taste of man candy."

For years, it'd been all I wanted. Only now that I'd gotten tangled up with Darren? I'd begun to want a whole lot more from him than a taste. I swallowed hard, refusing to think about something I couldn't fully define.

"But for now, we're just friends. He's helping me train."

"For what?" Kristen glanced up, pausing her top-coating at midtoenail.

"Well, originally, it started as a 5K. Now? I'm gearing up for a trail run race."

My two sisters fell silent, eyes blinking.

"What?" My tone turned defensive. I sat up straight, glaring at them. "I could do it."

"You were always the one ditching chores." Kristen shot me an accusing eldest-sister look.

I shrugged. "Why exert myself when the two of you had cleaning and yardwork down to a science."

"And it's…*sports*." Kendall jerked out an open hand in emphasis at the end, like that last word said it all. Probably because my sole passion had been art from the second I cracked open my first Crayola box.

"Mmm-hmmm…" Kristen folded her arms across her chest, doubt in her expression.

"Are you suggesting I'm lazy?"

"Uh…*yeah.*" Kendall twisted to fully face me on the edge of the couch. She and Kristen now physically formed a united front on the topic, practically shoulder to shoulder.

"Pffft. I'm not lazy. Just lacked motivation until now."

Hannah grabbed her drink, then abandoned her faraway perch on the wingchair to rest a hip on the arm of the couch beside me. She tilted her head toward my ear. "Like sex-on-a-stick motivation."

"No." I glanced at the traitor beside me. "For your information" —I stared pointedly at each of the three of them— "I downloaded the Couch to 5K app and bought my Vibrams months before Darren ever entered into the picture."

"And he offered to train you?" Hannah asked, arching a suspicious brow.

"Yeah. Challenged me actually."

"To what?" Hannah pulled away, turning to face me now.

"To be ready for the race with his methods."

And remain just friends while doing it. But they didn't need all the details.

"And what else?" Hannah prodded.

"How do you know there's an 'else'?"

"Gut instinct." She nudged me. "C'mon. You've got to have at least a *little* ulterior motive."

"Why?" Because a normal well-adjusted girl would? And really, I had. "Okay." I played along with what they wanted to hear. "Sure." I shrugged. "If he decides when I'm all hot and sweaty that he has to have me right then and there, I might cave."

Would totally *cave.*

"Not him…all hot and sweaty?" Kendall teased.

I groaned, closing my eyes as I pictured him at the gym the other day, all flexing muscles and glistening skin. "Not helping…"

"Okay. How 'bout we change the subject?" Hannah stood, then nudged between Kristen and me on the couch. I scooted far into my corner as she took a sip of her strawberry daiquiri.

"Yes. Please." I gulped down half of mine until a threatening brain freeze stopped me.

Hannah ran a finger along the rim of her glass. "Like, for example, why I'm drinking a *virgin* daiquiri…"

A heavy pause followed—due to four women collectively holding their breaths. A heartbeat later, high-pitched screams from Kendall and Kristen pierced my eardrums. I blew out an amazed breath, staring at Hannah. She did have a glow about her.

"You're pregnant." A slow grin curved my lips.

"Yep. You're all going to all be aunties." When she leaned in for a hug, Kendall and Kristen all tackled us into our corner of the couch.

When the excitement settled and everyone moved back to their respective couch cushions, I gently poked Hannah's ribs. "I can't believe you let me go on and on about my sore calves and sex-on-a-stick talk."

"Hey, now you owe me. I'm sure I'll have plenty of sore calves and…"

Fast as lightning, I pressed a finger to her lips. "Don't you *dare* utter sex-on-anything talk about my brother."

"We'll throw you an awesome baby shower!" Kristen pushed off the couch and grabbed her laptop. "I was going to touch base with you guys about party stuff anyway."

Low groans sounded out. Kendall snatched the laptop from Kristen. "This is supposed to be girls' night. No business talk."

"Not even about a 70's themed party?"

"Oh my God." My mouth fell open.

"No way." Kendall breathed out.

Hannah blinked, then glanced at each of us. "I don't get it. What's so shocking about a 70's party?"

I jumped up, balancing on my cushion. Kendall launched from the couch, then leapt onto the wingchair.

Kendall grabbed the stem of her daiquiri glass with a closed fist, holding it a few inches from her lips like a microphone.

I did the same, then glanced down at Hannah. "In junior high, we used to stand on our parents' bed, dressed in their old clothes, singing into hairbrushes to their disco record albums."

Kristen popped up onto her end of the couch.

Hannah sat where she was on the middle cushion, clapping and laughing as Kendall began to belt out Sister Sledge. We all joined in. "*We are family…*" I crooned into my almost empty glass.

"Wait." Kristen leaned forward, then planted a hand on the wall to steady her wobbly self. "Kiki, do you still have Mom's wig?"

I grinned. "Sure do."

Kendall shot a pointed hand up to the ceiling like John Travolta in *Saturday Night Fever*. "The 'fro!"

Yep. We were already set for the Industrial Grunge party tomorrow. And we would plan Hannah an amazing baby shower. But the 70's party? Would be epic.

My thoughts flashed immediately to Darren.

He would be there.

And that would seal the friends deal. No sex on a stick for me. Because after I let my inner 70's loose? He'd think I was certifiable.

12
NEW RHYTHMS IN PLAY

Darren…

Waiting? The worst part.

The audition yesterday had gone great. At least I thought it had.

But artists needed to mesh to work together. A rare magic flowed between the best musicians. Separated out the icons from the rest. And Dino Mathis was a rising star. So whatever *he* wanted? Happened.

Nervous energy cranked tighter. From only the audition?

I blew out a hard breath. Didn't even want to consider what else it might be.

Instead, I grabbed the brushes I'd auditioned with. Drove to Nick's. Opened the garage. Grabbed my favorite drumsticks from their case. Took a seat. Then took aim.

During the basic warmup, cold air chilled my bare arms.

But at some point after I walked in, I must have turned on the heater. It glowed red from across the garage. Must've tuned my drumheads too—always did. But I didn't specifically remember that either.

Eyelids falling closed, muscle-memory flowed through my arms and legs, translating into familiar sounds. Up, down, cross-over, cross-under, forward, back, crisscross, clockwise, counterclockwise. Single-stroke roll. Double-stroke roll. Buzz roll.

Though the tempo increased, my pulse began to calm as I ran through my ingrained patterns.

Then I set the sticks down and grabbed my brushes as yesterday's session replayed in my mind: slower tempo, more fluid rhythm.

With my left hand, brush held palm up, I marked time on the snare drumhead with an easy quarter-note pulse. I struck with my right, then drew back diagonally.

Left-hand tap.

Right-hand arc, sweep.

On and on the session played out.

Delayed eighth note after-beat.

Left-hand sweep.

Cymbal brush scrape.

Bass drum soft pedal.

Dino had been in the sound booth, arms crossed, expression intent—almost the entire time. He, his saxophone player, his manager, and the sound engineer had given me sheet music. I'd played it once through, then repeated by memory with my eyes closed, adding subtle improv elements where I thought the music could handle it.

When I'd opened my eyes, they'd leaned in toward one another, talking animatedly.

Then the manager stepped out to give me additional sheets of music. Faster tempo. More complicated changeups. And I demonstrated my skills all over again.

After a few rounds, Dino and his bandmate joined me. Well, actually, Dino began, and we joined him.

I exhaled, reliving the moment when I'd done my best to complement the jazz great.

Then the moment was over. The memory faded.

The garage grew silent.

But an electric buzz still hummed through my veins.

Kiki? *No. Not going there.*

I grabbed my sticks again. Only this time I unleashed a heavy rock rhythm. Needed to work out whatever had me on edge.

Before long, sweat broke out on my skin. I started breathing heavy. Muscles began to burn: shins, forearms, biceps, shoulders. Over and over, wood stick met drum skin, vibrations radiating up my arms, into my chest.

I *became* the rhythm.

So many things in my life would be better if Dino wanted me as his studio drummer. Graduating next year would be a technicality—wouldn't even need to finish if Dino wanted me right away. No more juggling two jobs to make ends meet; money would be a nonissue.

I could be home every night. Maybe things with Logan would improve.

There might even be a chance for a social life again.

Not a damn thing in my control about it now, though. I closed my eyes and gave myself over to the punishing rhythm. Sequences I'd practiced over the years flowed from my body through my kit and echoed off the walls.

Time warped. It usually did when I jammed by myself. What felt like a blink ended up being an hour, sometimes more. Years ago, I played for thirteen straight, not realizing it.

But my tight schedule didn't allow any room for not caring about time. Needing to stretch my legs, I stood from the stool, grabbed a water from the minifridge, then leaned over and pulled my phone from my jacket pocket.

When I clicked the side button, it lit up with the time, 4:27 p.m., and a text alert—from Kiki.

I stretched my neck left, then right, thinking about the rest of the night. I had just enough time to make it home, change, then head over to the new Eiselmann's Gallery for the setup of the Industrial Grunge party.

I stowed my favorite sticks into the box I'd made for them long ago. Cedar. Kept the elements away from the wood. And beat up as the sticks were, they were a part of my past: the original tools that helped me find what I loved about music. And I took care of them—I'd broken plenty of sticks, but never these—because they'd taken such good care of me.

Kiki's message remained in my phone. Unread. But it crept into my thoughts.

Still, I downed the rest of my water, then tossed the

bottle into the recycle bin. I punched the garage code into the keypad and waited until it closed securely.

Phone in hand, I took a lung-clearing breath before I walked to the end of the driveway. I crossed the street, opened my truck, then took a seat and shut the door. Its clang reverberated through the cab.

I stared through the windshield off into the distance. So much had changed in such a short period of time. And so much hadn't.

Past and present were colliding, morphing, becoming something new.

I'd driven to Nick's to get the anxious excitement out of my system. The new person in my life calmed me further, well beyond what the spur-of-the-moment drum session had.

Even from miles away, through the small electronic device I held in my hand, she quieted the racket in my head. And I hadn't even opened her text yet.

That's the power she'd begun to have over me. The simple fact that she'd thought of me, had taken the time to reach out.

Probably with some adorable smartass comment.

Finally, I hit the control button on the phone, opened the text.

What are you wearing?

I blinked. Then typed.

You coming on to me again, Flash?

She snapped back instantly.

NO! I meant to the party tonight?

I scowled.

Uh…don't GIRL friends do that? Trade outfit advice n shit?

Her reply came back:

It's what -I- do with my friends. Scared yet?

Shaking my head, I snorted.

Nope.

Another bubble. Another text.

Waiting…

I began typing as a grin spread on my face. The high I felt when being with her, even through texts, had become addictive.

Graphic tee. Jeans. Boots.

The usual.
Her reply fired back seconds later.

Boooring…

I ran my tongue over my teeth.

And you?

A pause, then her text appeared.

Not telling.

Figures.

Tease.

Her reply popped up.

You know it.

Wouldn't want her any other way.

Out of time, I tossed my phone down on the seat, then drove away from Nick's.

But as I headed toward my place with just enough time for a quick shower, excitement hummed through my veins. A different kind than earlier, though. A calmer, heavier anticipation warmed my blood.

All because of Kiki.

I let out a slow breath, unsure about the past and present colliding.

13
CLOSE TO THE CHEST

Kiki...

"**F**ind me something to do."

Guests had begun to arrive. Waiters with hors d'oeuvre trays rotated through the crowd. Music pulsed loudly around us, vibrating into my body—keying me up.

"There's nothing to do." Kristen glanced up from her clipboard, attaching her pen to the top edge.

I grabbed the clipboard and tugged it from her grasp.

"Hey!"

I ignored her and scanned the page.

Security? Check.

Decorations? Check.

Cake? Check.

Music?

I stared at the name beside the music slot: *Darren Cole.*

With a slow exhale, I lifted my gaze. There he stood, across the room, doing what he did at every party he'd been hired to work: jammed music.

No different than any other time.

Only tonight, *everything* felt different.

Kristen crossed her arms. "Well?"

When I turned, she arched a brow. I handed her back the clipboard. "Nothing to do."

She snorted. "Told you."

"We're running these parties too efficiently."

"Sounds like a great problem to have."

"Yeah." I slumped onto a barstool.

Cade walked up and stood beside Kristen. When he said nothing, I glanced at them.

He stared intently at me, but nudged Kristen. "What's with her?"

"If I had to diagnose it, I'd say she's lovesick."

I gasped so hard, a sudden coughing fit seized my lungs.

Cade hit my back with a couple of hard thwacks. "I concur."

With a shove to his shoulder, I pushed him out of immediate reach. "You're both delusional."

Amusement brightened both of their expressions. Kristen hugged the clipboard to her chest. "Sure it's us?"

Cade raised his arm and snapped his fingers, giving a short nod toward Ben who worked the bar behind us. "Something strong is in order."

Ben gave me an assessing once-over. "Vodka? Scotch?"

I let out an exasperated sigh. "A pomegranate martini will be fine."

Hannah sidled up alongside me, then leaned in, whispering, "What are we talking about?"

Cade nodded across the room. "Kiki and Darren."

I scowled. "No, not *Kiki and Darren*." A flashback of elementary school playgrounds and teasing kids hit my brain.

Leaning back a little, I rapped impatient knuckles on the empty bar top. "Martini?"

Seconds later, a cool glass stem slipped between my two fingers. I flashed a smile at Ben. He gave me a nod. Then I lifted the drink to my lips, touching my tongue to the sugar-dusted rim before taking a sip of the pink liquid.

"I dunnnooo…" Cade crossed his arms, then leaned toward Kristen. "Darren looks awfully 'busy' for someone who'd already laid down a soundtrack for the night."

Kristen cocked her head, casting me an appraising look. "And Kiki has been desperate to find something to do, on this side of the room, looking everywhere but somewhere in particular."

Curiosity got the better of me, and I finally darted another glance toward Darren.

He stared straight at me. His arms were braced wide on the edge of his sound board. His face was tilted down ever so slightly. Gaze intense. Fierce, almost.

Then one corner of his mouth lifted.

Sudden awareness hit me. I glanced right, toward Hannah. Then left, at my meddling brother and sister. The four of us formed an evident line—and stared directly at him.

My face instantly flamed hot with embarrassment.

Cade nudged me off the stool. "Go. Correct the poor guy. He probably thinks we're talking about him."

I stumbled forward a few steps, holding my martini high to avoid spillage. Then I shot a death glare back at Cade. "There will be retribution."

He grinned wide. "Counting on it."

Huffing out an irritated breath, I turned back around and worked my way through the throng of people who milled about in the center of the room. Two slower deep breaths later, and three feet from the raised temporary stage where the sound booth had been installed, I mustered enough courage to look up at him.

Annnd…he's still staring at me. With a smug expression. Like he enjoyed my discomfort.

I stepped up on the platform, forcing him to turn if he still wanted to look at me.

He leaned a shoulder on the exposed brick wall, not saying a word.

After another gulp of my sweet drink, I arched a brow. "Enjoying yourself?"

"Immensely."

"At my expense, it seems."

He gave a half-shrug. "Hey, I'm just an observer here."

"Good." I waved a dismissive hand out at the peanut-gallery-three who still watched us with clear glee. "Do not read into any of that. They're just harassing me."

"*Us.*" He gave a nod to our audience across the room.

Cade had the audacity to give Darren a mini salute.

I rolled my eyes. "Fine. *Us.*"

"Why would they do that?" His penetrating gaze remained fixed on me.

To stall, I scanned over the rest of the partygoers. The turnout exceeded even our estimates. Win for Invitation Only, win for the client. As the weight of the silence between us grew, I took another taste of the sugar edging my glass. Then I took a fortifying sip.

All or nothing. "They might have thought I was interested in you. At some point."

"Oh?" He swung his gaze toward them for a brief second, before landing it squarely back on me. "And what would've given them that idea?"

My pulse quickened. My breaths shallowed. He stood mere inches away, and I swore I felt the heat of his body, smelled the incredible scent of his skin.

"Ummm…" Yeah. Stalling didn't take the pain of humiliation away. It only prolonged it. When dealing with Band-Aids, experts recommended a brave ripping over cowardly peeling.

"I *might* have called you sex on a stick. Once."

His eyes widened. The corners of his mouth twitched. He pulled away from the wall, evening his weight on both legs… presumably to not topple over. Then he barked out laughter.

I frowned. "Not funny."

"Nope." He struggled to regain his composure. "That shit's hilarious."

On a huff, I turned away from him, squaring my

shoulders against the cold brick wall. Then I stared up at the high-raftered ceiling, searching for my patience somewhere up in those metal girders. "Was a long time ago."

"How long ago?"

"Ancient." Sudden déjà vu hit me. We'd had the same dialog. Only it had been about the last time I'd had sex. *Wonderful.*

"Nice outfit, by the way." His tone softened. The humor left his eyes but a steady warmth remained.

Pulling my drink away from my chest, I glanced down at my outfit. Chrome beading covered the thin strap of a tank top that disappeared under a faded black sweatshirt. My knees stuck out of the holes of acid-washed and majorly shredded 501's. I'd had to wear sensible black underwear that covered my ass, since another one of those shred-holes ventilated just under my left butt cheek. Strappy metallic-leather stilettos let my lilac-painted toenails peek out.

"Thanks." I let out a relieved breath, then smiled at him. "I was going for *Flashdance.*"

"Achieved."

For the first time all night, I appraised his outfit. The one he'd texted me about earlier. Tee, jeans, boots. Yeah. Not a damn thing boring about it. Probably because of who was in it.

"You look good too." Weak. My nonchalant tone sounded believable, though.

He didn't seem to care. Just scanned the crowd again.

The reprieve gave me a chance to collect myself: to try to be unaffected by how close we stood, ignore the butterflies dancing in my stomach—the slow heat spreading downward from my flushed face…settling between my legs into a delicious ache.

I swallowed hard. Then downed the rest of my drink.

"This would be a great place to show your art." He crossed his arms, scanning the room.

"Yeah." I'd initially thought so too. Relaxing back, with the ball of one foot propped on the wall, I examined the space from an artist's eye. Rusted I-beams supported the massive roof. The concrete floor had been burnished with an acid treatment, rich reddish-brown and black swirls covering the roughed surface. Exposed brick lined only the wall we leaned against. Along the back and across from us, ivory plaster served as a backdrop for giant black-and-white photographs that matched the industrial theme. All were prized collector pieces, historical photos from atop skyscrapers and bridges in various stages of construction.

"Don't sound so thrilled." He glanced at me, brows raised. "Aren't you in another gallery?"

I huffed out a held breath, wincing inwardly—I hoped. I felt as if my brave face was failing. "Yeah."

When Kristen had told me the party was for a new gallery opening, I thought I could handle it. No biggie. Been to plenty of art exhibitions.

My opening in December had been the high point of my life. Hopes and dreams had been pinned to that one night. And it had been a wild success.

But in the months that followed, it had twisted into the worst mistake of my life. Well, second worst. Trusting business associates apparently equated to trusting men. Inadvisable.

"Aren't you able to show in more than one?"

I gave a slow nod. "Sure." Wasn't the issue. Sticking my neck out again was.

He nudged me. "Go for it. They already have metalwork displayed." He nodded to one of the handful of pedestals arranged throughout the room. Small industrial cogs from much larger machines had been welded into a modern-yet-rustic piece.

"I suppose I could ask." Didn't mean I had to commit. Or even seriously consider.

"Look at the sculpture on the other side of the bar." He tugged on my arm, forcing me to push off from the safety of the wall. Both of his hands curved around my upper arms from behind. Then he tightened his grip ever so slightly and pulled me against him, holding me captive.

My body tensed, heart racing as his heat permeated through the threadbare cotton of my jeans. Warm gusts of his breath rustled the hair above my ear. The stubble of his jawline scratched along my cheek as he leaned forward.

Mouth gone bone dry, I swallowed hard.

Then I did my best to focus on what he'd pointed out.

Beyond an exquisite cake Hannah and her team from Sweet Dreams had designed that depicted a historic flour mill stood a polished steel replica of *The Illinois*, Frank Lloyd Wright's mile-high cantilevered vision that had never come to pass.

Mind scrambled by how close Darren hovered, I

stumbled on any intelligent words. "It's…nice."

"I've seen your mailbox."

A soft laugh escaped my throat, body relaxing against him before I realized it had happened. "So you're saying my random junkyard art will fit right in?

His hands released their hold on my arms. They moved forward, first landing on my hips, then sliding around until they locked together, pressed firmly against my belly.

I stopped breathing for a moment, closed my eyes, and basked in how good it felt to just let myself go and be held: warm, solid—sure. For the first time in longer than I could remember, I gave in, didn't fight the impulse to pull away and put on my armor.

And for the briefest moment, as Darren literally supported me with his intoxicating embrace, I pretended he was one of the good guys, would protect me no matter what might happen, that whatever had begun slowly unfurling between us was real—that *he* was real.

When he took a deep breath, his chest expanding and shifting me a fraction away from him, he quickly compensated, tightening his hold, pulling me closer.

"What do you have to lose?"

I let out a shaky breath.

Everything.

14

PLAYING WITH FIRE

Darren…

Three days. Sixty-nine hours and thirty-seven minutes, to be exact. Apparently, that was the amount of time it took for me to go nearly insane.

Just to be near Kiki again.

I'd never been so crazy about a girl before—never allowed myself to get that close.

Now, I could finally breathe easy again. Because she sat across from me laughing. Her hair was pulled up into a messy ponytail; pieces of her dark hair had escaped, framing her face. Pink brightened her cheeks. Long dark lashes blinked over bright blue eyes.

Beautiful. And she didn't try to be—seemed to have no clue she was.

We'd shifted our Tuesday run to late afternoon—at my

request. Then we ran a new longer trail that skirted the other side of town. On our way back, we hit up my favorite dive burger joint on the corner of 6th and Elm.

Her laughter at my weak joke died down, and she took a long pull of her near-empty beer. "So why the time shift?"

My attention had gotten stuck on her bra strap. It peeked out from under the collar of the worn gray T-shirt she'd changed into after the run. An inch-long band of white lace crossed her delicate collarbone before it vanished under the cotton. My focus lowered. And before I could stop the thought, I imagined the rest of the bra as I watched the tempting curves of her chest rise and fall with each breath.

"Heeellooo…" She waved a hand over the table between us, in my line of sight.

I cleared my throat. And my head. Not a damn thing I could do to clear the blood from where it had rushed. I shifted uncomfortably on the booth. "Had to sign an employment contract this morning."

Blinking, she clanked her empty bottle on the table. "You got a job?"

"Not just any job. *The* job. Dino Mathis, huge in the jazz world, hired me as his studio drummer."

"That's awesome, Darren. Congratulations!" She grabbed her already waiting refresher bottle and angled it toward the one I held.

"Thanks." We clinked bottle necks. "To new beginnings." As I stared into her eyes, hers widened a fraction at the toast, then softened as her smile grew.

"To new beginnings." She took a deep breath as she stared back, gaze intensifying.

How much of that toast meant *us* to her? To me, for that matter. I had no idea.

I sensed the hesitation she had around me. Hell, I had serious reservations about how close we'd already gotten. And we *had* made the agreement to be just friends.

Shit, I *needed* things to stay platonic. At least, I thought that was the right thing to do.

But with every passing day, the time I spent getting closer to her, I wasn't so sure.

We'd stumbled into a definite gray area, one where the closeness of friends had transformed us into some undefinable *other* thing. Deeper. And dangerous.

Because while I watched her, her gaze lowered to my lips. Her breaths quickened as she stared at my mouth with unmistakable want.

I sucked in a deep breath, arousal still lingering behind my fly.

My gaze dropped to her mouth too.

Those pouting kissable lips of hers parted.

My mind fuzzed out about the reasons we shouldn't be going there.

We leaned toward each other, forearms braced on the tiny table of our half-booth.

Our breaths began to mingle as inches of space disappeared between us.

Consequences be damned, we were about to kiss—throw the whole "just friends" thing out the window.

A loud clank startled us.

We blinked hard as two identical plates slid onto the

varnished wood, and we instantly pulled our arms off the table to make room. Both of us took a deep breath, gazes locked, as we reclined back to our respective sides.

She licked her lips, then tugged a side of the lower one behind her teeth. Her eyes darkened, lids drifting slightly closed, as if she could taste me even though we hadn't yet touched.

But we almost had. She'd wanted to. Fuck, *I'd* wanted to.

The air between us hung thick with tension.

I pursed my lips, let out a hard breath. "So, yeah." I raked a hand through my hair. "Seems like today is the day for it."

"New beginnings." Her words had gone soft, tone flattening them into a statement.

Because it didn't matter that we hadn't touched physically. A line had already been crossed.

On a deep breath, she finally broke our gaze, then blinked, glancing around as if she'd been in a trance. Then she looked down at her plate. Her brows twisted downward, expression growing doubtful as she leaned forward sniffing the air above it.

"Doesn't look edible." She poked at the mushrooms and onions with her fork.

And just like that, things between us lightened. Veered back into friend territory.

I let out a relieved sigh, comfortable with things staying safe between us. For now, at least. "It's good for you."

"What is it again?" She leaned left and tilted her head, examining it from the side.

"Chipotle ranch burger, no bun."

"How can it be a burger with no bun? It's ground steak, at this point."

"Try it. We've got all the food groups here. Fuel for our bodies."

She eyed her food with suspicion. "Since when is grease a food group?"

"Eat, smartass. Then you can judge."

Only after I took a hefty bite of my mushroom-and-onion topped burger, complete with its layer of grease and chipotle ranch sauce, did she venture a bite. She took a good sized one too.

Then her eyes drifted shut, head tilting back. She let out a low moan while chewing slowly.

Something hit me, low and visceral. Arousal, and more. I wanted to be the one to have that effect on her. If that was what one bite of a halfway-decent burger did to her? I wanted to explore every kind of reaction she had to pleasure.

Realizing my brows had lifted, I swallowed hard. Then I blew out a lungful of air, regaining *some* semblance of composure.

Get your shit together, D.

Her eyes suddenly blinked open as she swallowed down her food. She began fanning the air in front of her wide open mouth. "Hot! So hot!"

I choked out a surprised laugh; the woman had me on an emotional rollercoaster.

"Here." I dipped a sweet potato fry into her honey mustard dressing and handed it to her. "Puts the fire out."

Then I let out a long sigh and watched her devour her food.

Yep. Kiki Michaelson had me up and down. Turned on, then turned inside-out. Torture one minute—teasing laughter the next.

I'd never had anything close with anyone else.

In just a couple of weeks, she'd twisted my view of the world into something unrecognizable—scary and unpredictable.

Yet inadvisable as it was, I wanted it.

I wanted her.

The only problem?

I wasn't sure I had a right to want her—let alone have her.

15
HEIGHTENED AWARENESS

Kiki…

The vibration of the truck seat turned me on as the imported beer-and-a-half buzzed through me. And a sky that had been a smoky purplish-gray minutes ago finally shifted into full-on darkness.

We were in Darren's truck at night, him driving me home. Again. Alcohol obliterated my inhibitions. *Again.*

No matter how many lies we'd told ourselves between that last nightclub drop-off and now, no matter how afraid I was of the powerful attraction between us, what it could do to me…how it could devastate me…I wanted to get closer.

I wanted him. No amount of logic changed that fact: My body had an agenda completely separate from my heart and mind.

He shifted his leg wider, pressing a knee against mine.

Turned on beyond reason, the near-shock of the contact jolted an electric current outward. Upward. The sensation sizzled up the inside of my thigh until it reached right between my legs. My pulse throbbed there. Hot. Heavy.

I stared at the seemingly innocent spot where knee touched knee. Then I swallowed hard and sucked in a shaky breath.

Only after a slow, long exhale did I dare speak. "Is your skin prickling?"

He'd been a marble statue for the last few minutes, inches away, yet only moving his hands on the wheel to make slight driving corrections.

But at my comment, his low chuckle boomed out. Then nothing.

I pressed my lips together, fighting a smile. Because it wasn't funny. Even though it was. "It's like the air in here has supercharged."

"The air in here." His deep voice spoke the words slow and flat. Like he pondered each word, searching for hidden meaning.

I moved closer, pressing my entire thigh along his, making him adjust left for the intrusion. "Maybe it's not the air."

"Probably not." He stole a glance at me.

Even in the dim light, I caught it. Hard to miss. In that brief moment, with the supercharged air—that wasn't really the air—a spark ignited. White hot and glowing. Even if neither of us could see it, in spite of the fact that we didn't want to admit it, we both felt it.

A connection pulled taut between us. Always there, but undeniable and growing stronger.

Just like it had when we'd almost *kissed.*

His right hand released its grip from the wheel and lowered toward me.

On instinct, I reached toward him, wanting to grasp his hand.

Enough with the elusive thing we'd been dancing around, too afraid to embrace. Alcohol had dulled my senses. And I was tired. And lonely.

Maybe it wouldn't be so bad with him. Maybe he wasn't like other guys.

A buzz stuttered into the tense silence.

His hand froze in midair a mere inch from mine. He shot a quick glance at the road, then down at the carpeted floorboard. His phone screen glowed in soft blue up at us.

He leaned forward and scooped up the phone, pressing the side button to light it back up. "*Fuck.*" He spat out the word on a sharp exhale.

Without warning, he simultaneously spun the wheel hard and grabbed my forearm to prevent me from jerking toward my door.

"Gotta make a quick stop." His brows pinched together.

I straightened, sobering instantly.

The formerly heat-charged air? Iced over.

Lines etched into his forehead as he gripped the top of the steering wheel, wringing the leather-covered metal so hard it looked ready to bend under the crushing pressure. His chest expanded slowly, froze when he held his breath for a beat, then collapsed with a hard whoosh.

I frowned. "Is everything okay?"

Clearly it wasn't. I'd never seen him like this. Anger emanated from him. And something more. Something unidentifiable.

"No. But it will be. *Has* to be." The last three words were barely audible.

Unsure what to do to ease his distress, I put a hand on his knee and squeezed. Wasn't much. But when his next breath exhaled a little calmer, I was glad I'd made the effort.

"Want to talk about it?"

"No."

I shouldn't have taken the curt word to heart. His rejection wasn't personal. I got that. But we'd been so close only seconds ago. Now it felt like we were a million miles apart.

The moment the truck jolted to a stop alongside an old redbrick apartment building, he flung open his door and jumped out.

When I opened my door too, he popped his head back into the cab. He gave me a pleading look on a heavy exhale. "I'm sorry about the detour. But I need you to stay here."

I shot him a deadpan look. "You're kidding." I glanced out the windshield at the sketchy neighborhood. Trash clumped the gutters. A couple of vagrants wandered the streets.

"*Please.*" As he stared at me, he started breathing heavy. And bouncing. Like his legs wanted to sprint toward his undisclosed destination, but he couldn't race off until I fired the starting gun.

"Go." I couldn't stand to see his tortured expression. Not if I caused any part of it.

He pressed the automatic door lock and a loud click sounded before he slammed his door shut and ran off.

Inhale. Exhale.

My legs began to bounce too as nervous energy spun tighter and tighter inside me. I needed to tear off after him. I could convince myself he wasn't in his right mind and didn't realize that even with the doors locked, I wasn't safe against some thug with a gun or a baseball bat. But really, a need to somehow protect him from an unknown threat, and an overriding curiosity about the man who shared very little about his life, won out.

I jumped out, relocked the doors before shoving mine shut, then ran after him into the lobby. The elevator doors were just closing. I watched as each floor number momentarily lit up until the one farthest right stayed illuminated: 5.

Searching around the corner, I found the stairwell.

"Piece of cake," I muttered under my breath as I leapt onto the first step, then jogged upward. "Like a metal mountain."

Echoes bounced off the walls from my footfalls.

My thighs began burning between the third and fourth floors. On my way up to the fifth, my pace slowed.

An incredibly steep *metal mountain.*

Sucking serious wind, I reached the fifth-floor landing. But before I opened the door, I heard a low creak then a louder clang from somewhere above. I glanced up, contemplating. Only five floors total. That had to be the roof.

I inhaled deeply, trying to calm my breaths. Then I

grasped the handle and eased open the fifth-floor door. I leaned my head inside the hall. All was quiet. No hum of the elevator. No footsteps or voices.

I chewed on my lower lip, then stared upward again. I figured the odds were fifty-fifty. Darren either went to the roof, or a tenant was up there smoking a joint—or growing an entire marijuana garden. Hell, maybe on Tuesday nights, the building threw a rooftop barbeque.

Steeling my nerves, preparing myself for whatever unknown lay ahead, I pivoted on my heel and jogged the last flight up to the rooftop. I'd already gone rogue by leaving the truck. No point in wimping out now.

Cool air feathered over my face as I climbed the last few steps. The door stood ajar a few inches, propped open with a weathered red brick.

Muffled voices filtered through the crack as I pressed a palm to the cold metal door and pushed it open. The familiar creak sounded out again after I stepped through, but I gripped the edge of the door, preventing it from crashing into the brick.

I moved away from the door, creeping forward, drawn toward the voices. A dark figure came into view, beyond a cluster of vent stacks.

Darren. I knew his posture anywhere: wide stance, arms crossed, which broadened his shoulders and made normally large him seem even more imposing. His head tilted slightly, expression softening.

He inhaled a slow breath before letting it out. "Please, Lo. Get off the ledge."

My heart shot into my throat. *Ledge?*

A few more steps, and I reached the vent stacks. Five feet in height, they no longer hid me from view. Still, I hovered in the warmer air beside them, trying not to intrude.

"No, D." A female voice. "You don't need to save me. You can't. I just…needed you here."

Another couple of steps to the side, and I'd be able to see who "Lo" was. Well, her shape mostly. Two industrial lights on either side of the stairwell door behind me cast the pair hovering near the building's edge in hazy shadow. All I could make out was that she had tousled dark hair and wore a faded jeans jacket.

He opened his arms, reaching for her. "You're scaring me. I hate it when you come here."

"No!" She blasted an open palm toward Darren.

I froze, terrified of what she might do.

A broken sob tore free from her throat. "I…just needed to be here with her. And you."

One more step brought me a little closer. Then another. Some internal need drove me slowly forward, as if I could help more than just Darren.

A rock crunched under my shoe.

Both of them jerked around to face me.

"I told you to wait in the truck," he growled.

"Who's that?" The girl asked, brows furrowed. She twisted further around to face me.

My focus was stuck on her precarious position, and how she now had one hip hung over the edge of her perch. I'd done that. I'd made her turn, possibly worsening the situation.

In the dim light, her features struck me as familiar, but I couldn't place from where. I swallowed hard, already committed. "I'm Kiki."

"Sounds like a pet's name."

I let out a short laugh, mostly from nervousness. Then I clasped my hands together in front of my chin, silently pleading with her, Darren—the universe at large—that my presence in this unpredictable standoff would only be a good thing.

Darren narrowed his eyes at me.

I shrugged. "You asked me to stay in the truck. I took your request under advisement, then declined."

Lo snorted.

I dropped my hands to my hips. "And it *is* a pet name. Kiki is short for Katherine."

Darren recrossed his arms, continuing to glare at me.

"I'm Logan."

"And she was just about to come away from the ledge," Darren grumbled.

"No. I wasn't. Kiki was about to join me."

I was?

Unbelievably, his expression hardened further. "No, she isn't."

The challenge in his booming voice pricked the daredevil side of me.

"Yes, she is." I had no idea what made me say that, or why I stepped the rest of the way toward them. But I went with the crazy idea, heart pounding faster and faster as I approached the ledge on the other side of Logan.

When I glanced down at her, a flash of bright pink glimmered from amid darker locks of hair. Recognition hit. *The girl with the guitar from his garage band.*

Only back then, I'd thought they were close, romantically. Now, I didn't get that feeling. Too much irritation hummed in the air around us and none of it had to do with me being there.

Darren simply stared at me, jaw dropping with an incredulous expression, while I lowered myself down with tremendous care.

Yeah…no way in hell I'm biting it off the edge of a building tonight.

Logan gave him a put-out look. One that said *trust me.*

When Darren still didn't move, I tilted my head, giving him what I hoped was a reassuring look. "I've got this." I mouthed. Then I nodded toward where I'd been standing, where I'd been able to hear their conversation more clearly.

His jaw shut and he cast me a doubtful expression. But he finally moved away from us and toward the shadowed area of the vent stacks.

"Nice to finally meet you, Kiki. I knew someone had to be dragging Darren away." She leaned toward me, lowering her voice. "Bet he didn't tell you about me."

"No," I admitted quietly. "Didn't realize I was a secret either."

She shrugged. "He's pretty protective of me."

Everything began weighing heavier as information was revealed—against Darren's plan.

And as the seconds ticked by, a phrase he'd said more

than once kept repeating in my brain. *It's complicated.*

I had a strong feeling she was the complication. "Nice to meet you too, Logan."

She glanced at me, narrowing her eyes a fraction as if assessing my worth. Then her lips twitched and she gave a slight nod. Like she'd decided to induct me into the members-only club the two of them belonged too. "I'm Darren's sister."

Okay. That suddenly made sense.

I huffed out a breath I hadn't realized I'd been holding.

Then I waited. Because my gut screamed that it was *still* more complicated than that.

16

PAST AND PRESENT COLLIDING

Darren…

There they were. The two people in the world I was crazy about. Worried about.

Logan and Kiki.

Standing in an acoustical sweet spot, I could hear every word. Every frustrated sigh.

"I don't come here to jump, you know." Logan leaned back on straightened arms, her hands gripping the bottom edge of the worn brick.

"No?" Kiki glanced at her.

Logan shook her head. "*She* jumped."

There it is.

Felt like a gut punch every time.

A long pause followed. Almost a full minute ticked by. Finally, quietly, Kiki asked, "She?"

Tipping her head back, Logan exhaled hard. "Our mom."

Kiki gasped softly. "I'm so sorry."

My eyes never left the two girls most important to me, my sister, who my whole world revolved around, and Kiki, who'd unexpectedly breathed new life into it. But both leaned backward toward the building, sitting inches from one another. Safe, for now.

Logan let out a heavy sigh. "I come here to feel close to her."

Kiki glanced at her. "You do?"

"Yeah. She suffered on the inside. Me and D knew that. We tried to help. But depression wrecks a person. Makes them not be able to feel the good that everyone else tries to share with them."

After another long pause, Kiki swayed a little closer to Logan and nudged her shoulder. "Sounds like you understand her."

"I do."

"You suffer from depression too?"

Logan shrugged, took a deep breath, then exhaled slowly. "Yeah."

Kiki nodded. Nothing more.

"Sometimes the meds help. Most times they don't. But even when it gets bad, and I find myself up here, on the same ledge she stood on…in her last seconds…I still don't want to jump."

"Good," Kiki said. "That's good."

I blew out a relieved breath. A part of me had hoped that's why my sister often texted me from up here. She'd just needed me to be here with her, talk her away from the ledge. But she'd never opened up about the why's of it. Maybe I'd been too fucking scared to ask.

"Means I'm not yet as bad as she was. We didn't understand her." Logan's voice broke, and her head hung lower. Then she glanced up and sniffed. "Me and D didn't get how bad it was, or we would have done something."

My heart burned as I listened to my sister's version of the story I'd lived. She paused long enough for another sob to tear free from her throat.

Kiki instantly slung an arm around her shoulder.

Logan leaned in toward the comfort. She'd never let me get close enough on that edge to touch her. But Kiki, she let in.

And none of it mattered up here. Logan needed something and Kiki could provide it. Meant more than anything I could've done.

Logan's voice quieted to the point I had to take a few steps closer and strain to hear her above the wind. "I miss her. I miss…family."

Her pain shredded me. I'd been so busy juggling responsibilities, I'd slacked off on the one thing that mattered—the very reason why I'd never gotten serious with a girl. Yet it all still fell short. I hadn't been holding up my end of the bargain…taking care of my family.

Kiki squeezed her shoulder. "You busy this Sunday afternoon?"

Logan choked out a laugh. "Why? Wanna meet back up here in the light of day?"

"Nope. My brother, Cade, and his new wife, Hannah, are throwing a barbeque."

"I don't…I'm not sure." Logan eased away from Kiki, tilting her head. "How many people will be there?"

"You *have* to come. There won't be 'people' there. It's family. Not just Cade and Hannah, but Ben and Mase, his friends. They're like my brothers. And Chloe and Daniel are coming, they're the owners at Hannah's old bakery. And Ava, our dog."

The spot in the center of my chest warmed—not a burning hole like a minute ago, more like an ember glowing back to life. Kiki hadn't meant it's *her* family. She meant they were Logan's family too, our family, if we wanted to be included.

Instead of replying, Logan leaned back and swung her legs around to the roof side of the ledge, back to safety. She stood, then walked toward me. In the dim light, I saw dried blackish tear-tracks down her face, from all the dark mascara and eyeliner she wore.

But hope shone in her eyes as she lifted her brows. "Could we go?"

I roped an arm around her neck and kissed the top of her head, grateful as hell to have her by my side, safe and sound. "Yeah, we can go."

When I glanced toward Kiki, she stood and brushed her hands together, dusting them off.

"Thank you," I mouthed to her.

She let out a hard breath. Then a crooked half-smile curved her lips. She mouthed back, "You're welcome."

"Okay, ladies. It's cold as fuck up here. Can we go home now?"

Logan wrapped an arm around my waist. "You're giving me a ride home, right?"

"Damn straight, I am. With a lecture about walking this neighborhood at night."

Or at all. But I didn't say the last part. I got it now. Up on the roof, with Kiki to support her, Logan had shared more than she ever had with me.

And I'd thought bringing another person into the mix would be a bad thing.

Then again, Kiki wasn't just *any* other person.

17
EXPOSED

Darren and Logan didn't live far from the apartment building we'd just come from: an eight minute truck ride. And Darren had lectured Logan about walking bad neighborhoods—at night—all the way home. Logan had answered with heavy sighs and placating *Yes, D*'s when he wanted her to promise not to go there alone.

I'd insisted we go to their place first–drop Logan off and get her settled before he took me home. She needed that. And curiosity had me wanting to see where they lived…where he went at night to lay his head down to sleep.

I wasn't sure what I'd expected. But what I saw surprised me. The yard once had grass, but it had long ago died. Instead, a wasteland of dirt stretched between islands of brown matted plant-matter. Two dilapidated pots sat on the left side of each step that led to the front stoop. The cracked lower terra-cotta one had a faded garden gnome who had fallen on his back, cherub cheeks plumped into a smile. The deep blue glazed one held nothing more than dry soil. A wooden swing hung from the overhang to the right, its white paint cracking and peeling.

Logan pulled open a frayed screen door, the frame of which Darren held while she grabbed his keys from his outstretched hand. The wood door she unlocked was caked with years of dirt on its decorative trim molding. The windows were dark; cardboard secured by curling duct tape covered the bottom pane of the one behind the swing.

Once I stepped inside, my attention drifted toward the only light, where it had been left on above the stove. A white refrigerator had dozens of magnets on its side-by-side doors. A small round farmers table, with four spindled chairs tucked beneath, sat in the far corner near a large *intact* window.

"'Night, Kiki." Logan's flowery shampoo filled my next breath as she pulled me into a fierce hug, her tousled hair covering my face. "Glad I met you."

"Me too." I gave her a hard squeeze back.

Then she ran up a dark staircase. "'Night, D," she called out when she reached the landing, not bothering to look back.

"G'night." His voice was thready.

When I glanced over, he had a puzzled look on his face.

I frowned. "You okay?"

He blinked, then shook his head, his expression growing more bewildered. "Yeah."

"Bullshit. What's wrong?" Music suddenly blared from above, so loud it vibrated the ceiling.

"You mean, besides the fact I had to rescue her once again from a rooftop?"

"*We*," I pointed out. "And your sister didn't seem to need rescuing."

"And yet you did. You rescued her. Me." His eyes slowly widened as his gaze shot back up to the top of the stairs. "All this time I'd been keeping women away from here—away from her—because I thought she needed me. Thought she'd be upset or jealous of attention I paid to someone else."

"She does need you." I put a hand on his chest.

He tore his gaze from the staircase and stared down at me. "She needs you too."

The solemn tone of his voice startled me. And scared me a little. I backed away, then turned to survey the rest of the room. I gave a halfhearted shrug to divert attention, lighten all the heavy. "She's a kid. Kid's need love. How old is she?"

"Almost sixteen."

"She driving yet?"

"No. Hasn't shown any interest in it. When I offered to take her to get her learner's permit, she changed the subject."

I walked toward the fireplace, turning on a table lamp along the way. On the mantle, tarnished silver and worn wooden frames held photos of their family. All pictured the three of them. One was taken at the park. Another had them posing next to the Hershey's Chocolate World sign. I picked up a third that looked like it had been taken at a county fair; rides twirled in the background above their heads. Their faces? Stuck through the holes of a painted scene, attached to the caricatured bodies of farm animals—his on a big bull with a tiny head.

"Maybe she doesn't want to be that responsible yet." I thought about how Logan had pined for family. Then I replaced the picture; I didn't want to disturb their cherished memories more than I already had.

"Probably." His breath parted the hair on the back of my neck.

I jumped, knocking back into him, startled that he'd moved so close without me realizing it.

On a hard swallow, I stepped away from him. For some reason, I suddenly needed distance between us. Even though just hours ago I'd nearly jumped his bones in a diner, then later in his truck. The rooftop had changed that. And being in his home only magnified the enormous pause-button on my libido.

The rest of his living room confused me. A metal rod had been propped between the far side of the mantle and the outer wall of the house. On the makeshift closet rod, flannel shirts hung from hangers beside a winter jacket. T-shirts were slung over the back of a green upholstered chair; its cushion held three pairs of folded jeans.

To my right, a faded striped couch had been mostly covered with a pale blue sheet. A flattened bed pillow with a matching pillowcase rested on one end. The other end had a brown, yellow, and orange crocheted afghan bunched into a ball.

Blinking, I spun around, practically bumping into Darren again.

I spotted more clothes thrown over every piece of furniture. Shoes had been lined up by the baseboard. Textbooks were stacked on the end of a tall sofa table that had been pushed against a wall; its other end held the light I'd switched on earlier. A wooden chair, the same style as in the kitchen, had been tucked under it.

I stared a beat longer at the makeshift study desk, glanced at the clothes, then the sheet-covered couch. "You live down here?"

"Yeah." He gave a hard nod, then walked into the dark kitchen. "Want something to drink?"

"In the living room? But…why? Isn't there a bedroom for you?"

He didn't respond. When I twisted to face him, he stood half-turned in front of the open refrigerator, its inner light shining on his face. He raised a brow, then nodded toward the top shelf which was loaded with bottles of beer and cans of soda.

"I'll have a beer." The earlier two from dinner had worn off. And the event on the roof, plus all the new information, had amped me up.

"It was easier to move down here." He popped open both beers and let the lids skitter across the counter before they stopped at a wall of stacked mail. "When my mom…"

His voice cracked at the mention of her. Then his face screwed up in frustration as he handed me my beer.

I put a gentle hand on his forearm. "How long has it been?"

"Just over two years."

I took a fortifying few swallows. But then I put the bottle on the counter, suddenly deciding I needed to remain sober. We were venturing into unfamiliar territory for me: depression, surviving a loved one's suicide—dealing with that unimaginable loss.

My heart ached for him. For both of them. When he said nothing further, I stayed safe and stated the obvious. "You haven't talked about it much."

"Not at all." He gripped his beer with a tight fist around its neck, then chugged a good half of the bottle before coming up for air.

"It's okay if you don't want to."

"No." His eyes searched mine. "For the first time, I do. After it happened, I buried myself in everything I had to do to keep Logan and me afloat: made sure I was able to be her legal guardian, lightened my school load…took on more than one job to cover bills."

"That's amazing, Darren."

"I love my sister. Had no choice. No way was she going into foster care."

"And that explains this" —I gestured to his living-room-turned-bedroom— "how?"

The corner of his mouth tilted up just a little. "When she…"

He exhaled a sharp breath, took a few more swallows of beer. "After it happened, Logan was a mess. She refused to give Mom up. The house only has two bedrooms: Mom's and ours. One day, about a week later, I came back from work to find Logan had moved out of our shared room and into

Mom's. She'd dragged all of her clothes into there and locked herself in."

"Oh, wow." I couldn't imagine all of the memories that had to be in their mom's room. Her clothes. Her personal treasures. Her bed.

"*Plus* my stereo system and all my music," he grumbled.

"What?" I huffed out a laugh. "The music?" I listened as the evidence still blared loudly. "Alternative?"

He nodded. "Some jazz. Lotta blues and heavier rock too. She plays it nonstop. Mostly the depressing stuff. But… it seems to be her way of coping. So I let her be."

My thoughts drifted back to the rooftop, of his sister and her struggle. "Logan also suffers from depression?"

"Yeah. Runs in the family, I guess. We had a couple of nasty fights, with her a sobbing wreck halfway through. Then she would shut down completely—just stare at the wall. Whenever it got that bad, I couldn't get through to her. After practically begging her, I finally convinced her to see a doctor."

"Did it help?"

"Not really. The doc saw her for all of ten minutes. Gave her a prescription. The drugs only messed her up more. Then we went to a shrink the doc recommended: an easygoing middle-aged woman. But Logan seems okay with her."

"So she's a little better now?"

"Not sure how much better she is," he muttered. "She keeps ending up on that *fucking* roof."

"Right." I didn't know what else to say. I'd be shredded inside too if someone I loved hurt that much.

"She's on her fourth drug. Two mellowed her out too much. Third turned her into a rage machine. This one seems to be doing okay, so far. It's only been a week. But at least no windows are broken."

Ahhh…the cardboard and duct tape.

"And you don't feel like sleeping in your own bed?"

"Nah." He tipped up his beer, finishing the last of it, then shot the empty bottle sliding across the counter until it clinked into mine. "Even if I wanted to, who could sleep through that? Besides, she started to leave in the middle of the night to go to that damned roof. I need to make sure she doesn't sneak out."

"But don't you work at night?"

"Yeah. Have to. But we made a deal. She promised me she would be home, that I would know where she was at all times. For the two of us to make it a go on our own, it has to be that way. She understands." He sighed heavily. "Even though she sometimes breaks that promise."

"Good that she texted you. At least she's trying."

They had it rough. That they were on the same page, even with their problems, helped.

"Oh…my…" Something I hadn't noticed earlier grabbed my attention. I crossed the room, then lifted a small black T-shirt from where it had been carefully laid out on a far table in the corner. "This is…"

"Animal."

"I was going to say *adorable*." The shaggy Muppet character beamed his toothy grin at us, drumsticks raised high.

Darren smiled and took the tiny shirt from me, spreading his open palm under it. "Animal is the reason I became a drummer. I loved watching him, and Mom encouraged me. She bought me this T-shirt for Christmas when I was four. She bought me my first snare drum the following year."

"That's awesome." My heart warmed at the story. I gently plucked the shirt from his hand by its shoulder seams, then arranged it on the table exactly as it had been.

The song above changed again. This time into a thumping pulse that stirred my soul. "What is that song?"

He cocked his head, angling an ear upward. "That's 'Jungle' by X Ambassadors with Jamie N Commons. Another drag rhythm."

Like he'd been playing at the garage. And I now realized, Logan.

"C'mere." He tore the sheet off the couch and whipped it up in the air, letting it settle flat onto the floor. "Lay on your stomach. I'll show you."

I hesitated, narrowing my eyes.

He arched his brows, then grabbed my hand and tugged downward.

"Okay." I turned my head, watching him as I narrowed my eyes again. "But no funny business." The entire night had unsettled me.

"Trust me."

Unsure about whether it was him or me I worried about trusting, I stuffed down my apprehension and stretched onto the floor.

The moment I relaxed, firm hands pressed onto the

center of my back. They spread apart, one toward my butt, the other, my shoulders. Then he began drumming with the rhythm of the song. At first, a light patter. Then a heavier beat.

"There's the drag." He thumped down harder at the end of a set of four. "That last downstroke—it's as far as you can drag out the beat before you lose the rhythm."

The contact was intimate. Drumming was his passion. With those muscular forearms, he gently pounded the rhythm that flowed from his head onto my body. Warmth traveled from his touch. The thumping grew heavier, harder.

When he spread his hands wide during a pause, then brought them back in again, his hand slipped under my shirt. The calluses on his fingertips tickled as he traced lightly up my skin, dragging the material upward. Then he began drumming with greater intensity on my flesh. My shirt kept working up, exposing more and more of me.

His fingers slipped under my bra strap. Then he pulled against the stretchy fabric, pausing. "Skin-only okay?"

Unable to think straight or form a reply, I gave a quick nod.

Then with a flick, the tension slacked. I sucked in a ragged breath, mind blown that he'd taken the liberty—and I was letting him.

He smoothed his hands over my bare skin, then resumed drumming. As if he hadn't just partially undressed me.

The intimacy of the moment grew.

My breaths shortened with every thump of his hands.

The freshly bared territory that he used expanded, first

venturing up toward my shoulders, then down, all the way to the top line of my hips, lower over my ass cheeks. Heat flooded everywhere, arousal ratcheting up with every heavy beat of my heart.

The song ended. His hands stilled in the growing silence, resting on me.

And I felt exposed. Not just from the pulled-up T-shirt and unfastened bra.

From everything: the sister I hadn't known about; the story of their mom and his childhood; learning of his struggle, how difficult he'd had it, why he'd never let a woman get close.

I sucked in a hard breath, then shot backward onto my bent legs. I clutched my shirt and bra to my chest. "I…I need to go."

With big gulps of air, I tried to calm myself.

"Now?" Surprise tightened his features.

I nodded wildly, reaching back to refasten my bra. "Yeah. It's been a long day."

Filled with lots of unexpected events.

And one big revelation.

I'd let it go too far without realizing it—I'd let Darren get too close.

18
RUNNING IN CIRCLES

Darren…

Kiki had gotten spooked.

Normally a happy chatterbox, for the last day and a half, she'd pulled back to one-word answers in texts. Hadn't answered my calls.

Yeah, I got it. We were both trying to deal with new shit.

In fact, Tuesday night shocked the hell out of me. Not because of Logan being on the roof, but how my sister reacted to another girl anywhere near me. She'd been interested in Kiki, had drawn her closer, wanted to get to know her.

Which was a first. A complete one-eighty from the cold indifference or hateful glares that had happened in the past.

And yet, I was different with Kiki too. Maybe that was the reason.

But the sudden frostiness from Kiki? Not cool. And it ended today.

I couldn't wait until afternoon to see her. So last night, I'd requested a morning run.

Her reply?

Fine

When I woke up, I sent another:

Meet you at your place.

The same one-word gem fired back, minutes later:

Fine

Today I would push her. See what she was made of. Physically. Mentally.

Because I no longer wanted Kiki at a distance. Her as just a friend would no longer work. And I for damn sure didn't want her for only a one-night stand.

No. Kiki didn't know it yet, but if she wanted to run from me? I would chase.

I pulled beside her car, then shifted into park. But I didn't get a chance to cut the engine before she opened the passenger door and climbed onto her seat.

"Hi!" She fastened her seatbelt, then stared at me.

Her tone had an unhealthy level of cheer so early in the morning. And I hadn't had enough caffeine yet. When

I reached to the floorboard to grab the tray of coffees I'd brought, she bent down at the same time.

Our arms brushed, her left, my right.

The backs of our hands touched for a brief second. Our fingers tangled together. And we paused there, like the shock of the contact needed a moment to settle in, and we didn't want to break away, not yet.

Until we did. Suddenly. She yanked her hand back, curling it into her chest. Then she cleared her throat and with her other hand, lifted the cardboard tray.

We both leaned back, out of apparent danger.

She unscrewed her coffee from its holder, then lifted the tray, offering me mine. I stared at her the entire time while I grabbed my cup, waiting for her to say something.

Until she didn't. And I'd had enough of the awkward. "You okay?"

"Of course."

Flippant.

"Bullshit." Yep. I was calling it.

"I'm fine."

"No, you're not."

She inhaled a deep breath, then let out a heavy sigh, her upper body collapsing against the seatback. "It's too early to talk so much. Can't we just run?"

"No. We talk. And it's way beyond time for it."

"Fine." There was that word again—no better said than texted. "What do you want to talk about?"

"Us."

"There is no 'us.'"

I let out dry laugh. "Keep telling yourself that. Doesn't make it any truer."

She brought her cup to her lips, took several swallows while staring at the dashboard, then pulled the paper cup down to her lap. She stared at it, picking at the seam of the protective sleeve at the top until it pried apart.

In a quiet voice, she finally said, "There can't be an 'us.'"

"Why not?"

"There just can't."

"I'm calling bullshit again. Throwing a big yellow bullshit-fowl flag into the air."

"Haven't you ever been rejected before? You're not taking this very well."

"Not from a woman who wanted me."

"Do not."

"Do too." In the silence that followed, our words echoed in my head. "What are we, five?"

Amusement flashed in her eyes. "Apparently."

"What's the problem? You wanted me. I had roadblocks to that happening. They're gone now."

"Did you ever consider that I only wanted you when I couldn't have you?"

"That makes no sense."

"Sure it does." She crossed her arms over her chest. "You were fair game when I could have something only physical. Now it's too late."

"*Buuullshit.*" My new favorite word. But there was a big stinking pile of it between us, and I wasn't done shoveling yet.

"Truth." She gave a half-shrug.

"Maybe your misguided understanding of it. Look, Kiki. I haven't been able to have *any* kind of relationship with a girl since…since Logan bottled up and lashed out."

"What's suddenly changed?"

"She seems to like you."

"That's part of the problem." Her voice quieted.

"What? I still don't get it."

"That's the reason we" —she pointed a finger back and forth between our chests— "can never happen."

I narrowed my eyes. "*Why* is that, exactly?"

She stared at me, tilted her head a little, then exhaled a slow breath, compassion softening her expression. Her voice lowered. "Because I *like* you."

My chest felt heavy at the weight of her statement: the tone in which she said it, like that fact represented our beginning and end, and the way she stared at me, like she wanted me so badly but for all of our sakes had resigned herself to the fact that it could never happen.

Shit had gotten too real in here.

We were in serious need of some mood lightening.

"So you wanted to fuck my brains out when you *didn't* like me?"

The corners of her mouth twitched. "Pretty much."

"But now that I'm a decent guy, sex is off the table?"

"Not…quite."

Confused as hell, I shook my head, gripped the steering wheel, and put the truck in gear. So I was *close* to the reason, but no cigar. "Don't follow. Gonna need more."

We pulled out of her neighborhood, then onto the highway toward the longer trail I'd planned on tackling before she replied. "It's complicated."

I grunted. "Sounds familiar."

Yet my excuse thrown back at me didn't sit well in my gut.

"Sooo…do you need help with gear for the 70's party?" Kiki crossed her arms over her chest again.

"Nope." Yep. If she was going to shut down and change topics, I wasn't playing along. In fact, I thought as I sped down the highway more determined than ever, I wasn't *playing* at all.

19
A MOMENT OF GRAVITY

Kiki...

As Darren drove and the tension in his truck thickened, my thoughts twisted into a chaotic mess. My head began to hurt. It matched my aching heart.

Shutting him down bothered me, but I had no choice.

I couldn't handle more.

Fear had paralyzed me the moment I'd let down my guard on his living room floor—that I could want someone that badly, straight to my soul; that I might reach for it, let it happen.

And then lose it. *Lose him.*

Better to have loved and lost? My ass. Loss after love was devastating. It shredded you apart. It crippled your ability to trust in love ever again.

Or maybe that was just me.

But my heart felt heavy with guilt the entire ride to the trailhead. Darren's frustration radiated off of him. I didn't want to close him out, but letting him in wasn't an option.

The instant we parked, he shoved open his door. "Let's go, Flash. You wanna survive this race, we've gotta up your game."

I jumped out as his door slammed shut. "Up my game?"

"You started the training methods I emailed you about, right?"

"Yes. Even-paced trail runs. On alternating days, wind sprints on the uphills."

"Good. Today's a new trail, but this run's also for time. Four miles. Push your limits. Sprint the steeps. Run the straightaways."

Right. Punishment. "And the downhills?"

He dropped me a deadpan expression. "Use your head."

Don't fall on it, in other words. "Got it."

While he tightened his left shoe, I tore off, running toward the gentle incline of the trail. After nearly two weeks of running every day, I knew my upwards speed, knew when my muscles burned, knew how much I'd get from them before they gave out.

All I could hear were my own footfalls, my pulse pounding in my ears, the rasp of my breath from my parted lips. A brisk north wind chilled my face. The branches of the pine trees swayed.

As I fell into the rhythm of the run, all thoughts in my head melted away.

A slow burn warmed my muscles. But I pushed them

further. Not solely because Darren had challenged me. Also because I enjoyed the reprieve and didn't want to deal with him right now. Our early arrival at the remote trail—plus my head start—gave me a run in solitude.

And he was far behind me. Or so I'd thought.

On the first steep incline, he barreled ahead.

"Show off!" I accused as I pushed my legs.

"Keep up, Flash. Let's see whatcha got."

Resolve pulsed through me, fueling my drive to run harder. Sure, he had longer legs, hence a longer stride. And maybe he'd been running longer than I had.

But he hadn't been training daily.

And I had a sudden determination to best him. His actions reeked of him thinking he could win at this. I needed to prove to myself that I was in control, no matter the obstacles.

He remained ahead of me during the rest of the punishing incline. On the straightaway, I gained ground, but I slowed to catch my breath, pacing myself.

On the second left-hand turn, I passed him.

For the rest of the run, I never looked back.

I could feel him right behind me, though.

The new trail was glorious. Lots of surprises. Plenty of hairpin turns and challenging climbs. Two recent bends had moss-covered boulders that stair-stepped upward; one, I had to scrabble over its enormous granite surface.

The challenging run left no room for anything other than pinpoint focus on the task at hand.

On several downhill sections, I pushed my pace: not

quite walking, not quite running, but instead planting one foot after the other in a focused stair-stepping power march. A couple of times, an avalanche of small pebbles caused me to power slide several feet, but I never lost my footing.

The last turn came and went.

At the end of the four-mile loop, muscles screaming, breaths coming in ragged gasps, I pushed my body to its breaking point; I forced my legs to sprint toward the imaginary finish line, marked by the trailhead's large information board.

Still running over the packed-dirt surface, I shot my arms up into the air and spun around, jogging backward. "Haaa!" I shouted into the wilderness. My echo followed.

Darren jogged down the trail, a slight smile on his face.

As I ran in place, claiming my victory, my heel caught on something.

A split second later, the ground slammed into me. Hard.

"Ow." I groaned at a flash of pain in my head.

"Shit. Kiki, you okay?" He hovered over me in an instant, blocking out the sun.

I pressed the heel of my hand against my eyebrow. "Don't know yet."

He pulled off my sunglasses. "Open your eyes."

The moment I did, he stared into them. Clinically.

"Pupils are good." Leaning forward, he palpated my head, running his fingers over my scalp.

"Ow!" I winced as fresh pain lanced through my skull.

He eased the pressure, but still rubbed his fingertips over a bruised spot. "No concussion. But you're gonna have a good-sized knot there."

"Cade always says I'm hardheaded," I muttered.

"Your brother knows you well." He stared at me, amusement sparkling in his eyes.

I slowly dropped my head.

He cradled the back of it until it rested on the ground. "What about the rest of you?"

Still breathing hard from my finish-line sprint, I gingerly pushed myself up.

He nodded toward the straps of my Camelbak. "The water bag protected your spine." But my black yoga pants had dirt scuff marks on my right hip. He tugged down the waist of my pants until a bleeding scrape appeared.

I leaned forward enough to see it was superficial. "That's not so bad."

"Nothing a Band-Aid won't fix."

"Have one of those handy?"

He gave a short nod. "Got a first aid kit in the truck."

When he held out a hand, I took it, then winced as my elbow brushed against my side. After pulling both sleeves up, I found two more scrapes: a matching set, one on each elbow.

"Can't believe I bit it at the end. With all the sprinting up boulders and negotiating down rocky crevasses, I have to fall at the very end…jogging in place."

He let out a slow breath as he raised a hand toward my face. With a gentle touch, he held my chin with his forefinger and thumb. He searched my eyes, intensity shining in his steadfast gaze. "You let your guard down."

"Yeah." Exactly what I was so damned afraid of.

20
ENOUGH

Darren...

Saturday night. Another two days of silence from Kiki. Except for a text from her that morning:

Skipping run today

No explanation.

You okay?

About ten long minutes later, her reply popped up.

Yeah

Wasn't sure what irritated me more, my disappointment or her lame-ass reply.

"Fuck it," I bit out under my breath. I shoved off the couch and jogged up the stairs, following the sounds of Nirvana's "Lithium."

Logan had left her door open a crack. She never did that. Typically it was closed and locked. I flattened a palm on the center of it and pushed it halfway open.

I let out a slow breath and just stood there, watching my sister sit in the middle of the queen-sized bed, arms wrapped around her bent knees. Eyes wide open, she stared blankly at a spot on the flowery comforter two feet in front of her.

Loud music thumped around us, her on her bed, me in the doorway. I wondered how many times she'd been holed up behind a closed door, totally zoned out with music hiding her pain.

My heart ached for her.

I felt like an intruder. But maybe me barging into her space was what she needed, the open door a hint.

Unwilling to stand unnoticed any longer, I knocked.

Her only response was a heavy blink.

I cleared my throat, raising my voice a notch above the bass decibels. "Logan?"

A few more blinks followed. Then she grabbed the remote, turned down the volume, and turned her head toward me. "Oh, hey, D."

"You okay?" The themed question of the day.

"Yeah."

Oh, *hell* no. Enough with my girls and their pat answers. "Doesn't look like it."

"I'm good." She shrugged. "Just bluesy again."

"Again? What about the meds? And Doc Jamison? Didn't you say she was helping?"

"I stopped taking the new stuff. It made my heart race and my hands shake."

Fucking drugs. "So, you're off the meds?"

She gave me a nod.

Part of me was relieved. She'd burned through them with no real improvement. But the risky alternative scared me shitless. "And Doc Jamison? Does she know?"

"I'm going to tell her on Tuesday. She already told me if I couldn't handle it to lower the dosage. I just stopped taking it."

"And you're feeling better?"

She finally glanced up at me, her lips tilting into a half-smile. "*Define* better."

A little sarcasm. Good. "No more heart-racing and hand-shaking?"

"No more of that."

"But still the depression. As bad as a couple of years ago?"

Her brow wrinkled. "No. It feels different."

I leaned a shoulder against the doorframe. "Different how?"

"Less drowning in an abyss of despair. More…numb?" Her voice held a tone of humor, uncertainty.

I snorted. "Numb sounds better than 'abyss of despair.'"

I shoved off from the doorway and took a seat at the foot of the bed, checking out her room from the inside, for once.

The bed didn't have a chance to settle with my weight

before she scooted forward to sit beside me. When I lifted my arm, she nudged under it and rested her head against my shoulder.

"I like what you've done with the space."

The lamp had a blue scarf, one of Logan's, thrown over the top. On the wall above the bed, a strand of white Christmas lights hung over a collage of sorts: twine had been crisscrossed in a diamond pattern, magazine clippings and music CD jackets tucked underneath.

My attention paused at the low dresser beside the closet. On one side, a silver picture frame sat behind a small pewter box. Aside from the furniture, they were all that I could see of our mom's belongings—the only personal items.

"Thanks." Her gaze followed mine. "It's been a work in progress."

"We all are, you know."

"You mean I'm not the only one?"

I huffed out a dry laugh. "Hell, no. We're all screwed up. It's the great test of life: how strong we keep fighting no matter what the world throws at us."

"Why didn't Mom fight harder?"

Heart heavy, I tried to speak, but had to force a swallow past the lump in my throat. "She fought as hard as she could, Lo."

What I keep telling myself every day. Truth or not, was the only way I could deal with it.

Silence surrounded us. She wrapped her arms around my waist and took a deep breath.

Pain burned in my chest, and I let out a hard sigh, rubbing

my sternum with the heel of one hand while I tightened my other arm around Logan.

"*We* are fighting to survive. We have each other. All that matters."

"Will we…ever be" —her voice broke and she cleared her throat— "*happy* again?"

"Yeah, we will."

"How do you know?"

Because I've already caught glimpses of it. With Kiki.

"When we look for the good in this world in spite of the bad? *That's* when we find happiness."

She gave a slow nod. "Maybe just small things, at first."

"Sure." I thought about what I'd busied myself with. "Gotta put yourself out there when you feel ready."

"Would it be okay if I watered the lawn? Planted flowers in the pots?"

I coughed out a surprised laugh. "Don't need my permission."

"But can we afford it?"

"Yes. You buy all the flowers you want." Whatever it took. But then the real question she'd been trying to ask hit me—time with each other. "We'll go to the nursery together. Maybe tomorrow. Gonna need a whole lot more than water to revive our front yard. Probably some sod, the space is small enough."

My spirits lifted. It would be good to do a project with her.

When she pulled away, her eyes glittered with unshed tears. But her face brightened with a smile. "I'd like that."

"You know you can talk with me anytime, right? You can leave the door open and let me in. Doesn't have to be an urgent text from a rooftop."

"Yeah, I know."

"Good." At least I hadn't failed to let her know I was there for her. "We're family. I want you to know I've got your back."

"I do." She took a deep breath, then let it out. "You understand why I go to the roof, right?"

"I understand what you've told me...and Kiki." Which wasn't much. She'd said she wanted to be close to our mom. Yet being in her room felt like all of the best parts of Mom. The roof? Felt like the worst. "Scares the fuck out of me whenever you're up there."

"I'll never jump. That's the point. If I've inherited depression from Mom, I can't help that. But I can control what I do with it. It's like a test for me. That no matter how bad I feel, I'm never gonna jump. I feel like Mom sees me up there. And…maybe she's proud of me for knowing that."

I half-turned, then wrapped both arms around her, squeezing her tight. "*I'm* proud of you. And when you really need to go, let me know. I'll be there with you."

Logan sniffed. "Thanks."

Torn between my original mission and our recent epiphany, I just sat there and held her.

All of a sudden, she shoved at my ribs. "Okay. Enough of the touchy-feely."

When I pulled away, she wiped her fingers over her eyes, smearing her eye makeup, and sniffed a couple more times. Then she glanced around, confused, as if just now realizing

I'd entered her sacred space for the first time in over two years. "Did you need something?"

"Yeah. *My music.* Thief." I stood from the bed and pulled a CD from the lineup while scanning for more.

"*My* music," she corrected. "Possession rules. And there's a time limit on claiming your stuff."

"Whatever you tell yourself to keep your loot and sleep at night."

As I collected CDs, her head pressed into view under me. She folded her arms onto the desk, rested her chin on them, then glanced up at me. "What are you doing, anyway? Isn't your DJ music at Loading Zone? I thought this was your personal stash."

"Aha! So you admit it's mine."

"*Ours.*" She pulled the top CD from my hand, then flipped it over. "What. Are. You. *Doooing*?"

"Grabbing some music for Kiki."

"A playlist?"

"No. Not a 'playlist.' It's not a sappy romance thing."

"Doesn't have to be sappy or romance. And you're doing it all wrong."

I dropped her a deadpan look. "I'm doing it wrong." The statement bordered on ridiculous.

"Yep. Put those back. We'll burn a playlist." When I hesitated, wondering how we'd do that without the source, she grabbed them from me and carefully filed them back in their open slots.

She sat in her chair and powered up her computer. "I've got all your songs in a database. Which ones do you want?"

Amazed at how she'd perked right up at the thought of helping me, I sat back on the edge of the bed behind her. "'The Stroke' by Billy Squier, 'I Wish It Would Rain Down' by Phil Collins, and 'Pour Some Sugar on Me' by Def Leppard."

At the last, she glanced back, face contorted into an odd mix of revulsion and confusion. "You're kidding."

I arched my brows. "You helping or mocking?"

Her expression softened into mild amusement as she raised her hands in mock surrender. "Helping."

"Then load songs, no questions."

Halfway through the next ten minutes, as I gave her additional songs, Logan figured out what they had in common. She nixed one of my choices and added two others. Then she popped in a blank disk and began burning the playlist. "You sure she has a CD player?"

"No." I hadn't thought of that. *I'm a DJ for fuck's sake.* But apparently, my brain fuzzed when it came to all things Kiki.

"Give me your phone." She held out her hand.

Before giving it to her, I glanced at the screen to see if Kiki had sent *anything*. Nope. Of course not.

Lo grabbed it impatiently, and I was left staring at my hand. Then she pulled out a cord from her top desk drawer and plugged my phone into her computer. "Just in case."

"Thanks," I said, amazed at how quick she was to figure out the playlist theme. Then I took a second look at the way she'd organized my music CD's before my attention landed on her bass guitar leaning against the wall. "You're *really* getting into music."

"Yeah." She handed my phone back to me. "You love it so much."

"And?"

She'd been jamming with the band the past couple of months after I bought her the guitar for Christmas. She'd gotten a few private lessons from Nick. But every other time I'd asked about it, she'd been tight-lipped and shrugged.

But tonight, something had changed. Like enough time had passed, and we'd finally broken through the cloud of loss that had hung thick between us.

Her gaze grew unfocused for a second in thought. Then she smiled wide—the biggest smile I'd seen on her in way too long. "I love it too." Her tone had lowered, reverent.

"Awesome." Pride filled my chest. "Anytime you want help with it, let me know."

"Thanks. But I want to do this on my own."

I gave her an understanding nod. "Hey, you sure you're gonna be okay alone tonight?" My thoughts flew to the despondent girl I'd seen on the bed not twenty minutes ago. No way in hell would I leave her on a high note only to have her spiral back down.

"Yeah, I'm good. Trevor's coming over."

"Trevor?"

"It's cool. He's been here before."

"*He has*?" I ground out, unable to stop the shift in my tone.

"Relax. He's helping me with the tighter riffs I'm trying to play."

"Music. He's coming over for music. *Only*."

"Yes."

"No…sappy romantic playlists…"

"No." She gave me a stern look. "And no condoms either."

I let out a relieved sigh. "Good." I walked halfway out, then grabbed the doorframe, and glanced back. "No need for condoms with…Trevor? Or no need for condoms…ever?"

She burst out laughing as I struggled with the concept. "I *will* be having sex, D. Not yet, but sometime soon. And there *will* be condoms."

"Okay. Good. I think…"

She threw a small green pillow at me when I hovered in uncertainty for too long. "Go! I promise not to do anything but music tonight."

By the time I made it over to Kiki's, I had it all worked out in my head. I'd already barged in and broken through with one of the silent women in my life; how hard could it be to do it again?

After the third heavy knock on the front door to her warehouse however, I began to wonder if I'd misjudged. I tried to open it, but it was locked. No noise came from inside, yet her car was parked just a few feet away.

I scanned the front of the building. Then I walked a few paces and rounded the corner, checking out the nearest side wall. The only windows began twelve feet off the ground. Dim light glowed from them.

Halfway down, I heard a muffled thump, like an inside door closing.

"This is ridiculous," I grumbled, feeling like a stalker as I skulked in the shadows of her building at night. I tugged my phone out of my back pocket, then texted her.

Answer your door.

By the time I walked back around the corner to the front, metal lightly scraped as she unlocked the door. A narrow shaft of light spilled through the crack as she opened it.

"Darren?"

I pushed through, stepping past her.

She gaped at me. "Gee, come in."

"Thanks." Moisture lingered in the air, along with a faint scent of vanilla. "Hope you're hungry."

"Depends. What's for dinner?" She relocked the door, then turned and crossed her arms.

"Whatever kind of Chinese you like." I held up my giant brown bag.

"What did you do, rob the place?"

"Nope. Just ordered one of every special they had. Figured one of 'em had to be your favorite."

Her lips pressed into a line as she fought a smile. "That confident?"

"Yep."

She stared at me a beat longer, then turned. "Okay. C'mon, then."

In near-darkness, I followed her through her maze of metal sculptures. We passed the sitting area, with its couches draped in clothes. We walked by her worktable, covered in an array of unopened envelopes.

She led me to the metal staircase that connected to her overhead loft.

As we climbed the stairs, the soft curls of her hair glistened whenever we stepped into the occasional beams of light from above. She wore a long-sleeved black T-shirt and cotton-flannel pajama bottoms. The muffled clank with every step she took came from a pair of green-and-blue plaid slippers, their sheepskin trim peeking out each time she took the next step up.

"You're not sick?" No sniffles. She looked great, complexion full of color.

"No."

Okay. "But no run today?"

"No, I ran."

"Just not with me." I suspected it had to do with the other night, yet we ran on Thursday. And that seemed to go okay. Mostly.

"I just needed time to think. Alone."

When we got to the top, she opened the door and stepped in.

The inside of her loft looked nothing like the stark metal outside. Soft colors on the walls and furnishings made the space a cozy home. The kitchen in front had a good amount of cabinets, stainless steel appliances, and a square butcher-block island with two barstools. Beside it sat a modern dining set with a pale gray lacquered top and four white wooden chairs. Under our feet spanned polished wooden floors.

As I looked toward the open bedroom area that was only a few feet away, she took the bag from me.

"The floor's not real wood. It's tile."

"Really? Fooled me." It looked like authentic tongue and groove, varying grains and all.

"Cheaper and more durable." The crinkle of the bag sounded out from the kitchen.

Suddenly, a brown furry head popped out from behind her light blue bed pillows. Its eyes blinked heavily.

"And the bed?" I admired the dark curving headboard while I patted the bedding. Chipmunky bounded out from his hiding place, then stalked my hand before crouching down in the center.

"Reclaimed mahogany."

Its low-slung style was simple, almost Asian.

I lifted the end of the comforter and slid my hand under it, then swept it quickly back and forth once. Chipmunky's eyes darkened. He dropped lower, back twitching. I arced my hand slowly to the right. He tracked my movements, then pounced, landing on it for a solid second, before jumping away and crouching down again.

"You're big into reusing items." Made sense with how she repurposed items to create her art and the decorating she'd done at Loading Zone.

"I am." Additional bag-crinkling stole the kitten's attention and my hand was abandoned. I followed the bounding cat into the kitchen.

Kiki pointed a fork toward the space above the dining table. "Salvaged the chandelier from a hotel demolition. The bathroom's sliding barn door came from a local farm. Cabinets from an old church. Corkboard on the walls for sound."

"Where'd the cork come from?"

"*A tree*?" Her lips twitched into a smirk.

Ahhh…smartass. Well, it was a helluva lot better than the recent silent-and-avoid treatment. Since she'd already arranged the takeout boxes in the center of the table, I took a seat.

She tossed the large paper bag into the air over open floor space. The instant the bag settled, Chipmunky darted into it. Then one section of the bag punched outward. Seconds later, another punch in a different spot deformed the bag and it collapsed.

She opened her fridge. "Want a beer?"

"Sure."

"A fork? Chopsticks?"

"Fork."

She brought two bottles over, dropped one in front of me, then stabbed two forks into a couple of random containers. The Styrofoam soup cup already had a spoon sticking out of it.

"So…you're not avoiding me." I grabbed the nearest fork, then bit a sweet and sour pork chunk off of it.

"Oh, I am." She leaned over, surveying the cartons, then forked up some almond chicken.

I chewed, then swallowed. "You suck at it."

"Apparently." She dug into a different carton, popped another forkful into her mouth.

"Why?" I knew what had pushed her, just didn't understand it.

"I don't do well with…commitment."

"Hence the one-night stands."

She pointed her fork at me with a nod. "He catches on quick."

"But why? Who hurt you?" It was the only explanation.

"Not talkin' about it." She laid her fork down, lifted the spoon from its cup, blew on the steaming liquid's surface, then slurped it down. She followed with a couple more spoonfuls before moving on to another container, another forkful.

She didn't look up from the food. *Silent again.*

"Okay." I had experience with protective walls with Logan. You didn't push too hard with emotional shit. You waited until they were ready.

"What about you?"

"Me?" I glanced up from digging into the nearest container to find her staring intently at me.

"Why no girlfriend?" She scooped up a forkful of shrimp fried rice into her mouth.

I grabbed a spring roll, dipped into the mustard then the sweet and sour before taking a bite. "It's…"

"Complicated," she completed. "I remember."

"Yeah. Lot to do with Logan."

"Hey. No need to explain."

Good. Because the reasons had begun to fade. And things had gotten a whole lot more complicated. All to do with the girl sitting in front of me.

"So, which is it?" I arched a brow at her.

The corner of her mouth quirked up. "Which Chinese dish?"

I nodded, then I stuffed a spoonful of beef and broccoli into my mouth.

"I dunnooo…" She surveyed the spread. "You sure you got one of everything?"

Blinking, I stared from box to box. "Moo goo gai pan. Egg foo yong. Egg drop soup. Sweet and sour pork. Chicken dumplings."

She twirled her fork into the shrimp lo mein. "Sure you didn't miss anything?"

"Okay. I didn't get *everything*. But I got the most common dishes. I figured you weren't a chow mein girl. And anything with lobster sauce seemed like overkill."

With an amused expression, she stuffed the fork-load of lo mein noodles into her mouth. Not a timid little bite—a huge mouthful of food.

After she chewed, swallowed, then took a long draw of her beer, she dropped her fork and pushed her hands against the edge of the table before settling back in her chair.

"Well?" I arched my brows, stabbing my fork into the fried rice container.

She swept another glance across the Chinese takeout buffet. "Undecided."

"Fair enough." Wasn't why I'd come tonight. "You got a place to play music?"

Her face scrunched into an adorable confused expression. Then she got up and began folding closed the few cartons that had leftovers. I stood, then cradled the boxes in my hands before helping her load them into the refrigerator. The shelves inside were neatly organized, glass containers of food with plastic lids stacked on every shelf.

"You know, a music plugin?" I pulled my phone from my back pocket, then held it up, shaking it back and forth.

"Oh." Her eyes widened slightly.

Okay. She was still spooked.

"Listen, about the other night, I—"

"No. I'm good. Let's not make a big deal out of it."

aka: I don't want to talk about it.

Tough shit.

She reached for my phone, but I pulled it back at the last second.

Unable to stop her forward momentum, she crashed against my chest. Her breaths quickened as her hands spread wide. Then she slowly glanced up.

Fear shone in her eyes. Desire too.

I brushed a damp lock from in front of her eyes, then tucked it behind her ear. Damn, she was beautiful. No makeup, hair messy, cheeks pinked, and looking at me like she wanted me—but was terrified to go after what she wanted.

"It *was* a big deal. And I'm sorry." I'd crossed an unmarked line. I knew that now.

She sucked in a hard breath, tears welling in her eyes. Then she scrunched her brows, blinked several times, and swiped the phone out of my hand while she pushed out of my reach.

"Thanks," she said softly as she took backward steps away from me. "And apology accepted."

She smiled, holding up my stolen phone as if she'd won her prize, had escaped my grasp.

I twisted my lips into a smirk as I watched her back away.

Go ahead, Kiki. Run.

When I really catch you…I'm never letting go.

21
FINDING THE UNDERTONES

Kiki…

Darren stared at me with heat in his gaze. His breaths slowed, intensified.

I backed up, caught too deep in a danger zone I hadn't seen coming.

Girls can't have guy friends. I'd heard people say it. But had never believed it. Mase was my friend. So was Ben. Stood to reason I could be friends with Darren too.

Only I couldn't. Because Darren was…well, Darren.

Unable to form any useful plan to get me out of my uncomfortable predicament, I spun around and walked the last few steps to my nightstand. Without turning, I answered his question about music. "Bose SoundDock."

"Will it fit?" The sound of his voice had grown closer.

Not sexual. His comment was not *sexual.* My heart picked

up speed anyway. I blew out a steadying breath, forcing my body to chill.

With laser-beam focus, I studied the phone, examining the port on the bottom. "Not sure. We both have iPhones, but mine's older." After I popped open the rubber cap at the bottom of his cover, I shook my head. "Your receiver is too small."

"Did the Bose come with any adapter cords?" He pressed in, watching over my shoulder.

The heat of him being right behind me fried my brain. I inhaled a slow breath through my nose, savoring his masculine scent. Then I blinked, shocked at how easily I fell prey to him.

I yanked open the nightstand drawer. "Help yourself."

Stuffed inside was a tangle of power cords. To everything. Laptop. Tablet. Phone. If there was one for the Bose, it'd be there. Thankfully, my vibrator was in the *other* nightstand.

Darren stared into the drawer, brows drawn slightly in concentration, as if unaffected by the mess. He plucked the end of one up, shook his head, then tried again. "Got it."

As he worked to untangle the cord, I kicked off my slippers before settling on the far side of the bed. He organized the remaining cords: pulled them out one by one, rolled each around his four fingers into a bundle, then tucked the ends and replaced it before grabbing the next.

I watched him, captivated by the focus etched into his face: the stern brow, the pursed lips. He was strikingly handsome in the dimmest portion of my room, shadows defining his dark features, emphasizing his strong jaw and high cheek bones.

My private observation time vanished once he shut the drawer and plugged in his phone. He scrolled across the screen a few times, then pressed the control button.

"This one should be familiar."

The song that had played at his house—when he'd been thumping a rhythm on my back—streamed its deep haunting bass through the speaker. "'Jungle' by..." I paused, unable to remember the artist.

"X Ambassadors. And it's my way of apologizing. Again. I didn't mean to make it sexual."

But it had gone there nonetheless. And so much more. From my end, anyway. I stared into his eyes, searching for a clue. It was there in the softening of his eyes. The intimate moment had been much more for him too. Whether or not he wanted to admit it. It made me wonder if it was the real reason why he'd come tonight.

"Don't. It's cool." And it was. For now. At least what I kept trying to believe. I'd made myself safe for the moment anyway: me on the far side of the bed, body turned upside down with my ass just below one pillow and my head near the middle.

He swept his gaze from my head up to my planted feet on the wall. "Uhhh...this how you listen to music?"

"Is tonight." I didn't elaborate, merely stared at my bent legs as I slid my socked feet farther up the wall. Nothing sexual...*or more*...could happen that way. I intended to make certain of it.

He pressed his lips together, amusement sparking in his eyes. "Okay."

I watched as he toed off his shoes, sat on the edge, then in one motion, swung his body around to mirror mine. Of course, with his long legs, his feet reached a good foot higher than mine, white socks pressed against my cork wall.

Unthinking, I stared at his large feet and blurted, "What size shoe do you wear?"

He bent his legs slightly. "Thirteen. You?"

My face flamed, but he appeared oblivious to my faux pas. He simply bent his legs further, pressing his feet flat on the wall and lowering them. I lined my heel up with his, trying my damnedest not to think about his broad forearms, large feet, and various other body parts that were bound to be correspondingly sized.

"Six and a half."

The song shifted. He began to drum his thumbs and pinky fingers onto his thighs. Every strike he made gave a muffled thump on the faded denim.

"This is a great example of drag rhythm," he explained, diving right into the topic of music. As if we hadn't been comparing body parts. As if my mind hadn't guttered.

Several other songs played. With each, he gave a blow-by-blow commentary of the rhythms and where they dragged.

A long pause happened after the most recent song ended. His quiet voice filled the sudden silence. "You know, you don't have to be afraid of us. Of you and me."

"I don't?" I pressed my hands up my pajama pants as "The Trouble With Love Is" by Kelly Clarkson began to play.

"No."

"What makes you think I am?" Had the word CHICKEN been stamped on my forehead?

"I don't *think* anything."

"Oh." My heart began to thump harder. I took a deep breath, trying to calm it.

"I *know*." He turned his head toward me.

I didn't reply. Couldn't really refute the truth. Instead I met his penetrating stare, searched his eyes for some sign that he really was a good guy. I felt he was. I sensed a girl could surrender, become engrossed in him—yet never truly lose herself. And still, I hid behind the enormous protective wall I'd erected years ago.

I glanced back up at the cork wall above us. At my striped socks and his athletic ones. I thought about how we'd met at a nightclub, were brought together by Invitation Only business, then had grown closer through a sport I'd decided to pursue.

His excuse about why we had to be "just friends" popped into my head. *It's complicated.*

"Do you miss your mom…think about her a lot?" The question came from nowhere, but it seemed like the right one to ask. And after being in his house, and our closeness while side by side on my bed, it felt like we'd gotten to the point where we could be random and it would be okay.

"Yeah." His tone quieted. "I hide it. Helps to stay busy. Gotta be strong for Logan." His voice started to crack and he cleared his throat.

I turned my head a little, watching as he stared up at the metal rafters above us. As the soulful music played, I thought about the words. About loss and love. "What's your favorite memory?"

The tiniest smile tugged at the corner of his mouth. He shifted to tuck his hands behind his head and crossed his ankles, one heel still touching the wall. "Thanksgiving."

When he was silent after that, I arced toward him, nudging his shoulder. "Tell me about it."

He let out a slow breath, like the memory was cherished and he didn't want to rush it. "All we could afford were turkey sandwiches. But Mom got the good deli meat, cranberry sauce to slather on, and crusty rolls from the bakery. The best part? We were together."

After a long pause, he continued, "Was the only day of the year we got to spend the whole day just us. Logan would clang pots if we weren't up in time for the parade. The two of us kids would make a giant mess in the kitchen with our feeble attempt at pancakes while Mom sat on the couch. She'd hold her cup of coffee and coach from the family room."

"It sounds like a fantastic memory. Only Thanksgiving together? Not Christmas? What did your mom do?"

"She worked at a grocery store, but it was more like a convenience store. And Thanksgiving was the only day they closed for a full day. She worked weekend days, most weekdays, and took a double shift every chance she got."

Wow. My privileged life had been nothing like his family's struggle. "No dad?"

The song changed and heavier rock streamed from the speakers again.

He shrugged. "Not really. We have the same father, but he was a traveling salesman: never married her, home only long enough to knock her up but never long enough for me to remember him well or miss him. When I was seven, and Lo was just a baby, I realized he beat my mom." He let out a heavy breath. "One day he left and never came back."

"I'm so sorry, Darren. That's a horrible home life." On top of it all, he'd lost his mom.

"Don't be." He gave a headshake. "Wasn't that bad. Lo and I came out all right."

"At least you have each other."

"Exactly."

Talk of family made me remember the invitation I'd extended to his sister on the rooftop. "You and Logan able to make the barbeque tomorrow?"

He finally glanced my way. "Yeah. Logan's looking forward to it."

"Only Logan?" I arched a brow.

His gaze held mine. "No. Not just Logan."

Loud music streamed through the powerful speakers behind him, but the moment seemed quiet, tense and frozen. His eyes searched mine as he inhaled a slow breath. "What about you?"

"Me?" The barbeque?

"Your favorite memory."

"Oh." Because, yeah. I was looking forward to the barbeque too.

I rolled my body the other way again, relaxing onto my back, staring at our socked feet pressed to the wall. "Mine is a holiday too. Christmas Eve. Is it weird that it doesn't actually involve anyone else?"

When I glanced at him, he had partially propped onto

his side and stared at me. "Depends. What are you doing?"

I relaxed my head back and closed my eyes. "I'm standing outside. If I'm lucky, it's snowing. One winter, I think I was sixteen, it was the first snow of the season. I was standing out in our backyard and these big fat flakes floated down from a bottomless black sky. An excited hush fell over everything and everyone. I almost stopped breathing it was so beautiful: nature coating the world in pristine white; the wound-up energy underneath it all of kids going to bed, parents wrapping presents, lovers tucking a special gift into a stocking."

The rock song ended as I thought about that moment of pure happiness. Every year I had a ritual of standing outside, thinking of the snow, hearing the hush.

Silence stretched for a beat. Then another.

Right as a new song began, he cleared his throat. "You had a lover at sixteen?"

I didn't need to look his way to feel the weight of his stare. I knocked the back of my hand into his hip. "*No.* But I was a dreamer. A romantic. And I wanted to have one—imagined it happening."

Finally, he settled again beside me. His hand brushed against the back of mine, then stayed there. "Seems like you've always been a glass-half-full person."

"Ever the optimist. That's what Cade always says about me. I get caught up in the falling snow, not how it clogs the streets. And I think about the glittering presents, not some hideous sweater bound to be waiting under the wrapping."

"Like your art." His hand rubbed up, over my knuckles.

When it settled, the tips of his fingers tangled with mine.

An electric hum buzzed between us at the small contact. I flexed my hand open until the pads of my fingers brushed his. Heat spread across my skin, warming every nerve ending in a spreading cascade. A low ache began to flare between my legs.

On a hard swallow, I struggled to focus on what he'd said. "My art?"

"Sure. You find beauty in rusted scrap metal." He tightened his hand, trapping my fingers in his grasp.

"I do." My quiet admission held conviction. I stared up into the dark rafters over my carved-out home in the middle of a warehouse. I saw the world with a different perspective. Always had. And it floored me that Darren saw *me*—the girl beneath it all.

The moment hung on that note, heavy and right. We stared up toward my roof and listened to song after song. On each successive one, he pointed out the drag.

"There, do you hear it?" He thumped the thumb of his free hand hard on his thigh, marking time with the lagging beat.

I nodded, watching his thumb snap the faded denim surface, mesmerized by that one beat made all the more intriguing because of how it nearly strayed off course.

Without thought, I closed my eyes, lulled by the intoxicating sensual rhythm.

Excitement charged the air around us. My pulse thrummed, heart nearly stalling with each drag beat. Our hands remained connected, fingers loose, barely touching.

But something seemed to be happening between us, this thick unnamable thing growing more intimate with every heartbeat.

The playlist ended.

Only the sounds of our breaths remained.

His. Mine.

I swallowed hard, not opening my eyes. The anticipation, the unknown, the strange beauty of the unexpected filled my heart with a warmth I didn't want to end.

A metallic ping echoed. Then another. In the next few seconds, a thousand tiny raps tinged out against the metal high above us.

"Oh, shit." I bolted upright, blinking hard. "Is that rain?"

"Sounds like it."

Heavier raps followed, like machine gun fire, and I flew off the bed and sprinted across the room. "I left my car windows and roof open!"

Bare-socked, I raced down the stairs. His louder footfalls clanged on the metal steps right behind me.

Blinding light flashed through the south-facing windows as I swiped my keys from the corner of my worktable. A second later thunder boomed, rattling said windows.

"What's the big deal?" He nudged my shoulder once we'd cleared the last of my metal sculptures. "It's just a little rain."

"Says the man whose windows are up. Are you even listening? The sky just cracked open."

I unlocked the bolt and opened my front door a crack. The wind caught it and tore it from my grasp, slamming it against the metal wall with an echoing clang.

He reached for my keys. "I can—"

Dodging his hand, I pointed my car remote. "So can I."

Cold fat drops pelted my face as I watched for some sign that my remote had worked. "The signal's worked from here before. Think the rain's interfering?"

In a flash of movement, he snatched the key from my hand, then bolted into the downpour. I gaped, unable to say anything. He had no jacket. No shoes. Only a black T-shirt that plastered to his body in an instant, jeans, and once-white socks that browned as he ran through muddy puddles.

Halfway there, he held out his arm. My car suddenly blinked its lights. The glass began to close. He stood there, waiting until my car sealed up tight before he turned around.

Still shocked that he'd done that, I shook my head. "You're crazy."

"Better me than you." He slogged past me through the doorway.

"Why's that?"

"Because I'm bigger." He dropped me a look, one that dared me to argue.

I scowled, closing the door. "How is that even an answer?"

"Bigger body mass equals more body heat. I'm good. You'd be a Popsicle by now."

"You're a dripping mess. And don't tell me you're not cold."

"I am."

"Well, c'mon. Let's get you outta those wet clothes."

"Exactly what I hoped you'd say."

I blinked, then glared at him. "Underwear *on*."

"What makes you think I'm wearing any?"

My heart jumped into my throat, mind flashing to images of his large feet and corresponding equipment lurking behind his fly. "*Please* say you're wearing underwear."

"I'm wearing underwear." His reply was quick.

"Are you really?" My eyes narrowed a fraction.

"Yes."

"Boxers or briefs?" My cheeks flamed at the bold question. But I wanted to prepare myself.

"Boxer briefs."

I blew out a hard breath.

He didn't move. Just stared at me. Dripping. Waiting. Like he wanted to see what my next move would be.

My breaths quickened as the seconds ticked by. My gaze drifted down from his intense stare to the pulse at his throat, then to the shirt stuck to his body, defining so beautifully every ridge and groove of the muscles beneath. The image before me would make an incredible sculpture.

He lowered his head a fraction until I glanced back up at him, met his gaze.

"I'm not taking my clothes off." His tone had quieted.

I blinked again. "You're not?"

"No. I have to go. Need to check on Lo. She's got a boy over. Need to make sure *no one* takes their clothes off tonight."

"Right."

"It's important to be ready for a big step like that." He cast me a serious look.

He wasn't just talking about Lo. My thoughts scrambled at the new information I hadn't prepared for. Could I take that step? Would I *ever* be ready?

"Maybe a towel though?" He arched his brows "And my phone and shoes?" An easy smile suddenly warmed his face.

"Yes. A towel." *That*, I could do.

And as I ran back up the stairs, grabbed two of my fluffiest from the linen closet, and pulled his phone from the cord before hooking my fingers into the back of his running shoes, I pushed aside my fear about the rest.

As I'd learned in the last couple of months—with everything in my life—the only way to keep moving forward when monumental things worried me was to ignore them until I was ready to deal with them.

By the time I dropped his shoes beside him and handed him the towels, he'd already shed most of the water into a puddle on the concrete. And the unexpected storm still raged outside.

"Take those with you." I nodded to the towel he'd tucked under his arm while he rubbed the other over his head. "You may need them by the time you make it to your truck."

"Thanks." He'd taken his socks off. Must've wrung them out, because the soggy never-going-to-be-white-again things were half-tucked into the waistband of his jeans.

I stared above them at a narrow strip of exposed skin, a ripple and shadow of one of his abs, then swallowed hard.

"Tomorrow. Noon?" He wrapped the towel around the back of his neck.

"What?" I blinked, confused. My thoughts had gotten stuck on his hidden body again.

"The barbeque?" He held my gaze as he worked his feet into his shoes.

"Right. Yes." I nodded, brain finally unsticking. "I'll text you the address."

"We'll be there."

As he stared at me, indecision flashed in his eyes for a split second—like he didn't want to leave.

I pressed my lips together, unsure of what to do. I couldn't have him stay—needed him to go. But a growing part of me wanted to take a crazy risk, invite him to take those clothes off, see where it could lead.

Common sense overrode what I wanted, what he wanted.

I made the choice for us, giving him a stern look as I opened the door. "Tomorrow."

22
OPEN FLAME

Darren…

The following day, I sat on my couch and stared at our latest exchange, all eight texts, one more time. Kiki had started sending them a couple of hours ago. I'd found her first one thirty minutes after my earlier shower.

> **Thanks for the talk last night.**
> **And the songs.**
> **And the Chinese.**

I'd replied.

> **Welcome.**
> **You never picked a favorite.**

Her response fired right away.

Song?

I'd volleyed it back.

No. Chinese dish.

After that, her replies had come through slower. The next, about twenty minutes later.

Not one of them.

An instant additional text popped up.

All of them.

I smiled now. Rereading with anticipation for the next part. My response had been basic. Smug-laced from my point of view, but basic.

Good.

Her last text still stunned me.

My favorite of the 3? The talk.

The talk. I stared at her words.
She might have been spooked before. But now? She

seemed to be inviting me over to her side. What side was that exactly? A one-night stand had been out from the beginning—she knew that. Was she ready for something more than friends?

"Better prepare yourself, Kiki," I muttered.

I checked the time on my phone again, then glared up at the ceiling, impatient. "Logan! You ready?" I shouted. "It's a *barbeque* not prom."

"Coming!" She rounded the top banister corner before bounding down the stairs. "Oh, good. You're wearing jeans too. I had on a summer dress and cardigan, but looked like a preppy housewife. Then I put on shorts and a tank top. But that felt too casual."

I roped an arm around her neck and planted a kiss on the top of her head. "You look great. Perfect for a barbeque. And they'll love you no matter what you wear."

With a grin, I let out a relieved breath. It felt great seeing her want to impress others. It meant that being accepted was important to her—that the world seemed worthwhile and she wanted to be part of it again.

I was also glad I wasn't the only nervous one. Did I know everyone there? Sure. We were all loose friends through Loading Zone and Invitation Only parties that Kiki and her family ran.

But this was the first time I'd be going as something more. Someone Kiki had attached herself to—even if she didn't know it yet.

The drive over lasted only the two-and-a-half hard rock songs Lo had chosen.

"Turn right here." She glanced up from reading the map on my iPhone. "Whose house is this?"

"Hannah's." I found an empty spot along the curb and parked. "Well, now Hannah and Cade's. Kiki said this was the house Hannah grew up in."

A sign on the front door said *OUT BACK* with a long arrow underneath pointing left. We walked along the grassy side yard and through a wooden gate. We were about fifteen minutes late. Which apparently was right on time.

Down on the backyard lawn, Mase and Ben raced back and forth, playing keep-away with a barking and chasing German Shephard. Mase caught my gaze and tossed me a chin-up greeting. I replied with a slight nod as he lobbed the ball toward the far corner of the yard before the dog raced after it.

Beyond them was an aged wooden dock that led to a waterway. Houses stretched along the opposite bank. A few boats and kayaks glided over the water's surface.

Someone nudged my hip. As I turned, Kristen pulled me into a hug. "Hey, Darren. Glad you could make it." When she let go, she leaned in, lowering her voice. "Got any grilling skills? My husband thinks he's King Barbeque. If you can humble him in any way, *please* do."

I glanced at Jason who manned the massive grill. "Uh, I've flipped burgers. Burn hot dogs every time."

"Great." Defeat flattened her tone. "He'll impart his searing wisdom to yet another victim." She put her hands on my shoulders and gave a light push. "Go."

I half-turned, hesitating as I glanced at my sister.

"You must be Logan. I'm Kristen, the oldest sister. I'm very happy to meet you." She wrapped a gentle arm around Logan's shoulder. "He's got grill duty. What are you good at? Salad tossing? Table setting?"

When I didn't move, Kristen shot me a glare. "Go."

Logan arched her brows, amusement in her eyes.

I held my hands up in surrender. "Going."

On my way to the grill, I scanned the backyard for Kiki. *Not on the grass. Not on the patio.*

When I turned toward the house, the back door swung open. Cade stepped out with a large yellow bowl balanced on each hand. Hannah followed, gripping a brightly striped platter loaded with rolls.

And right behind them, her short yellow-and-green skirt gently fluttering in the breeze? *Kiki.*

She glanced my way, then beamed me a huge smile.

I swore my heart tripped.

"Ready to sauce?" A mason jar appeared in front of my face, brush sticking out of it. Jason nodded toward six sizzling racks of baby back ribs, blond spikes of hair that poked through his backwards baseball cap bobbing.

"Sure." I knew jack shit about saucing. "Light coat?"

"Yep. Got another jar if you need." He pointed his barbeque tongs at a spare jar on the shelf to his right. "Give a good swipe down each rib."

I obeyed, brushing on a thin coating.

While I smeared on sauce, I kept glancing toward the house, where Logan had disappeared with Kristen. Logan had been excited about coming, but I wanted to be sure she fit in okay—felt comfortable. Kendall came out the back door, two large pitchers in hand, one looked like iced tea, the other lemonade. Logan and Kristen immediately followed, each holding armfuls of large glasses stuffed with green napkins and silverware.

And Logan wore another one of those big smiles that I'd been missing the last couple years.

"Beer?" Jason popped open a small fridge down below.

"Yeah." I coated the last rack, then grabbed the opened bottle he offered.

He took a long pull from his, then swallowed, staring at me the whole time. His eyes narrowed a fraction, then he nodded toward the picnic table. "So you and Kiki."

That obvious?

I took a healthy few swallows, unwilling to admit anything. "We're friends. Was cool she invited us."

He flung a loose arm around my shoulders, gave the far one a gentle slap, then a squeeze. Those hair spikes bobbed repeatedly as he slowly spoke, "Awful lot of sparks flying for just 'friends.'"

He'd noticed that from where he stood at the grill?

Or maybe their close family had talked about it.

Had Kiki?

He released his grip, then began loading the ribs onto two platters.

I shrugged, acting unconcerned. "Friends attracted to each other." Truth. It had ventured far beyond that. But the simple explanation was enough to satisfy the hanging question without him digging further.

Over the next five minutes, everyone gravitated toward two picnic tables joined end on end. Platters lined the center, two with the baby back ribs, another loaded with burgers. Bowls held coleslaw and a regular garden salad. One plate held a couple dozen deviled eggs. Another had rolls piled high.

Kiki sat across from me, wearing a yellow top with thin shoulder straps, her dark hair pulled into a high ponytail. Her blue eyes sparkled in the bright midday light.

She stared at me for several beats, smile widening. Innocent. Happy.

In those heart-stopping seconds, deep emotion began to burn in my chest for the girl who had no idea how big of an impact she'd begun to have on me. And Logan.

Then my gaze swung toward Logan as she settled right beside her.

Kiki suddenly lifted her knife and clanked it on her glass of lemonade. "Introductions are in order. Some of you have already met her, but she's my new friend and Darren's sister." She wrapped an arm around Logan whose cheeks began to flush with embarrassment. "Everyone, this is Logan Cole. Logan, this is Jason, Kristen's husband. Cade, Hannah, and Kendall, who you met in the kitchen." Kiki pointed her knife as she went down the line while each person nodded or waved. "Ben, Cade's best friend since kindergarten. Mase, Cade's roommate, well, former roommate. He still lives in Cade's old house."

"Uh…for now." Mase interjected from the end of the table, grabbing a rack of ribs.

Cade's expression darkened. "What do you mean for now?"

"Oh, are you moving in with Laura?" Hannah's brows lifted as she plucked a deviled egg from the plate handed off to her.

"No." He passed Ben the bowl of coleslaw. "Laura and I broke up."

Hannah's brows fell. "Oh, I'm so sorry."

Mase gave a hard headshake, his long dark-blond bangs falling over one eye. "Don't be. She got a position with a law firm in Chicago. Wants to work hundred-hour weeks for the next few years to make junior partner. We'd been growing apart while she studied for the bar anyway."

Cade grabbed a roll and tossed it onto his plate that was piled high with food. "What's that got to do with you moving out?"

"Just got back from the South Pacific. Won a couple of windsurfing competitions down there. Might travel the globe and compete. See where that takes me."

Cade dropped his beer down with a hard clang. "You're not moving out. You will always have a room there."

Mase pegged him with a hard stare. "Thanks."

Kiki leaned over the table, looking beyond Kendall to see Mase. "That where you got the new tattoo?"

Mase nodded, lifting the cuff of his T-shirt higher over his right biceps. Clear plastic wrap covered a tribal tattoo that wound around the widest part of the muscle. "Yeah. Got it in Tahiti, day before yesterday."

A loud bang echoed and everyone snapped their attention toward the house.

"We're here!" Two voices called out in near unison.

Kiki nudged Logan. "That would be Chloe and Daniel."

"Are we late?" Chloe dressed rockabilly today: 1950's pinup-style makeup with dark arching brows, fire-red hair pulled back in a wide black headband, black-and-white polka dot dress with red neck straps and matching petticoats. Classic louder-than-life Chloe.

Daniel approached the table and turned his head left and right, surveying the spread. "Did we miss anything?" His jet-black Mohawk quivered back and forth, and his ear, nose, and brow piercings gleamed in the sunlight.

"Chloe and Daniel, this is Logan, Darren's sister."

"Nice to meet you, Logan." Chloe gave her a half-hug, then planted a bright red kiss on her cheek before taking a seat at one of the two empty place settings.

Daniel held a hand out to Logan. "This bunch of rejects behaving?"

Logan shook his hand, lips pressed into a firm line as she fought a smile. Then her expression hardened further. "Hell, no."

"Good." Daniel lumbered toward Chloe. When he sat beside her at the end of the table, he swept a casual hand toward the rest of us who all still stared at him. "Carry on."

For the next hour, lunch turned into layers of conversations. Nearly everyone had an opinion about the new ballpark going in at Fairmount Park. Hannah and Cade shared the progress of their upcoming restaurant along the Schuylkill River. Ben, Mase, and Cade analyzed the latest baseball games and debated which teams would make the playoffs this year. I got sucked into a conversation with Daniel and Chloe about the lineup at this year's Gettysburg Bluegrass Festival.

Through it all, Logan seemed to come to life. Kendall sat on her other side, Kristen opposite her, next to Jason and me. And Kiki and her sisters kept pulling Logan into every one of their topics: shoes, shopping, favorite cupcake flavors… shoes again. Logan would glance at me every now and then, broad smile on her face.

I kept staring at Kiki. Didn't care one bit if anyone noticed. Each time she caught me, she would draw in a deep breath, then exhale slowly, her smile softening.

"Who wants pie?" Kristen pushed up from the table.

"Duh." Mase said, standing with her. "Who doesn't want pie?"

Plates were cleared, everyone lending a hand by carrying something into the kitchen. Then three kinds of pie were served: cherry, apple, and strawberry-rhubarb.

Kiki didn't sit back down, however. Plate of pie in hand, she nodded toward a seating area off to the side while the others dug into their desserts at the picnic tables.

I followed right after her.

We ended up leaning against a three-foot high brick planter, watching the others as she forked small bites of cherry pie into her mouth. She'd sidled up next to me, her arm pressed against mine. The contact felt both innocent and intimate.

I put my half-eaten apple pie on the brick beside me. "Thank you for inviting us, Kiki. Logan's having a great time."

She speared a lone cherry with her fork then popped it into her mouth. "You're welcome."

"Me too." My whispered words felt heavy. But I needed her to know how much it meant.

Kiki put down her fork, then swept a slow gaze at each person.

"Friends mean everything to me. You included." She glanced at the brickwork under our feet. After a few seconds, she lifted her head and stared off into the distance. "I don't want to do anything to jeopardize that."

Fear edged her tone, and I put a gentle hand over hers. When she finally looked at me, her lower lip trembled.

I touched a finger under her chin, tilting her face up. "Hey. I don't want that either."

Disappointment tightened her face. "You don't?"

"I don't want to jeopardize our friendship."

"Oh, right."

"Maybe…you could trust me."

She sucked in a deep breath, searching my eyes. Then she let out a heavy sigh. "Maybe…"

Who hurt you? What I wanted to ask, but didn't. Something had happened to her. She'd gotten burned by a guy. Bad enough to cause her to be guarded with all others.

Logan and Mase strode into our line of sight, Mase's arm slung around her shoulders, his large black sunglasses on her face. He leaned his head toward her, mouthing something unintelligible. She burst out laughing.

"Hey!" Kiki put her plate down, then glared at Mase. "No corrupting the innocent."

"You heard the lady." He gently shoved Logan away from him. "Go easy on me."

Logan shoved him back. He roped an arm around her neck again then rubbed his knuckles over her head. She elbowed him in the ribs.

I grinned at their playful roughhousing. "What were you two laughing about?"

"Guys." Logan nudged his hip.

My smile faded.

But before I could ask, Kiki crossed her arms, leaning toward them. "What *about* guys?"

Mase gave a nod. "Told her guys were pretty much assholes until thirty."

"Hey." I snorted. "That makes us all assholes."

Logan pushed the borrowed sunglasses back up, then lifted her nose a little higher to hold them in place. "He said 'pretty much.' Not always. Or all guys."

"You misunderstand, young *padawan*." He glanced down at her. "*All guys*. All guys are assholes until one proves himself worthy."

"Exactly!" "Yeah." Kiki and I agreed simultaneously, hers voiced many decibels louder than mine.

Cade walked up right as Logan wrapped her free arm around Kiki. Then Logan and Mase began to drag Kiki away. She threw me a helpless look. Then she sighed and her expression turned serious. My thoughts flashed right back to our conversation…her fears.

As Cade leaned against the planter beside me, I remembered his warning at the club a couple weeks back.

"What did you mean when you said to be careful with Kiki?"

He took a deep breath, then let out a sigh. "She's more vulnerable than she lets on."

"Yeah, I got that."

"Keeps secrets close to her chest. She thinks I don't know. I may not know exactly what they are, but I know they're there."

"Got that too. Tough being an older brother. Gotta figure out how to protect them but still give them space."

He took a swig of beer, then gave a nod. "Wouldn't know about the older brother part. I'm the youngest."

My jaw fell open a little. "Really? Kiki seems so much… how old are you?" I pegged Cade mid-twenties, at least. Kiki seemed younger than me at twenty-two.

"Just turned twenty-five."

"And Kiki?"

"Twenty-seven…almost twenty-eight. Kendall's between Kiki and me. Kristen's the oldest."

"Huh. I had no idea Kiki was five years older than me. She seems so…"

"Young."

I nodded.

"Part of her vulnerability. I think she hasn't wanted to grow up."

Her one-night stand proposition haunted me—the way she'd been casual but determined. Had I taken her up on her offer, she wouldn't have let me stick around long enough to be at her family's barbeque, finding out more about her.

Something lay at the heart of why she didn't want anyone close.

All guys are assholes.

Kiki had reacted to Mase's comment. Enthusiastically agreed.

A burning question began to surface: Would she make an exception for me?

23
THE GREATER THE FALL

Kiki...

Over the last week, I'd gotten daily running down to a science. Once faint morning light beamed through my high windows, instead of rolling over and burrowing deeper under the covers, I'd stretch. That goal of a runner's high got my sluggish body out of bed—even if only half-awake.

Total miracle.

After a loaded protein shake down the hatch and tights pulled on to keep the spring chill out, I'd be off, driving at the early-morning hour toward one of a dozen trails I'd found on Darren's advice.

Darren.

I gripped the steering wheel. My heart leapt at the thought of him. On a deep breath, I tried to ignore that fact.

But no matter what I did, he kept edging into my mind.

Until Darren, I'd only been a "me." Solitary. The sole person in my head…in my world. Now, ready or not, I'd become a "we" in my head—in my tiny existence, one I'd carved out to protect *me*. The sudden plurality of my perspective threw me.

My stomach churned each time I analyzed the unsettling development. But then, as if planted there by hackers in my subconscious, memories of little things about him tipped the scales heavily in favor of the "we."

Could I trust him to be different?

I didn't know.

Five days ago at the barbeque, he'd hinted that he would be—that I should have faith in him. From that patio wall, I'd stared at clear evidence that men who loved their women became their unwavering heroes: Cade was for Hannah, Jason for Kristen.

But not all guys were wired the same. And girls didn't find out a guy's true worth until said guy opened up all of himself. When did that happen? Usually when the girl had already sunk all-emotions deep into him.

I parked, then began running the trail's gradual climb, mentally and physically preparing myself for its rocky steep terrain. It would demand all my concentration not to stumble.

Every footfall was calculated, each breath a cadence, as my mind let go of my worries and my body gave itself over to the exertion. An easier bend in the trail led to a challenging staircase of granite boulders ahead.

Sudden resolve bubbled up from my gut, like a last-ditch effort to settle the matter once and for all. "It's simple, Kiki," I muttered. I took a deep breath, then blew it out.

"Don't let yourself fall."

Afternoon dragged into evening as I became engrossed in my latest sculpture. Another bit of metal held with the pincers, another throw of the flame, sudden bright light filtered through the welder's helmet, and… *BAM!* The last petal of the drooping tulip-shaped flower hung in place.

I lifted my helmet to get a fresh look at it.

Rough. Delicate. *Perfect.*

With a satisfied sigh, I pulled the helmet off and set it on my worktable. Then I grabbed a chilled green tea from my minifridge under the counter and took several swallows. A bead of sweat rolled down from my hairline onto my forehead, and I wiped it with the back of my arm as I sat on a barstool.

The towering stack of unopened bills on the far corner stared expectantly at me.

I narrowed my eyes, glaring back.

Hard to play by society's rules when you got screwed by them at the same time.

Ignoring the situation didn't make it go away, but I didn't know what else to do. Denial seemed to be working—so far. But a countdown clock ticked louder and louder as the end of the month approached.

My phone buzzed, dancing a few centimeters across the table as it vibrated. The screen lit up with a number I didn't recognize, so I let it roll over to voicemail.

When it bleeped a voicemail alert a good minute-and-a-half later, I retrieved the message.

> *"Hey, Kiki. It's me. Logan. Is it okay that I called you? Hope so. Anyway…wanna hang? I could really use someone to talk to. A* **girl** *someone. If you get this in the next little bit, you know where to find me."*

I did?

The roof!

Panicked, I scooped up my keys and purse, grabbed a sweatshirt off the end of the couch, and pulled it over my head as I jogged out to my car. Then I drove off in the general direction of town I remembered being in last time and wondered if I should call Darren.

But Logan would've called Darren if she wanted him there. For some reason, she'd called me.

A red light snagged me, and I waited at the longest streetlight ever, bouncing an impatient leg. *Call him? Don't call him?*

In the end, I decided not to call right as the light turned green. I took it as a sign that I'd made the right decision.

The tall brick apartment buildings all began to look the same. The streets were one-way, and I ended up looping around in a circle. Twice.

My phone buzzed beside me. I glanced down to see the same number light up.

I turned it on and hit the speaker button.

Logan chuckled, "You've almost got it."

"How can you tell?" I craned my neck and stared out my windshield, up toward the rooftops.

"You're the only car driving five miles per hour down the street." Movement flashed back and forth up along the edge.

"Do *not* wave at me!" I growled, worried she'd fall.

"Chill. I kicked a leg out. Parallel park out front."

I yanked the wheel right, then parked behind a newer black SUV, making me feel slightly better about the sketchy neighborhood. Then I swiped a credit card into the meter for an hour's time. Hopefully we wouldn't be up there longer than that. I didn't need a bird's-eye view of my car being towed.

This time, I took the elevator. The doors slid open at the fifth floor, then I bounded up the flight of stairs to the roof and burst through the door that had been propped ajar by a brick again.

There, on the edge, sat Logan. Half-turned my way, she waved.

"You're waving." I arched my brows as I walked toward her.

She rolled her eyes, then shot me an exhausted look. "You gonna lecture me all night?"

"Depends." I curled my hands under the hem of my sweatshirt.

"On?"

Good question. I had no experience dealing with depression. But maybe I didn't need any. Logan clearly didn't think so.

"Whether or not you're gonna throw me attitude all night."

She ran her tongue over her teeth, assessing me. Then she reached back and plucked a bottle from a cardboard six-pack. One was already missing.

I took the bottle, staring at the label. "Beer?"

The fifteen-year-old with alcohol arched her brows at me.

Right. Lecture equals attitude. Got it.

Without another word, I carefully settled beside her, then popped the top of my beer with a twist. After I took a healthy gulp, I lowered the bottle to rest on my thigh. "So what's the occasion tonight?"

"What makes you think there's a reason?" Her voice softened by a small degree.

I gave her a half-shrug. "Hunch."

She didn't respond right away. In fact, for the next five minutes or so, we stared at cars driving by. Most flowed in from the direction of the highway a few blocks back. I figured the drivers were going home from their jobs in the city.

"Did Darren tell you about our mom?"

I nodded slowly as I took a swallow, then pulled the bottle from my lips. "A little."

"Aren't you curious?"

"I didn't want to pry." And I got the sense he dealt with things in his own time. Logan too.

As she began to pick at the label of her bottle, I leaned back, propping my weight on my free arm. Sitting at the edge wasn't all that dangerous, as long as one respected the need to get safely situated—and no high winds blasted us.

When she didn't respond, I glanced at her. "Do you want to talk about it?"

"No." Her clipped tone carried bite. Then she exhaled slowly. "Yes."

"I'm here. Anything you want to talk about, I'll listen. No judgment. Possibly advice: if I can and you want it. And all it will cost you is…"

When I didn't finish, she turned her head arching a brow.

I rocked my beer back and forth in my hand with a grin.

She cracked a weak smile. "Deal."

Silence continued for the rest of my full beer. The moment I put my empty down, she grabbed a refresher, popped the cap, then handed it to me.

Not wanting to offend her, I took the cold bottle. "I have to drive, you know."

"So don't slam it."

Riiight. Because I can down half a six pack and still blow under legal limit. Instead of drinking more, I propped the new bottle on my thigh, doing the responsible thing. She'd been nursing her same quarter-full beer since I'd sat down anyway.

Then, as if she'd sensed my analysis of her alcohol consumption, she chugged the rest of hers down and popped open another.

After she took a few gulps, she glanced at me. "It's kids at school. They don't…get me."

I remembered high school: the struggle of fitting in, pretending not to care what everyone thought of you, swallowing down the hurt when you were the butt of their joke.

"No one got me either." My voice quieted.

"Really?"

"Yeah. Think art student. Then stretch your mind to imagine a girl trying express her art through fashion."

She scrunched her face, as if trying to imagine it. Then her eyes slowly widened.

"Yeah." Novelty didn't go over well in my private school.

I didn't want to talk about my teenaged nightmare, though. We were up on this roof for her. Staring at the faraway skyline of Downtown Philly, I watched the lights begin to glitter as night darkened.

She exhaled heavily.

I waited, taking the first sip of my second beer.

"It was my *mom's* suicide." Her voice broke at the last word. After a long exhale, then a catch in her breath, she continued, "But I'm the one paying for it."

24
ROOFTOP REVELATIONS

Darren…

"**T**hat goddamn *roof*," I growled. My phone-tracking app pegged Logan there. *Again.*

I slammed the door and floored the truck, pissed the fuck off. At the world. No matter what I did, my family ended up on that goddamn roof. I'd lost one. I would not lose another.

Seven-and-a-half long minutes. I'd clocked it. The time it took to get from our house to that roof took forever. Every single time.

No rhythm chattered in my head. My thumbs didn't drum the steering wheel. Only gut-wrenching terror filled my brain, pressed down on my chest, rushed hard past my eardrums.

I skipped the building's slow elevator and pounded up

the steps. One flight. *Two. Three. Four.* Each passed faster and faster as adrenaline pumped, fueled by frustration and anger.

At the fifth flight, I slowed, catching my breath as I approached the final climb to the rooftop landing. She didn't need to see my rage. I took a couple of lung-clearing breaths and paused, waiting until my pulse slowed.

There. Nice and calm. Like Logan needed me to be. Her rock. The one holding it together. As long as she believed that, everything would be okay.

Unable to wait any longer, I put my hand on the door, leaned my head down, then paused. Mild relief coursed through me when I saw the same brick propped against the doorframe. It kept the entry point two-way. Meant she'd planned to come back through it. Finally, I pushed the door open.

Then I blinked, confused at what I saw.

Two dark figures sat on that ledge.

Keeping to the shadows, I walked forward. Did this boy *friend* of hers—I struggled to remember his name—have long hair?

Two voices carried my way. Two *girl* voices.

I narrowed my eyes and came closer, moving behind the vent stacks. I didn't feel one damn ounce of guilt for spying on Logan. She was my responsibility. And she'd promised not to come up here anymore alone. I'd meant *not without me.*

A gust of wind caught the other girl's hair. She turned. Smiled.

Kiki.

My whole body shuddered from the shock of seeing her. Then relaxed just as fast, my stomach dropping, as the realization hit me.

Logan had called Kiki—not me.

I moved in front of the vent stacks, shielding myself from the wind and searching for that acoustical sweet spot from the other night. They were partially turned toward each other, their faces in profile. If I squinted, I could barely make out their features.

"…don't know what to do." Logan paused. "I like him. I mean *really* like him. But I'm not ready for that. Not yet. It doesn't feel right."

The hair on the back of my neck raised. *No* him *better be pressuring you to do anything, Lo.*

"Trevor isn't *just* a guy." Kiki tilted her head. "He's a senior? So he's what, seventeen?"

Trevor. That's the punk's name. The one Logan had sworn needed no condoms—*no sex.*

"Eighteen." Logan leaned to the side, then dropped an empty bottle into its carton with a clink.

Kiki gave a hard nod. "Not just a guy. A *hormonal* guy. Guys in high school think with their dicks. It's impossible for him to understand." She tapped Logan's temple twice with her finger. "He has no blood up here to think with."

Listen to Kiki, Logan. Guys are dicks.

Logan adjusted, facing Kiki more fully. "I just wish I didn't like him so much. Sometimes I think the heavier depression was better. I was lost in a huge haze that I couldn't see out of. But at least I wasn't up and down like this, worrying if he'll like me if I push for us to wait." She let out a heavy sigh. "I think about him all the time."

"Wait." Kiki's voice had a stern edge.

Yeah. Wait.

"Then what? How will I know?"

Kiki's gaze dropped and she stared at some point on the roof. "Hell if I know. I made the mistake of *not* waiting. I liked a guy so much in high school. I thought when he started paying attention to me that he liked me. Instead, I think it was more I wanted him to like me, accept me. With everyone in school snickering behind my back, and then him suddenly listening to me, paying attention to me, I thought someone finally *got* me. And it wasn't just *any* someone. It was Kyle, the one guy I'd been crushing hard on."

Kiki shook her head. "Idiot me didn't suspect that maybe he noticed me because I stared at him every chance I got. I was the girl blushing and turning away when he'd look up and catch me staring."

Logan leaned forward, edging more into Kiki's space. "What happened?"

Yeah. What happened? Was Kyle the guy who spooked you?

"He said he liked me. A lot. And he made it a point to tell me it was because I was different." Kiki turned now, crossing her legs underneath her.

I blew out a tense breath, worried as fuck that the two most important women in my life were both sitting too far out on the edge of a five-story building. My heart jammed into my throat as I began to obsess about the fall. A *deadly* fall.

This building takes things.

With a hard swallow, I forced the lump back down. I closed my eyes, took a deep breath, then opened them. Kiki and Logan were fine. They didn't seem bothered by the height.

If they aren't worried, I shouldn't be.

"He met me every day at lunch for weeks," Kiki continued. "We went out to a couple of movies. Bowling once, just him and me. Then he asked me to prom. And I lied to my parents, saying I was going by myself. I didn't want them to meet him. Which was weird, because I shared everything with them. Cade and my sisters didn't even know about him."

Logan nodded her head. "I get that."

That bothered me. Knowing Logan would want to keep anything from me. But that she shared her issues with Kiki helped. Maybe Logan needed a girl to talk with. I let out a relieved breath, grateful that Logan had felt close enough—safe enough—with Kiki to open up to her.

"Anyway, I told my parents I was staying at a friend's house. We really went to a hotel room. We didn't even stay at prom an hour. What I didn't know until that point was that I was the main event for him."

"Were you a virgin too?"

Kiki nodded. "He told me he loved me. I believed it, because I loved him. I had no idea at the time that I wasn't in love; I was infatuated."

"You had sex?"

Kiki paused, taking a deep breath. "Eventually. That night I had my first kiss. My first attempt at a blow job. My first sex. Second sex. And before we left in the morning, another blow job under his direction, then my third sex. He dropped me off at the curb in front of my house." She paused, then took another breath. "Didn't call me after that."

"*Motherfucker*," I bit out under my breath, scowling.

"Oh, wow. That's horrible." Logan crossed her arms over her middle, hugging herself. After a long silence, she sighed. "Trevor told me he loves me." Her voice hushed.

"Look, I've never met Trevor. Maybe he's one of the rare ones. How long have you two been seeing each other?"

"*Define* seeing."

Yeah. I leaned closer, glad Kiki asked every question I would have.

"Just hanging out in my room. Or at school, in the music room."

"How long have you been 'hanging out'?"

"'Bout a month."

"*Wait*, Logan." Kiki dropped her head down, then glanced back up. "If he really cares about you, he will wait. If he won't, then he doesn't. Real love doesn't need sex."

"How do you know?"

Kiki's expression changed, her face relaxing. The corners of her mouth lifted into a smile. "Because I've had sex. Not a ton of it, but enough to know all I've ever had is 'sex' with guys." She took a healthy pull from her beer.

"Have you ever been in love?"

Kiki pulled the bottle away and licked her lips. She stared hard at Logan. "Yeah. With the one guy who wouldn't have sex with me."

I wondered who that guy was for five idiotic seconds. Then it hit me.

Me. I'm the one guy.

Air sucked in and out in short bursts as I struggled to breathe.

Then I silently backed up and escaped through the rooftop door.

25
GRIPPED BY THE PAST

Kiki…

My head spun a little after the talk with Logan and not all of it from the slight beer buzz. As I drove through the gate of my property, still processing everything she'd shared—what I'd shared—Darren's truck came into view.

He leaned against the back fender, knee bent with a foot propped on the tire, arms crossed over his chest. He stared at me with a dead-serious expression.

Busted. Somehow he knew. Everything about him seemed coiled, pissed. Had Logan called him after I left… or before?

I parked in my space and got out. "Hey."

"Hey."

Nothing more. Only the intensity of his stare.

"I just came from—"

"I know."

"You do?" I frowned, hoping he'd elaborate.

"I was there."

Okaaay…not at all what I expected. I hadn't seen or heard him. Had Logan known? My mind raced over what I'd revealed. Too many private things. "How much did you—"

"Enough."

He knew.

My face flamed with heat. Great. Yet another guy who knew how deeply I felt about him. That knowledge changed the game for guys. Shredded hopes for girls.

"He's a *motherfucking* asshole."

I blinked. Clearly we weren't talking about the same thing. "Who, Trevor?"

"Maybe Trevor, too."

Confused, my brow wrinkled.

"Kyle." He bit out the name.

It stung my ears. Like it always had. Then I winced, realizing he'd heard plenty.

Before I processed the movement, Darren collided into me, arms wrapping behind my hips in a gentle hold. "Not all guys are like that."

"No?" My cheek pressed against his solid chest as I breathed out the question.

"No." His tone held finality as his arms tightened.

Several heartbeats later, when he eased his grip, I slipped my hands between us, pressing on his chest.

He only let go enough to allow me to look up into his eyes, but not to break away.

His gaze intensified. "*I'm* not."

I opened my mouth to argue. That it didn't matter. That I couldn't take the chance. That I liked him too much… but then, if he'd heard about Kyle, he might know that my feelings ran much stronger for him than "like."

No words came out, humiliation sucking the air from my lungs. I frowned, head tilting down until my forehead pressed to his sternum.

A gentle finger touched my chin, tilting my face upward until our gazes clashed.

He stared down at me with renewed intensity. "You will give me a chance. *Us* a chance."

"I will?"

"Yes. So you're scared. Suck it up, Flash. When you run, if you stare at the rock, you will hit the rock. Keep your eyes on the trail. What we could be is just around the bend."

It sounded amazing—the tiny bit of unknown hope that we could be something.

Worry sank in an instant later. My brows furrowed and I opened my mouth to ask about every little thing that jammed into my brain.

His expression darkened. "No. You don't get to shoot this down before it happens."

I took a deep breath, exhaled slowly. Then began chewing on my lip.

His tight embrace—his entire essence—was unwavering. And I liked being in his arms. It felt warm there, strong, safe.

I wanted to believe. The little girl somewhere deep inside me—the one who hadn't become jaded—wanted to believe there was a good guy for her.

"Say it. Say you'll give us a chance."

I tried to visualize what that might be like, but failed. "I don't know what that means."

"You don't have to."

"That makes no sense."

"Not everything does, Kiki."

And still, my brain shut down at the idea.

"Remember the first trail run I took you on?"

A smile tugged at my lips. "Yes." *That*, I could visualize.

"Do you also remember hanging by a branch, almost falling into a ravine?"

My stomach clenched as I remembered that harrowing moment. I gave him a short nod.

"Then what happened?"

"You said I was almost there. To trust you."

"I'm telling you to trust me again." His eyes narrowed. "You're hanging by the branch again, afraid to let go. I'm asking you to let go. I won't let you get hurt."

"You can't promise that." Love and hurt went hand in hand.

For the first time since I'd returned home tonight, amusement lit his eyes. His lips twisted into a smirk. "I can promise whatever happens will be worth the pain."

I slapped his chest. "Confident much?"

He didn't relinquish his iron hold. "I'm serious. Say it."

On a hard swallow, I considered what he offered. More than a one-night stand. More than friends. I'd be risking it all on what I'd been afraid of for years. But then, *my friend* wasn't promising me a guaranteed happy ending, just that it would be different—better.

Could I take that chance?

My heart raced. My whole body began to shake. I tried to push out of his hold, scared to death that I wouldn't be able to handle it. What if my own fears screwed it up?

What if I…lost…him?

"That bad, huh?" His voice quieted as he tightened his arms around me.

I nodded, tears springing to my eyes.

"He really did a number on you."

"Yeah." My breath stuttered as I tried to pull air into my lungs. "I was crushed. It wasn't just him. All the kids who'd ostracized me knew. Like I'd become some puzzling endangered species they stared at and whispered about until he flushed me out of the jungle one day and conquered me."

"He was an asshole. They all were."

"Yeah." I sniffed.

"I'm not."

"I know." And yet fear still gripped me.

When my lips parted, all the reasons why I thought it was a bad idea ready to tumble off my tongue, he pressed a gentle finger to them.

Fierce determination glittered in his gaze.

"Don't. Don't say no. Don't answer now. Don't even think about it—about us."

He huffed out a frustrated breath, brows furrowing. "All I'm saying is, don't fight it. Don't be afraid of us. If we are meant to happen…just let it."

Then his eyes softened.

And my resolve crumbled on a whisper. "Okay."

26
TO THOSE WHO WAIT

Darren…

O*kay.* Twenty-four hours later, Kiki's soft-spoken word still echoed in my head.

So did the memory of her shoving gently against me, trying to break free of my hold—trying to deny…us. Which had only made me tighten my arms and my resolve.

No way was I letting her fears make her run.

I'd loved her pressed against me, all soft curves and hard determination. Black hair wild. Cheeks pinked. Fiery spirit masking a tender heart.

Before I'd had a chance to call her, she'd texted at 11:08 a.m. Saturday morning.

Okay if I run on my own today?

The gentleness of her request had floored me. She needed space. Time.

Of course. See you at the party tonight?

Her reply had pinged right back.

Definitely. I'm looking forward to it.

No afternoon had ever dragged slower.

Saturday night finally came. Set-up happened as usual. Cade played point man, like he typically did.

But the party started without his sisters showing up.

Minutes ticked by. *Twenty…thirty…forty-five…an hour.*

Nervous excitement buzzed through me.

Just to see Kiki.

I busied myself manning the sound booth. Colored lights pulsed onto a boogying dance floor. A rotating disco ball glittered over their heads. The low hum of conversations filled the space between notes of loud music.

The next time I glanced up, there she stood. In the middle of the dance floor.

I instantly abandoned my booth and strode through the crowd toward her.

She broke into a wide smile the moment her gaze fell on me.

My steps slowed as the hilarity of her outfit finally made it past my need to be near her.

"What…are you wearing?" I blinked, turned on in a shocked kind of way.

"It's my 70's getup." She danced backwards, one step for every beat, shoulders and hips working the rhythm. "Do you like it?"

"Yeah." My voice broke as my gaze roved downward from the foot-high bobbing Afro wig on her head.

"Amazing how fashion comes around. These are my favorite yoga pants."

My favorite too.

Bell-bottom cuffs let her purple-polished toenails peek out. But the black fabric snugged in at her knees, clung to those sexy hips and thighs, then tucked inward at her trim waist—a waist I hadn't seen before. Slight defined vertical cuts began somewhere under the waistband of those pants and ran upward, toward her ribs.

"You're staring at my boobs."

My lips quirked up. "Can't help it. They're bouncing."

Yep. Hidden from view only by a clingy band of sparkling silver held up by two tiny straps.

"It's vintage."

Coolness edged her tone. As if she had no effect on me. That my throat hadn't gone dry. That my cock behind my tightening jeans hadn't grown hard. For her.

"Can't believe I found it in a thrift shop," she continued, oblivious. "Only needed a few extra sequins sewn on." She talked about the bangles on her wrists. Then she described her other thrift-shop finds while showing off her shoes.

I'd stopped actively listening. Because it was her face, the glow in her cheeks and the bright shine in her eyes, that had stolen my attention.

Until she nodded her head so hard her outrageous hair shifted halfway down her forehead.

She pressed her lips together, fighting a smile as she straightened her wig.

"Kiki!" Kristen called out to her, waving.

Her face fell, like her sister had spoiled her fun. "I have to go."

"Me too." I hiked a thumb back toward the sound booth.

We parted ways, Kiki to her event duties, me to mine. During the next hour, I stole glances at her while she danced around and mingled with guests.

I'd been watching her solidly for the last few minutes. She stood with her sisters and Hannah as her body bounced to Kool & the Gang's "Ladies' Night."

The moment I changed songs, Kiki broke away from the girls and jumped up onto a low table. Her hands flew into the air as the first electro-funk bars of The S.O.S. Band's "Take your Time (Do It Right)" blared out. Yeah, it hit the charts the summer of 1980, however I wasn't a 70's purist and it was close enough.

But had I known what the song would do to Kiki? Would've been the only one I played all night.

Another huge smile broke out on her face.

She stared at me the entire time she mouthed the words to the song.

And in that moment, it struck me. *She* struck me. A bolt of realization shot from the essence of who she was through my chest, straight into my heart. It thudded hard. For her.

I didn't remember leaving the sound booth.

The crowd on the dance floor parted as I worked my way through dozens of gyrating bodies.

She tracked my every move as I stalked her.

Her gaze at me intensified as I came within touching distance. "One life is all we have to *liiive*," she belted out.

On a deep breath, fully committed, I reached up and wrapped my arms around her thighs, lifting her from the table.

Her eyes widened a fraction as I let her slowly slide down my body.

As she lowered, when the inside of her elbows reached my ears, she wrapped her arms around my head. Her fingers combed through my hair before clasping behind my neck. Her lips parted as the song continued on without her.

Then on a whisper, she repeated the last verse, "*Our love is all we have to giiive...*"

She swallowed hard and stared into my eyes. Those words hung between us, heavy with importance.

I blew out a slow exhale. "I want you."

The corners of her luscious mouth twitched. "It's the getup. I'm rockin' a deadly 'fro."

"No." I sucked in a deep breath, gaze hardening, never more certain of anything in my life. "I *want* you."

Her expression sobered. "You do?"

She trembled in my arms.

I tightened my hold around her. "Not for one night. All the way, Kiki. Starting tonight...more than friends."

When her mouth opened, I sensed a protest coming. So I kissed her.

A tiny squeak escaped from her throat before her lips softened.

The kiss was brief, but effective.

I left her there, staring at me with a stunned expression, her lips slightly parted. She looked amazing. Good enough to devour. But the party pulsed on all around us. Our time together would have to wait a little longer.

The night dragged on. Each time I felt like another hour had passed, I'd check my phone to see it had only been another thirty minutes.

Song after song, I watched her dance. Occasionally, she'd mingle through the crowd with a pink drink in her hand. A wide smile brightened her face every time she glanced my way—which was often. Every now and then, her sisters would pull her away to talk to a partygoer or handle the cake cutting.

When midnight loomed close, Cade dropped by the sound booth. "You look anxious."

"Do I?"

"Yep." He tipped his beer bottle back, took a long pull.

I shrugged and forced myself not to glance Kiki's way.

"Don't suppose it has to do with your eyes glued to Kiki every chance you get."

"That obvious?" No way was I going to deny it.

"Lil' bit."

"I'll do right by her."

"Don't doubt it." Cade gave a short nod.

"Good." His blessing meant something to me.

"Party's wrapping up. No point in you hanging around.

I'll man the booth and lock it all up after."

"You kicking me out?" Best news in hours.

"Somebody better. We only do PG parties. Go."

I hesitated, staring at him. "So, you're okay. With me… and Kiki?"

He shot me a deadpan expression. "You two have been fooling no one but yourselves. Kendall and Kristen all but ordered me to come over here and talk some sense into you. We know you and Kiki were meant to be more than just friends. *Go.* Do something about it."

A relieved breath whooshed out of me. Hadn't realized I'd held it. "Thanks, man."

By the time I turned around, Kiki faced me from the other side of a thinning crowd. Her sisters formed a wall behind her. Then she stumbled forward, like they'd given her a gentle shove. Her eyes narrowed and she glanced back toward them, but she was laughing by the time she faced me again.

Body vibrating with anticipation, I crossed the floor with determined strides.

Her smile widened as she reached out, then grasped my hand. "We're being kicked out." She pulled off her wig, then handed it to Kendall as her hair tumbled down over her shoulders in loose waves.

I tucked a stray curl behind her ear. "Guess we've been bad."

She stared up at me, her beautiful blue eyes darkening. "Or about to be…"

Yeah. I led her out of there, holding her hand tightly. We burst out of the double doors at the entrance into the dimly lit parking lot.

When I turned us toward the truck, she tugged on my hand. "Mind if we walk?"

I calculated the distance. Her place was three and a half blocks away. Then I glanced down at her high heels. "You sure?" A few minutes by truck. About twenty by foot.

"Yeah. There's a place on the way I want to show you."

Make that maybe an hour, or more. I took a deep breath. I'd been waiting a very long time for Kiki. Another hour? I could do.

The night was mild as we walked hand in hand down the cobbled sidewalk. Without warning, she dropped my hand, skipped ahead, then popped onto the curbing around the last lamppost on the street. A breeze stirred the ends of her softly curled hair, then calmed again as she wrapped her hands around the wrought iron pole.

She stared off into the darkness of a neighborhood park as tree leaves rustled overhead. "This is perfect." She scanned the sky. "It's a moonless night."

Didn't argue. Any night with her was perfect.

With a slight squeal, she grabbed my hand and rushed forward. The clicks of her heels disappeared the moment we hit grass.

I couldn't see jack shit, but I jogged after her, barely keeping up. "Don't step into a hole."

"There are none. I've snuck out here every night this week." She stopped so suddenly, I crashed into her. She giggled, then half-turned as she reached up, lifting the end of a branch. "Be careful, low bridge."

Intrigued by what would capture her attention for a whole week of nighttime visits, I ducked under the branch. We picked our way through thick bushes and low-hanging limbs. "A wilderness hike?" This part of Glenhaven was on the outskirts of town, bordering forest land.

She slowed her steps, then stopped altogether. "Close your eyes."

"Seriously?" I snorted. "Can't see a damn thing."

"Close them."

Her stern tone made me smile. "Fine. They're closed."

She led me forward while insects chirped and sang in the trees around us.

"Okay." Her voice dropped to a whisper. "Now open."

I did. Then I blinked, not quite processing what I saw. Thousands of greenish lights glittered against a black backdrop.

"Wow." All I could say. "Fireflies?"

"Yep. Aren't they amazing?" She leaned against me, touching her head to my chest, just below my shoulder.

"Can't believe they're here this early." I rested my hand on her hip.

"Right?" She glanced up at me, then back out again. "Must be the really warm early spring. It's the first time I've ever seen them in April."

In silence we stared at the spectacle. Tiny lights blinked on and off. If you stared in one spot, the lights would dance, swaying in a ripple anytime a slight breeze would catch them.

"It's like the miracle of a first snow on..." Her voice turned breathless with wonder.

"Christmas Eve." I remembered.

I now felt it too, understood firsthand what she'd meant—that quiet moment of *before*, when anticipation wound tight inside, about to explode.

She let out a sigh. "This is *our* Christmas Eve."

I wrapped my other arm around her, brushing my lips along the top of her ear. "Please tell me I get to unwrap my present tonight."

She shifted in my hold, then stared up at me with dark wide eyes. The weight of the moment crackled with intensity as she pressed her hands to my ribs, then ran them up my chest. In the light of the fireflies, her halo of dark hair shimmered pale green around her face.

"That depends," she whispered.

"On?" My hands tightened, pressing on her back.

I stared at the incredible girl in my arms. Soft tempting curves. A heart full of wild wonder. One whose first wish tonight was to share her secret miracle. With me.

Nothing on earth had ever made me feel so lucky.

"On whether you're bad or good."

I dropped my head, pressed a kiss to her temple, then dragged my lips to the top of her ear. "Bad," I growled. "I plan to be very bad."

Her entire body shuddered in my arms. "Good answer."

I eased back and savored the moment, staring down at her.

Over the rustling of leaves and singing of insects, only our heavy breaths were heard. I swallowed hard. She licked her lips.

Then she bit the plump lower one as she stared up at my mouth.

I lost it. Dipping down, I captured her lips with mine. The kiss was hungry. Insistent. She exhaled a sigh into my mouth as I thrust my tongue forward. She tasted sugar sweet, remnants of those pink drinks she'd been holding.

Groaning, I buried my hands into her soft hair.

Her weight leaned against me as she relaxed in my hold. Our tongues explored, mine dragging alongside hers, hers tangling over mine.

My hands fell lower until they gripped her hips. Unable to stop myself, I ground against her.

A *fucking delicious* little moan came from her throat.

Then a shudder tripped through me, the impact of our kiss shocking me down to my bones.

When we pulled apart, she blew out a slow breath through pursed lips. "Wow."

"Yeah."

"Ready to open your present?"

"*Fuck* yeah."

I scooped her up into my arms. "Which way to your house?"

She kicked her feet, fighting my hold. "I can walk, you know."

"No. I'm about to tear off at a dead run. Those heels will only slow us down." I shouldered past the low-hanging branches, turning her away to shield her. "Direction. *Now.*"

Laughing, she gripped my shoulder and biceps and nodded her chin up the street. "Next block up. On the right."

With a quick toss of her slight weight, I adjusted my grip then made good on my word. Holding her tight, I ran the fifty yards to the nearest street corner.

She pressed her face into my neck. "A right here. Second drive."

I already spotted the white picket fence. Aimed for the alley before it. At the corner, I paused and leaned against a lamppost, catching my breath.

She smirked. "Out of shape, big guy?"

I grunted. "Need to work in hundred-pound girl carries."

"You'll be carrying no other girls. And it's a hundred and seventeen."

"No wonder."

She smacked my pec loud enough to sting.

"Need your stance on condoms."

Her brow furrowed. "Right here?"

"The info, yeah." I straightened from the lamppost, hoisted her up, letting her slight frame leave my touch for a fraction of a second, then caught her again. "'Cuz the second we hit your place, all rational talk is out."

"I like condoms," she blurted when I crossed half the distance down the alley.

"Any other birth control?"

"I'm on the pill." Her voice lowered.

"Ever go without condoms?"

"No." A whispered word.

"Me either. Got tested in March. Clean bill of health." My words were clipped. All I could manage with blood rushing south.

"Me too. Last November."

She hadn't been with anyone since then. Almost two years she'd said.

"No condoms, then." Her voice had a breathless thoughtful tone.

An excited breath gusted out of me—at the thought of skin to skin, her wrapped around me with nothing between us.

Everything from that point on blurred. Didn't even remember passing through her gate. When I lowered her to the ground, she fumbled with her keys at the front door. Then we were inside. The metal clanged shut, the bolt thrown.

A few lights had been left on; their dim glow from farther inside cast shadows on the expansive warehouse. But I saw Kiki clearly, my gaze pinned on her.

She tugged at the bottom of her skimpy silver top, taking backward half-steps away from me. "Do you want to do the unwrapping?" A tiny smirk twisted her lips, her hips swaying as she automatically sidestepped around her metal sculptures.

I swallowed hard and shook my head. "No. You."

Her pace picked up once we cleared the metalwork and stepped into the wide-open main room. As we passed her living room, she tore off her top then tossed it onto the sidearm of a couch.

Then she paused.

I stopped walking. Stopped breathing.

A light blue lace bra cupped her breasts. Dusty pink nipples showed through, erect.

She reached back, stretching the barely-there fabric. Her fingers slipped under her waistband at her hips, but paused. Her head tilted, a single brow arched. "Now you."

Fuck yeah. No slowing down now. I gripped the back of my shirt and yanked it over my head. Jeans and boxers were stripped off together seconds later.

She blinked, staring at my body. "Oh. My."

"Five seconds," I growled. "Naked. Or I'm tearing off the pretty wrapping."

Her eyes widened. Her breaths quickened. But she didn't move.

"Four."

I could practically see the gears turning in her head as her pupils darkened.

"*Three*." I stalked forward, closing the distance.

She squealed when I came within reach, stumbled a few steps back, then dropped her pants, jumping out of them before running toward the metal stairs that led up to her loft.

My mouth went dry. The barest scrap of blue lace stretched over her hips, then disappeared between two glorious butt cheeks.

"Damn," I breathed as I watched her run up the stairs.

Flashes of her breasts bouncing etched into my brain.

I raced up the stairs two at a time and reached the middle landing as she paused at the top. When she opened the door, a flash of brown fur blurred by, brushing against my leg. Focus trained only on Kiki, I jogged up the rest of the stairs, pushed the closing door open, then strode inside, letting it slam behind me.

At its banging echo, she turned right as she reached the edge of her dining room. Then she backed up a step, bright smile on her face, chest heaving from her exertion.

Two quick strides and I had her in my arms.

Her hands planted on my chest. "Don't you want me to finish unwrapping your gift?" A slender brow raised as she slipped a finger under the delicate lace at her shoulder.

"No," I growled.

I gripped her shoulders, guiding her until the backs of her legs were stopped by the bed. Then I kissed her, devouring her lips, her mouth. I explored with hungry sucks and gentle bites.

Her body grew limp, little whimpers sounding out with every exhale.

When we'd both gone breathless, I pulled back to take a good look at her.

Her eyes glittered with lust. Kiss-roughened lips were plump and parted.

I gave her a gentle push, and she fell backward, landing on the bed with a slight bounce. Creamy skin taunted me. Dark wild hair framed a beautiful face that smiled up at me.

My chest grew heavy, warm. With…

Gratitude.

Then something snapped inside. Raw need rippled through me and a low growl rumbled from my throat. "*I* get to rip those pretty ribbons off you."

27
LETTING GO

Kiki…

arren looked fiercely beautiful as he towered over the foot of my bed. His entire demeanor tensed with determination: dark brows lowered, defined jaw clenched, lean muscles of his sculpted body twitched.

And a provocative dusky line of hair, low in the center of it all, led downward. My gaze drifted along that path of temptation, drawn to the impressive thick erection pointing my way.

The weight of it bobbed as he shifted and crawled onto the bed. His intense gaze held mine for a beat longer, then his attention trailed down my body, pausing at my chest before landing at the juncture of my thighs.

I blew out a nervous breath. Even so, no fear remained about us moving forward. I wanted this—wanted him.

Knees planted on the bed, he leaned his weight back, resting on his heels between my parted legs, then swallowed hard. After a deep breath, he hooked his thumbs under my thong straps on either hip and tugged, gradually dragging the lace down over my thighs. When he'd pulled the material as far as our closeness would allow, instead of moving, he yanked the fabric up and my legs with it. His hands caught under my calves, spread over the muscles, then pressed forward until my legs straightened in front of his chest.

Once the scrap of lace cleared my ankles, he tossed it over his shoulder. But his gaze never strayed from that private space between my legs. My chest heaved up on a breath, excitement thrilling though me as I lay before him, vulnerable, wholly exposed.

"*Fucking gorgeous.*" The words growled out from his throat, guttural.

A smile curled my lips. "*You* are."

And he was.

It wasn't just the wild beauty of his face, the lustrous dark hair that framed it, and his primed athletic body. His mind challenged me. His heart captivated me. The soul of a man dedicated to helping others before himself riveted me.

Everything Darren was…had become all I'd ever wanted.

With gentle movements, he leaned forward and lowered his body over mine. Dipping his head down, he planted a soft kiss above my navel. Another landed between my breasts. His face turned to the side, his lips running over the transparent lace of my bra. When his mouth reached the peak, he exhaled warm breath over my nipple.

Ache pinged there then snapped through me in a split second, firing into a sharper twinge between my legs. I gasped at the erotic sensation.

Another low growl rumbled from him right before his mouth captured it between his lips.

My awareness shattered as pleasure sparked through my whole body. On a ragged groan, I arched off the bed, but he shifted his upper body weight, pressing me back down. Small tugs as he suckled became harder nips. Each one wired directly to the sizzling pulse that throbbed between my legs.

With a loud pop, he released the captive nipple. Then he nuzzled my other breast while his hands reached behind my back; deft fingers unfastened my bra with a single twist. He eased backward, pulling the lace free with both hands to expose my breasts. He stared at them, transfixed with a held breath, before tossing the bra behind him too.

Then his gaze clashed with mine. "Perfect."

Warmth bloomed in my chest—that he thought so with a meaning that reached far beyond skin deep.

He lowered back down and seized my lips. My breath caught at the intensity of the kiss, different than before— tender and deliberate. Every gentle sip and slow suck held the weight of heavy emotion.

When he pulled back, I brushed a thumb over his cheekbone. The flameless candle on my nightstand flickered, making his skin sparkle.

I almost laughed. "You have body glitter on your face."

"I'm about to have body glitter all over me."

Without another word or any warning, he lunged

backward until he dropped between my thighs, his wide shoulders spreading them. I watched the top of his head for a brief second, until delicious heat licked a broad path over my center. Then my head fell back on a strangled cry when harder sucking pressure speared hot ache through me.

My breaths reduced to shallow pants. Blood rushed through my ears as the ache intensified. When the sensations became too great, my body arched bowstring tight off the bed. I hung there, on a precipice of pain and pleasure. My hands flew to his shoulders, nails digging in as I gasped for breath.

He slowed his movements, easing the pressure—toying with me.

The edge of my orgasm hovered just out of reach.

"*Pleeease…*" The graveled plea rasped from my throat.

Warm air fogged over the sensitive skin as he pulled back, denying me.

My clit throbbed.

One heartbeat. Another.

I groaned as the exquisite pressure grew to be nearly unbearable.

Then all at once, hot and fast, he covered me with his mouth, lashing me with his tongue.

I gasped, then burst into sizzling sparks of pleasure on a scream. Hard pulses ravaged my body as he continued to lick and suck with renewed force. Wave after wave crashed through me, over and over, as I became lost to the demands of his talented mouth.

Then he relaxed his movements, his tongue licking in slow, reverent strokes.

My body fell limp, every muscle boneless.

His head fell to the side, his soft hair and the warmth of his cheek resting on my inner thigh.

After long seconds, when he didn't move, I glanced down. He stared intently at me, pride in his eyes. A smirk tilted one corner of his mouth up.

Lost in a dreamy haze, my lips curved into a lazy smile. "Well done." The only words that came to mind. Of his performance. Of my sated state.

"Just getting started," he growled.

His expression grew wild as stark need painted his features. But in the intensity of his gaze, behind those dark eyes, I saw more than sexual hunger. Raw emotion fired brightly there.

I sucked in a slow breath, briefly stunned by the depth of his passion. Then warmth spread through my chest. Because I felt it too, the incredible pull, our solid connection strengthening with not only our physical act…but by finally letting go.

Gaze locked to mine, he turned his head, then pressed a soft kiss to my inner thigh. He shifted his position, arms suddenly bracketing outside my legs, and placed another kiss along the seam where thigh met hip. The scruff of his face scratched a little as he brushed his chin over my hipbone; but his slow exhalation cooled the skin seconds before warm lips caressed the dip below it.

Up he wandered, dotting kisses in a random path to mark the exploration of my body. The brush of his nose under the curve of my breast. The slow lick of his tongue under the other. In the valley between them, he peppered tiny kisses while he inhaled; his eyes rolled back as they drifted closed, as if he drew in our intoxicating scent. The next long, hot exhale worked its magic over my collarbone, then fogged up the side of my neck.

My entire body shuddered. Renewed sensual warmth spread outward to my fingers, my toes. Every nerve ending awakened again, alive and zinging.

His hips settled between my thighs, pushing my legs up and out to make room for him.

The rigid length of his erection pressed against sparking nerves. I sighed as he settled over me, pressing down, arching his pelvis against mine—right where I throbbed the most.

He stared into my eyes, searching.

I smiled up at him.

"Hi." He let out a shaky breath.

"Hi."

"Ready?" His gentle questioning tone surprised me.

I *almost* gave a cute quip in reply.

But then it hit me: Our coming together was as immense for him as it was for me. He'd never allowed anyone into his world—anywhere near his heart–until now.

And I'd not let anyone in either: no one real, no man worth my heart. Until him.

"Yes." I ran my hands around his waist, up his back. "I want you. *All* of you."

Nothing less would do.

After all. He now had all of me.

Joy shone in his eyes seconds before he dipped down

and brushed his lips over mine. With a sigh, I melted into him. Grateful for so much, for him, for our finally taking what we'd been denying ourselves—a chance at happiness.

He pressed forward.

I pulled him closer, wrapping my arms and legs around him, holding on tight.

Solid pressure nudged at my entrance.

I pressed a kiss to his neck on a slow exhale, relaxing my body, letting him in.

And in he came. One slow powerful stroke stretched me wide, took me completely. I gasped at the overwhelming feeling, nerve endings sizzling to life once again.

We were one. As he flexed his hips, forward, then back, retreating then surging, I met him in the middle, thrust for thrust, holding on for the ride. Every move he made, I made, together—harmonious.

Pressure mounted with each passing second. Ache intensified with every stimulating undulation. Our bodies instinctively curved and arched, hitting all the right spots, causing pleasure to spark, then grow hotter. A low moan escaped my throat as erotic fire sizzled deep inside me. He groaned, swelling harder, driving deeper.

I gasped, hanging on the edge of pleasurable pain.

He paused, his entire body going rigid in my hold.

Then he plunged deep on an animalistic growl.

I screamed as a second powerful orgasm whipped through me.

Time warped as every tiny thing claimed its split second of awareness. Another powerful spasm of pleasure. The warm solidness of him deep inside me. Our hearts pressed together, beating a frantic rhythm, mine with his. Our labored breaths, mine at the base of his throat, his ruffling the hair above my ear. Everything chaotic had fallen into perfect balance.

As our racing hearts began to slow and our ragged breaths grew more even, he leaned to one side, but tugged me with him. He wrapped a leg over my hip, secured an arm around my back, and pressed a kiss to the top of my head with a long sigh.

Imprisoned in his embrace, I smiled, then burrowed deeper into his hold, seeking all he had to offer. In that rare, blissful, utterly complete moment of happiness with him, no part of me wanted anything else.

At some point in the dark early-morning hours, after a headboard-banging round three, he curled onto his left side with a satisfied sigh and I spooned behind him, sliding my hand under his arm and across his chest. He clasped my hand, then pressed a kiss over my knuckles. His lips lingered there, brushing across my fingers while my attention strayed to the thick curving lines of ink on his skin.

"Tell me about your tattoos."

His mouth left my hand, then he pressed my palm to the center of his chest and held it there, over his heart.

"One tattoo. They're my family," he rasped out, voice just above a whisper. "Mine is the larger crescent. Mom's is the one that wraps around my back. Lo's tucks under my arm."

"All connected." *Like family.*

He gave a slow nod. "And protecting…watching over… each other."

"When did you get it?" The question felt personal, yet too important not to know. I wanted to understand him.

He gripped my hand tighter before pressing down on it again over his rapidly beating heart. "When Mom died."

Silence followed, him holding my hand to his chest, me curled behind him, tucked against his body.

And in that space of honesty and vulnerability, I traced my lips along parts of the dark lines: his downward, his mom's, his sister's. In the center where they all met, I pressed a tender kiss.

He let out a heavy sigh before his breathing fell into a deep rhythm.

I settled my head on the pillow, tightening my grip over his heart.

Nothing on earth would take his pain away entirely, but I planned to do my best to ease it.

I blinked my eyes open to bright light, then instantly pinched them shut to block out all things *way* too-early morning. But when I tugged the covers to pull them over my head, they didn't budge. When I turned, a solid, warm wall met my face.

"Mmm…" With a sudden flash, recognition hit me. Then

I pressed a small kiss on Darren's ribs and snuggled closer to his warmth, resting my cheek in the indentation just below his collarbone.

I inhaled his scent as hazy memories drifted in. His smile and raw laughter. The intense expression on his face when we'd connected deeper, in every way. How the emotion glittering in his eyes matched the unnamed feeling I'd been harboring but hadn't fully admitted to myself, until then.

I'd fallen for him. Or at least, had begun to, as much as my protective armor had allowed.

The large hand that cradled my hip drifted higher, rubbing lazily up my back, then down. His other arm moved under my shoulders, until they locked together and squeezed, holding me with near-crushing force.

A low growl rumbled above my ear, rustling my hair. "Let's stay here forever." The deep timbre of his voice soothed me, but the words themselves prickled worry up my spine.

They reminded me of time—something I didn't have.

My ticking bomb of an envelope, rigged to blow, didn't allow us a forever. Not here, anyway.

I draped my leg over his hip and drew circles over his pecs with my finger as I let out a sigh. "Do you have the power to make that happen?"

Maybe he did. What if other forces in the universe, the ones that had pushed us together in the first place, had a hand in my fate?

What if Darren could work a miracle with just one wish?

He pulled back, searching my eyes, studying me. Then something sparked in his and one corner of his mouth twitched up. "Watch me."

With a low growl, he grabbed my waist and flipped me to his other side, in the center of the bed. My squeal rang out, echoing around us.

His smug grin was the last image in my mind before he kissed me senseless. Then he worshiped my body with methodical precision and absolute reverence.

Anxiety about the future? Banished.

28
HIDING UNDER THE COVERS

Darren…

I drifted in and out of consciousness. Lazy. Happy.

Kiki's soft body stretched, then pressed up tighter against me. She let out a satisfied hum as she planted a kiss below my collarbone.

My stomach answered with a grumbling roar.

Her muffled laughter vibrated into my skin.

"Feed me." I tightened my arm around her, briefly squeezing.

She stretched out an arm, her flattened hand rubbing in a slow circle before it landed on my hip. "Thought you wanted to stay here forever."

"I do." I grunted, pulling myself upright. "Food first. Need energy."

She wearily collapsed into the dent I'd abandoned. I bent

down and kissed the nearest patch of forehead under her messed-up hair.

Then I stared at her for a minute. Her creamy skin glowed a healthy pink. Her normally wild hair had that well-fucked look.

Gorgeous.

Unusual happiness swelled in my chest. That I was lucky enough to have her. That she trusted me enough to take a chance with her heart, to rely on me to guard it—protect her.

I didn't kid myself, though. She wasn't the only one I needed to safeguard. The forever I wanted wasn't possible. Not yet. But maybe moments with her here and there could add up to a forever for us someday.

When I stepped into the bathroom and lifted the seat, a thought hit me. I finished, washed my hands, then popped my head back out. She'd abandoned the bed.

I wandered into the kitchen. Then my mind totally blanked. The counters were already covered with bowls and spice jars…and she hadn't yet put any clothes on.

Best woman ever.

"What are we making?"

"Apple pancakes with bacon."

"Aw, damn. I just drooled." And not only because of the food.

"Good. Peel." She handed me a slab of bacon strips, then pointed to a tin-foiled baking sheet. She began adding ingredients to a bowl filled with flour.

"Naked baking." Yep. Master of the obvious.

She giggled. "First time for me."

"Me too."

She plopped a spoonful of coconut oil into two large frying pans, then clicked on the burners beneath each. "Pretty sure I'm never baking any other way again."

That made two of us. She looked incredible. And a unique energy buzzed from her.

As directed, I peeled off thick strips and lined them up side by side onto the foiled baking sheet. "You doing anything tomorrow night?"

Her brow crinkled as she scooped a fourth dark spice into a measuring spoon, then dumped it into the bowl. "Monday…" She shook her head. "Nope."

"Wanna come watch me play?" Finished with the bacon, I washed my hands.

She paused in the middle of dry-whisking her ingredients. "Your and Logan's garage band?"

"No. With my new boss. Even though he signed me as a studio musician, he plays live a few times a month. It's a jazz ensemble. Dino, his guy on sax, and me."

A wide smile brightened her face as she glanced up while pouring almond milk from a measuring cup into a green bowl. "I would love to come."

"I have to show up early, so I can't pick you up, but I'll text you the address."

"Sounds great." A timer beeped, then she turned it off. "Can you man the fort for a few?" She pointed at the bacon-covered baking sheet. "That goes in the oven for thirty. Mix the dry ingredients into the liquid batter, then pour into each pan. I'm taking a quick shower, but should be back in time to flip them."

"Sure." I grabbed the large spoon she held, wrapping my hand partially over hers, and gave her a soft kiss. When we broke contact, she stared at my lips, breaths accelerating, before her lust-filled gaze met mine.

"You're insatiable." I muttered.

She didn't release her hold on the spoon. "You're addictive."

Less than thirty minutes? Not even close to enough time for everything I wanted to do to her. Repeatedly.

"Go." I gave a nod over her shoulder, toward the bathroom. "Food now. Sex later."

As I mixed, then poured, the rightness of the moment hit me. I stood in her kitchen cooking. She showered, humming a lighthearted melody, after an incredible night where we'd tested the limits of her bed frame. We'd finally taken the leap of faith to be together—as in my *first relationship ever* together—and the world as I knew it hadn't caved in.

The whole thing seemed unreal. Made a guy say things like "Let's stay here forever."

Like clockwork, she returned, towel wrapped around her, hair damp and smelling of tropical vanilla. I gave a quick glance at the stove; the pancakes had little bubbles popping open on their uncooked side.

When she tried to sidle in front of the stove to take care of them, I held a barring arm out and gave her a headshake. "I got these." One by one, I shook each pan until its giant pancake slid freely, then on an arcing upstroke, I slipped the spatula under and flipped it the rest of the way over in one fluid motion.

"Bravo." She clapped.

"Not my first time in a kitchen." Or with pancakes. My mind flashed to those cherished Thanksgivings with my mom and sis. What an amazing thing to share pancakes now with Kiki.

The scent of cooking salt and fat wafted around us with eight minutes remaining on the oven timer. I used fifteen seconds of it tugging on that fluffy towel wrapped around her, pulling her close, then kissing her thoroughly. By the time we broke apart, we'd both gone breathless.

Her eyes were wide, shining an electric blue in the bright light angling in from the upper windows. She grabbed the spatula from me then pointed it toward the bathroom. "Go. Shower."

"Yes, Ma'am."

The only soap and shampoo in there were the tropical ones she wore. I used just enough to suds myself clean, then rinsed with a lot of hot water. After I toweled off, I grew fairly confident that I would leave smelling only *a little* like her. Then maybe I could convince her to go another round and leave smelling exactly like I wanted: a little like Kiki and *a whole lot* like our sex.

When I walked back out, towel tucked around my waist, food had already been doled onto two large plates. She grabbed both, handed me mine, then headed toward the door.

I followed. "Where are we going?"

"Downstairs."

"Why?" I reached around her, opening the door.

She glanced over her shoulder. "Coffee."

"Ahhh…good answer."

Thank God she stepped through the door first. The furry one had crouched on the landing just outside the door. I smiled at the cute little guy. "I wondered where the cat was."

"Hey, Chipmunky!" Kiki rubbed the ball of her foot over his back before stepping over him.

He sprang up and lunged a shoulder across one of her bare legs, then darted between mine. I had to pause midstep to avoid tripping over him.

"He watches over the warehouse at night." She made three short kissing noises to get his attention.

"Guard kitty?" When we reached the middle landing, he raced ahead, a bounding blur of fur.

Her soft laughter drifted up as she trotted down the stairs after him. "Something like that. Anything amiss, he howls. If something's really wrong, he'll come up and scratch on the door. I leave food and water near the worktable and his litterbox in the far back corner."

"Has anything been really wrong?" I frowned. My imagination exploded with thoughts of that side alley and the industrial nature of her property.

"Not really." She shrugged, sliding her plate onto the worktable. Then she grabbed a freshly brewed pot, righted a couple of mugs that had been resting upside down on a towel beside it, and poured us each a steaming cup. "Once some vandals broke into my car. Stole the radio."

"Better than breaking into your house." I muttered.

"Warehouse," she corrected, taking a seat on a metal

barstool. "Rusted metal outside. Not many people think anything valuable would be in here."

I pegged her with a hard look. "*You're* in here."

Her gaze held mine a beat. Then another as she took a deep breath. Her lips curved into a smile as she tilted her head in a slight nod my way. "Fair enough. I promise to be careful."

Only partially calmed by her promise, because it did *fuck all* to actually keep her safe, I sat on the barstool beside her and dug into my breakfast. We ate for a few minutes in silence as I watched her cut tiny little triangles, one at a time, along the edge of her plate-sized pancake.

Fascinated to learn how she ate, I arched a brow. "I've seen you eat burgers, ribs, and Chinese."

When I didn't elaborate, she smirked. "This a weird bucket list of yours?"

"Maybe. Do you always cut food on a plate into uniform pieces? Or is it just pancakes?"

"Pan*cake*. One. And I've never had a *giant* pancake before. So I don't know."

"How do you normally eat pancakes?"

"In a stack."

Smartass.

"A perfectly uniform stack?" *Back at ya.*

Her lips twitched. Then she huffed out a laugh and shook her head. Her cheeks still held a pink blush. Her eyes sparkled with amusement. I'd had a hand in both and I wanted to do it again. Often. She was beyond beautiful when she stopped thinking and let herself enjoy life.

Remembering how bad her coffee was before, I took a tentative sip. It tasted…good. "Mmm. Different brew?"

She nodded. "Kendall gave it to me. She said she was trying to save me."

I choked out a laugh. "I didn't have the heart to tell you."

"That's cool." Her brows arched as she glanced at me. "I'm open to java suggestions and donations." She popped a folded piece of bacon into her mouth.

My eyes wandered as we ate, then landed on the stack of unopened mail still sitting on the far corner. One envelope had been pulled out from the rest. Bright red block letters had been stamped across the front of it: FINAL NOTICE.

Curious about the dire warning, I glanced at Kiki.

She stared at the envelope, must have caught me looking at it. Her entire demeanor had changed. Her body had gone rigid, shoulders tensed toward her ears. Breathing that had been calm and easy had now shortened to rapid breaths.

"Kiki?"

She didn't respond.

I put a hand over hers, tangling our fingers together. "Kiki, look at me."

After another couple of short breaths, she finally inhaled deeply and blinked, as if pulling herself from a trance. Then she turned her head, finally meeting my gaze.

"What's in the envelope?"

She let out a huge breath and angled a wary glance at the envelope again, like the damn thing had teeth. "It's my eviction notice."

My heart sank. The warehouse wasn't just her home;

every square inch of it emanated parts of her. It *was* her.

"When?"

"End of the month."

"*Nine days* from now?"

"Nine days, eleven hours, seventeen minutes from homelessness."

"But..." My mind froze at how wrong it was, none of it made sense. "What about your art? Didn't you have a successful showing?" I hadn't been to her opening exhibit, but the crew at Loading Zone had heard all about it from Cade—proud brother bragging.

"Those exhibit sales are what I rented the place with. The very first thing I did. That money covered the security deposit plus first and last month's rent, with enough left over to renovate the old office" —she pointed at her loft above us— "some furnishings, and a few art supplies."

"You haven't sold any pieces since then? It's been...five months."

A hard laugh huffed from her. "Oh, I did. Sold two more in January, one in February. Big pieces, too. Would've paid my rent through summer."

"What happened?"

"The gallery owner turned crooked. Or maybe she always was; I didn't verify the sales prices with what the buyers paid. Maybe she shafted them too."

Anger welled up from my gut. "Shafted?"

I dropped my fork and shoved my plate away, appetite gone.

She took several gulps of coffee. "Yep. Got excuse after excuse for the delays on payment of the additional sales.

Then my calls weren't being returned. When I finally got pissed off enough to go there to stand in front of her and watch her cut me a check…it was too late."

My eyes narrowed. "Too late how?"

"Gallery locked up with a small notice on the door. Closed by order of the IRS."

I blew out a harsh breath. "Tax evasion."

"Yep. My calls to the IRS were a joke. The money for the sales of my art was sitting in accounts the government had frozen. They don't care about contracts, or receipts of sale, or starving artists. All they care about is the money. And the money in those accounts? Pennies on the dollar for what the bitch owed on back taxes."

"Damn, Kiki. I'm sorry."

"Don't be. What I get for being so trusting."

"Wasn't it a reputable gallery?"

"Yep. Been there for years. The same years she'd been falsifying her taxes. She owes them almost seventeen million."

"*Fuck me.*"

"Exactly." She glared at the envelope. "But you know the worst part? I have eight other sculptures sitting in that gallery unsold. Big pieces that would fetch a lot of money. And I can't touch them."

I frowned. "Why not?"

"Because the IRS didn't just freeze her accounts. They froze her physical assets, the gallery."

"But those sculptures aren't hers, they're yours."

She heaved me a weary look. "Tell that to the IRS."

"Wait…doesn't your landlord live in the house up front, the one you housesit for?"

"Not exactly housesit, more like watch over. But yeah." She shrugged, poking a fork at the half-pancake left on her plate. "She doesn't call the shots. The property management company and her accountants do. They've already given me two extensions at her request. I've blown past all my deposits and been living here rent-free for two months. They can't do any more for me without all the back rents paid up and then some."

"Why not ask your family for help? Surely they'd lend you some money."

"No." She gave a hard headshake. "I don't want help. I want to do this on my own."

"Okay. So what's your plan?"

She slumped down to the table, folding her arms under her chin. After a long pause, she glanced up at me. "Denial?"

I stared at her for several long seconds. Her eyes had lost their fire. She wasn't being sarcastic, she'd just run out of steam. And hope.

She might not want help from her family, but she would get it from me. No way would I let her lose everything she'd worked for. All her dreams had been poured into her warehouse.

I pulled her up from the table, and her towel slowly unraveled, then fell away, but neither of us grabbed it. I folded my arms around her, pulling her tight against me.

On a slow sigh, she nestled into my hold. Bared. Trusting.

I pressed a kiss to the top of her ear. "We're gonna come up with a better plan."

29
DEEPER CONNECTIONS

Kiki…

B y the following night, Darren hadn't come up with a plan. Neither had I. Because you can't plan your way out of a mess you had no control over.

None of it was fair. But that was life.

I turned out of my neighborhood, heading toward the address Darren had given me, thinking about my situation and what he'd suggested. I'd already contemplated asking my family for help. My brother and sisters would lend me money in a heartbeat. My parents too.

Any of them would give me a roof over my head. And in another eight days, it may come to that.

But going to them meant admitting failure out loud—to a family who always succeeded in anything they'd tried. And I was the artistic one. Although they'd never done anything to discourage my passion, I still felt a heavier burden compared to them to prove my worth.

Besides, those ideas were nothing but temporary Band-Aids to my greater ailment.

Stuck in a place of anger and frustration—in my denial—I hadn't formed any kind of back-up plan. No safety net.

For some idiotic reason I kept thinking, one more phone call to the IRS. Or maybe after ninety days, they'd open the gallery and release my sculptures. Maybe they'd listen to reason.

But why would they? I hadn't listened to my own self with how ridiculous that sounded. Or admitted to myself what dire straits I was actually in.

A part of me had faith that it would all work out. Even though I had no reason to believe it.

"Is that what you are, Darren?" I whispered into my car as I followed a curve, then turned into the parking lot in front of a posh resort. "Are you my miracle worker?"

He had been so far. He'd turned out to be more than I'd ever expected.

Which scared the hell out of me. Too much faith in someone left too much room for disappointment.

I blew out a slow breath, calming my nerves. Then I opened the heavy lobby door, whispering. "It will all be okay."

The optimistic mantra had been said so often, it soothed me—even if it didn't solve anything.

My high heels sunk into a plush Oriental rug, but I didn't make it to the polished marble on the far side of it before Logan came rushing in from the side.

"You made it!" She gave me a fierce hug.

I blinked, surprised. "I didn't know you were going to be here."

An iridescent-green dragonfly barrette clipped her pink streak above her ear and she wore a blue paisley peasant-style dress, making her seem much younger and more feminine than her usual jeans and cap.

She rolled her eyes. "D apparently keeps everything about me secret."

I looped an arm through hers. "Show me where we're going."

"Just down here." She steered us along the edge of a massive round table, then leaned over and plucked a fork and a dessert plate of chocolate cake from a display laden with them.

Tilting my head toward her, I murmured conspiratorially. "Do we need to stockpile food?"

She glanced left, then right, before arching her brows. "If they're offering, I'm taking." Holding up the plate with one hand, she gave a decisive nod as she speared the fork through the densely frosted back corner. Then she paused in the middle of the hall and offered me the first bite.

The moment the rich dark chocolate exploded on my taste buds, I moaned. "*Oh. My. God.*"

"Right?" She gave me a secretive look. "This is my second piece."

I laughed as she stuck a heaping forkful into her mouth. Then she guided us down a hall, left, right, then led us into a tiled gallery.

Through a set of french doors to the left, a hostess stood at a podium with menus in her hand, then directed a young couple farther into a candlelit dining room. We went to the right, down two wide steps, into a lounge area where the sultry sounds of jazz music already drifted into the air. I tried to spot Darren by the windows, but too many people standing and dancing blocked my view as we worked our way inside.

Across the sizable room and along the far wall, stretched a stately bar area furnished in rich, dark woods. On my right, a half dozen cozy seating areas had been created with squared-off leather club chairs and matching ottomans. Candles flickered on low tables.

In the center of the space, three couples commanded a wooden dance floor, mesmerizing the audience with their twirling moves and gyrating hips. My brain tried to place their dance: Samba? Rhumba? As a kid, I hadn't paid enough attention to the country-club mandated ballroom dance lessons to remember.

We claimed one of only two available seating areas left. I relaxed back into a butter-soft brown leather club chair with an unimpeded view of the musicians who were positioned near the right corner of the dance floor.

My gaze finally landed on Darren. His dark hair was its usual: messy but stylish. His black short-sleeved T-shirt exposed the flexing muscles of his forearms.

"Another bite?" Logan asked, lifting a second piece of cake toward me.

I shook my head. "No, thanks."

My focus remained riveted on him. He had his eyes shut. With the slightest movements, his whole body undulated in a rhythm that transformed into sound through his hands to the various percussion pieces of his drum set. His left hand remained low, pulsing a soft beat over the center of a snare with what looked like a brush. His other hand hovered a matching brush over the top cymbal of a pair that had been vertically mounted on a stand.

"That's a hi-hat." Logan nodded toward Darren's left.

"The cymbals?"

She nodded. "Yep."

"What's he using on it?"

"A brush." She put her empty plate on a side table. "It's made of thin wires. Gives a softer sound for jazz and ballads."

"You play guitar, right?"

"Bass guitar." She slouched down into the chair until her head rested on its low-slung back. "I like losing myself in the deeper tones."

I mimicked her posture, relaxing back with her.

The song changed, shifting the music to a much slower tempo. After a moment, all three couples vacated the dance floor, heading in the direction of the bar. Two other couples, perhaps encouraged by the experts' absence, migrated to the floor and began swaying to the romantic strains.

My attention drifted back toward Darren.

My breath caught when I realized that he stared directly at me, gaze smoldering.

A sensual smile curved my lips as a heated flush worked its way outward from my heart, both up my chest, neck, and face and down through my belly, lower, into more scandalous regions. *Connected.*

"You're into art, right?"

I blinked, suddenly aware there were others in the room. "Yes. I'm a sculptor."

Darren broke eye contact, closing his eyes once more as he played.

"Ever teach a class?"

"A class?" I glanced at her, confused about the topic changeup, wanting to be sure I hadn't missed something during the seconds I'd been entranced while staring at her brother.

"Yeah. Art."

"No." I'd only graduated in the last year myself. "Why?"

She gave a one-shoulder shrug. "I go to meetings on Tuesday and Thursday mornings at the community center."

I didn't follow. "Meetings? Don't you have school?"

After a deep breath, she glanced my way, then stared hard for a few beats. "SSL. Survivors of Suicide Loss. And yeah, I go to school in the afternoons on those days."

"Oh." Made sense. I would be a wreck if someone I'd loved died, let alone by suicide.

"My therapist made me go. At first it was horrible. Total nightmare having to listen to everyone else's stories. Then I'd go home and relive my own. Eventually it started to help."

I put a gentle hand on her arm. "I'm glad."

"Anyway, art is supposed to help. Their budget from donations allowed for art supplies. All the stuff was bought, and they'd lined up a teacher and everything. But he was transferring in from out-of-state for his paying job and his move got cancelled."

"What kind of supplies?"

"Not sure. It looked like a case of metal boxes of colored pencils. Another case had paints, I think. Drawing pads and about a dozen small canvases.

Drawing and painting were different than sculpting—and each other. It had been years since I'd done either: high school and first-semester art school. "I've never taught art before." Or anything, for that matter.

"No biggie." She glanced back at her brother. "Just thought I'd ask."

My heart ached for her. *For them.* "Well, I suppose if there's no judgment, I could learn as I go."

"Really?" Excitement buzzed in her tone.

"Hey, now. I'm not promising amateur to Monet, or anything."

She snorted. "I suck at all things on paper. You keep me in the lines? You're a success."

"When? How often?" Then a thought occurred to me. "Any pay involved?"

"After our meetings. And no. I'm pretty sure it's volunteer. That okay?"

"Yeah." I leaned over and looped my arm through hers. "It's totally okay." And it was.

After all, I'd sought something outside of my art to brighten my spirit and had found trail running. Darren had gifted me that. The least I could do was give them something in return.

As I sat in the posh hotel lounge, arm in arm with Logan, Darren glanced my way. Only this time, instead of my body responding with a sexual heat, a different kind of warmth surged through me. And instead of spreading outward toward erogenous zones, it flowed inward, settling into a heaviness right in the center of my chest.

Love.

Incredibly, I didn't fear the emotion. I welcomed it.

I tightened my hold on Logan as I stared intently at Darren. I watched as his expression transformed into something that resembled pride.

And for the brief moment in time, while he immersed himself into his passion for music, in front of those he cared about and sought to protect, a part of me began to believe he could protect me—that *he* was my miracle.

30
SYNCHRONICITY

We wrapped up the second set by 10:00 p.m. I stowed my gear, then led Dino and Gordie, our sax player, to introduce them to Logan and Kiki.

Pumped from one of the most surreal experiences of my life, I couldn't wipe the shit-eating grin off my face. I'd been cool and relaxed while playing; the music took me there.

Now? My hands began to shake. My mind still couldn't wrap around it.

I'd played with *Dino Mathis.*

And we'd been awesome. Like we'd jammed for years.

To ground myself, I stared at my girls who had nothing but pride all over their faces. "Logan, Kiki, this is the *great* Dino Mathis."

Nervousness buzzed inside of me, only for a new

reason now: I hoped Kiki liked the music. And that she felt comfortable with my new crew—guys I'd be working with for months on end.

A throat cleared beside me. "And his lowly sidekick, Gordie."

I blinked. "Oh, dude. I didn't mean it like that."

"Don't sweat it." He arched his brows. "You're now the *lowlier* sidekick."

Dino shook the girls' hands. "Ladies, it's an honor to meet you." His southern drawl oozed charm. "Darren didn't tell us how beautiful you both were. Which one's Logan?"

"I am." She crossed her arms. "But don't be getting any ideas, Dino. I'm jailbait."

"Me too." Gordie batted his eyes at Dino.

Everyone burst out laughing. Because even though Dino was closer to my age—twenty-five to thirty tops—Gordie had to be pushing sixty. Not that anyone cared. Music knew no age.

When the chortling died down, Dino clapped his hands. "Who's hungry?"

"Me!" Logan thrust both arms in the air.

Kiki's jaw dropped. "You polished off—"

"Shhh!" Logan shot Kiki a glare. "No one needs to know the details. I had a *tiny* appetizer. Growing girl. High-speed metabolism."

Dino gestured forward with the broad sweep of his arm. "After you, my lady. This swanky establishment has offered us dinner on them. And *I* am famished."

I grinned, then roped an arm around Kiki, whispering

an educated guess about Logan's appetizer, "Danish?"

"Cake." She wrapped an arm around my waist as Dino and Gordie flanked my sister on the way to the restaurant.

"Chocolate?"

Kiki gave a nod.

"I bet she had two."

Kiki glanced at me, then Logan. She pressed her lips together, but amusement twitched the corners. "Not telling."

"So what did you think?" I had an amazing time, but jazz wasn't for everyone. A split second after I asked, anxiety pinged in my gut. I wanted her to like our sound, my playing, more than I'd realized.

"I loved it." Her face brightened with a wide smile.

I blew out a relieved breath, then nodded with a grin as warmth spread through my chest. "Good." Fantastic, actually. Meant we had yet another thing in common.

She moved in front of me, following our group as the hostess led us toward a more private table on the back patio. Before we made it out the doors, we paused while an older couple got up from their table, her with a walker, him with a cane.

"Sir" —I reached down to pick up a dark coat still draped over the back of his chair— "I think you forgot something."

The old man turned, then smiled, weathered face crinkling. "Oh, thank you, my boy. I'd have been mighty sore to lose that."

The woman appeared by his side and nodded. "I gave that to him on our fifth anniversary. Sixty-five years ago."

"No problem." I held out the coat, helping the gentleman put it on.

We watched the couple as they carefully negotiated their way through the tight tables of the dining room until they disappeared.

When I turned, Kiki stared at me with a dumbfounded expression. "Do you rescue everyone you come in contact with?"

"Nope." I corralled her into my arms. "Only the destitute and the elderly."

She poked a hard finger into my ribs as we stepped through the open french doors. "Ow! Okay, okay. I *do* have a soft spot for gorgeous metalwork sculptors who mistakenly think they need one-night stands."

On a heavy sigh, she leaned into me. "*Sooo…*I need *more* than a one-night stand?"

I stared down into her eyes. A tender vulnerability shone back at me. And I wondered what I did to deserve her. I gave her a tight squeeze, then dipped down, brushing my lips over hers. "You need the whole enchilada."

Laughter erupted against my lips. "Do *not* talk about sex and food in mixed company." She sighed as we walked to the table, joining the others. "Great," she muttered as I pulled out the chair beside Logan for her. "Now I'm thinking about a very *big* enchilada."

"*Ooo…*" Logan flipped a page in her menu. "Do they serve Mexican?"

Kiki glared up at me.

I kissed her temple. Then hovered my lips over her ear, whispering. "You started it, Flash. *Sex on a stick…*"

That quieted her down. But all through dinner, between

the jokes and laughter among old friends and new, she kept darting secretive glances at me loaded with heated innuendo. Like even though we were in mixed company, her thoughts kept straying to when we'd be alone—when we'd put something else altogether on the menu.

My attention drifted toward Logan as the servers began clearing the plates. She wore an easy smile and had engaged in razor-sharp banter several times during the meal. And yeah, we were out late on a school night, but taking a rare break out together and seeing her enjoying herself was worth a few hours of missed sleep.

Dino took a long pull of his beer after his plate was taken. When he put the bottle down, he glanced at Kiki. "So, tell me about your art."

She snapped her head up from staring at the spot on the white tablecloth where her plate had been. "My art?"

"Sure." He gave a nod toward me. "Your boy tells us you forge metal?"

She glanced at me, her eyes sparkling and smile widening. And although her art did that to her—made her glow from the inside out—I got the feeling it had more to do with Dino calling me her boy.

And damn, if that didn't make my chest swell.

"I do." She fingered the corner of her napkin, staring at it a moment. "Some are sculptures made of found metal objects. Originally, I forged botanical sculptures out of bronze. On each piece, I add a mineral pigment to the molten metal, turning one small element a color."

In the relative quiet around us, with no other guests

seated on the patio and everyone at our table listening to her, her voice softened as she spoke, clear passion about her art coming through in her tone.

Dino tilted his head a fraction to the side. "Why don't you work with bronze anymore?"

"Oh, I do." She took a deep breath, expression growing serious. "I mean, I will. I've just finished one. Money's tight. Need to sell a few pieces in order to buy more of the good stuff."

"Hand me your phone." Dino reached over the table, palm up.

Kiki's brows furrowed. "My phone?"

"I'll put my number in there. When you have time, text me pictures of some of your pieces. I'm closing escrow on a pad in that new downtown skyscraper next month. Penthouse takes up the entire top two floors."

Kiki's eyes remained wide as she pulled her phone from her purse. "You like art."

Dino pushed a button on her phone, then typed as his expression grew amused. He handed her phone back, giving her a pointed look. "I'm a musician, Kiki. Of course I like art."

Gordie made a disgusted face. "I'm a musician, but I don't like *art*."

The entire table fell silent. The last weighted word hung in the air, like it held judgment. Everyone darted glances at everyone else, but for several seconds, no one said anything. Maybe because they couldn't tell if there had been some private joke we'd all missed.

The longer the silence dragged on, the heavier an irritation uncoiled in my gut. He'd just insulted my girl. Brand-new bandmates or not, I didn't give a shit about my lowlier sidekick status.

I sucked in a deep breath, ready to rail on him, but someone beat me to the punch.

"What don't you like about *art*, Gordie?" Logan's words oozed venom as she shot a pointed look at him.

I stared at my sister, shocked she'd jumped into the minefield.

Gordie blinked, suddenly looking uneasy under the heated scrutiny. Then he glanced at Kiki. "I didn't mean any offense."

I leaned back and crossed my arms over my chest, narrowing my eyes at him. "Then what did you mean?"

"Yeah." Dino turned to fully face Gordie. "What's wrong with *art*?"

Gordie swallowed hard. "It's just all the…nakedness."

"Nakedness?" Kiki's voice squeaked. The corners of her lips twitched, her expression incredulous.

"On the sculptures. David hanging his junk out there. Not even sizable junk either. And those warped paintings of women with their eyes in the wrong place on their faces."

"Michelangelo and Picasso." Kiki folded her napkin, her gaze never leaving Gordie's as amusement sparked in her eyes. "Total opposite spectrums of style. But those are only two examples of many of the greats. You should expand your horizons. Maybe we'll go to the museum. I'd be happy to show you around."

"Uh…" Gordie shifted uncomfortably in his seat, then cleared his throat. "No, that's okay."

Dino shoved his shoulder hard enough that Gordie had to plant a hand on the table to prevent himself from toppling out of his chair. "Clear your ears out, Gordie. And straighten out your head. Kiki said she sculpted *botanicals*. You got a problem with her making *naked* flowers?"

Kiki finally burst out laughing.

Then everyone joined in but Gordie, whose cheeks reddened with embarrassment. "Sorry, Kiki. Didn't mean to insult you. I'm sure you make pretty flowers."

"It's okay, Gordie." Kiki's expression softened at him. "You play beautiful saxophone." Then she glanced at Dino before her gaze landed on me. "You three have an incredible sound. I'm honored to have had a chance to hear it tonight."

Pride swelled in my chest again. That she'd loved our music so much. That she and my sister had stood their ground to these guys, and the guys respected them and me enough to fix the awkward art conversation. The night had gone better than I'd hoped.

"You should come to her class." Logan arched a brow at Gordie.

"What class?" I frowned. Had I missed something?

"Oh, we just decided while you were playing," Logan continued. "Kiki's agreed to step in and teach an art class at the community center a couple times a week."

"Really?" I glanced at Kiki, unable to believe it.

Not that I doubted my sister. Just…I'd been so afraid that bringing any woman into the mix of my chaotic life would spin it out of control. Apparently because that woman was Kiki, my life had not only begun to calm, but the benefits reached out and grabbed hold of Logan too.

"Yeah." Kiki smiled up at me and gave a little shrug. "They need someone." Her expression fell a little. "And I might have some free time on my hands soon." She muttered, "And maybe need a place to stay."

Determination roiled inside me. I leaned over and whispered fiercely. "You will *not* have free time on your hands soon. I plan to keep you *plenty* busy. And you will *always* have a place to stay."

Her expression lightened with the tiniest bit of hope and a small smile. But then it faltered.

On a growl, I kissed her. Didn't care about the audience. Didn't matter about her worries of the impending deadline she faced.

Something in my gut told me we would figure it all out.

After all—we made it this far.

31
SAVING ME

Kiki...

The next day, when I showed up at the community center for my first art class, it all clicked why the address Logan had given me after dinner looked so familiar. It was the same place where Darren worked out. We'd run for the first time on the track out back, done stadiums together.

Apprehension of the unknown—that had clenched my gut the whole way over—began to ease a bit as I stepped through those outer metal doors. And although Logan had instructed me to take a right at the first hallway, I kept going straight, then took a left, drawn toward the gym Darren had been in.

Would he be there now?

It struck me that the time of day was similar: Tuesday morning, 9:30 a.m. Same day of the week, nearly an hour later. Plus I'd shown up about thirty minutes early to take stock of my surroundings and the art supplies I had to work with.

But first, the propped-open metal door at the end of the hall held my interest. On occasion, a heavy grunt would filter out. When I stepped into the room, a guttural growl vibrated through the air, and my gaze shot to a guy on a weight bench who powered through the middle part of a bench press, arms shaking. A spotter above him barked unintelligible words at him until, with a low shout, he pushed the barbell all the way up. Then his spotter guided it onto the rack.

As I loitered in the doorway, my attention drifted toward the far corner. My breath caught the moment I saw him.

Eyes closed, Darren stood motionless, ear buds in his ears, arms extended at shoulder height out to each side, hands gripping the handles of his sand-filled metal pails.

I watched him, mesmerized. This was where he went to push his body, to calm his mind. For me, that was running. Maybe running did that for him too.

After several seconds of standing there, I felt time press in on me. My class was in twenty-five minutes. I turned around and backtracked down the hall, then took the turn toward the rooms Logan had told me about.

On the left, a closed door had a vertical window above its handle. Through the glass, I saw a group of about twenty people sitting in chairs that had been arranged in a circle. Logan sat on the far side with her black newsboy hat on. She faced my way, but a teenaged boy across from her kept her attention.

Breath held, I eased the door open and stepped inside.

"...so I'll keep on with my journal," the boy said. "Not sure if the meds are helping. But I'll stick with 'em until I see the doc next week. And my mom...still trying to get her to come to a meeting. And that's all."

"Thank you for sharing, Henry," the group said in cadence.

Several hands went up. Henry pointed at a man who looked to be about forty. The man lowered his hand and took a deep breath, wiping his hands once down his jeans. "Hi, I'm Will."

"Hi, Will," the group replied.

"I'm...this is my first time sharing." He closed his eyes. "I've been here eight times. It's only been five weeks since..." His hands trembled. He sucked in a shaky breath, brows furrowing. "My wife, Diane..." His voice broke. Then his eyes popped open, wild and unfocused. "I can't. That's all I've got."

A big guy to his right put a hand on his shoulder. "It's more than enough. We're here to help any way we can. When you're ready."

The entire group nodded, eyes shining with intensity. "Thanks for sharing, Will."

When Will dropped his face into his hands, shoulders racked with silent sobs, the big guy's hand stayed on Will's shoulder while he nodded to a woman who began to raise her hand.

"Hi, I'm Carrie."

"Hi, Carrie," the group responded in chorus.

"It's been twenty-one months since my son Justin..."

My heart ached for this brave group of souls, survivors trudging through the muck of emotions everywhere they turned. Carrie told a heartbreaking story, one of trying to do all she could for her son, but he'd been pulled under by depression, unable to claw his way out.

Maybe I could help these people. At the least, show them distraction with a new endeavor. Running had done that for me and more. My distraction had set me free from my solitary life.

Zoned out for the moment, rapid movement caught my attention. Logan waved, then got up and crossed the room.

She pulled the brim of her hat down a little over her right eye, then tucked one side of her hair, part gloss-black and all of the pink streak, behind her ear. "You're early."

I nodded, stuffing a hand into my jeans pocked. "I hope that's okay. Wanted to set up. Get comfortable." As much as was possible on a first day.

"That's cool. It's the room across the hall."

At her chin-nod in the direction over my shoulder, I glanced back toward an identical door with a vertical window slot.

"Thanks. This" —I tipped my head in nod behind her— "seems like a good group."

"It is. Tough as hell at first. But if we stick it out, it helps. Takes time."

"Like for Will."

"Yeah." She turned, glancing the man's way. "He'll be okay. Ron's gonna sponsor him."

"The big guy."

Logan nodded. "Ron's my sponsor too. Will…he'll make it through okay."

I didn't even want to think about the alternative. Clearly the group held a vital role in their recovery. And if artwork would help a little more? I was all in. "I'll let you get back. Just head on over whenever you guys are ready."

"Thanks, Kiki."

She gave me a quick hug, then crossed the room, skirting the chairs toward her own. When Carrie began to wrap up, Logan raised her hand while she took a seat. Carrie pointed at her.

And as Logan began to talk, my feet remained rooted where they were.

"Hi, I'm Logan."

"Hi, Logan," the group chimed.

"It's been two years and three months since my mom took her life." She sucked in a deep breath. "My mom committed suicide. I can finally say that out loud now. I'm starting to understand that she felt like she didn't have a choice. Not a day goes by that I don't think about it.

"And I'm still struggling with depression. Some days I lose time: I find myself zoned out and hours have whizzed by since my last clear memory. When my body feels too heavy, each breath torture to pull in, and the whole world closes in on me, I seem to shut down. But the last few weeks, that's been happening less and less."

As I listened to Logan share her innermost secrets, a small part of me felt guilty for eavesdropping. But a bigger part overrode the guilt. I'd eavesdropped on that roof, which is how I'd met her. She'd invited me onto her ledge. She'd also invited me to her group, to be a part of the private healing happening between these walls—wanted me to be a part of it.

And if understanding Logan and learning about her peers helped me do that, then it had to be okay.

Logan adjusted her hat again, tugging it up a little. "Some things are helping. I'm finally opening up to people. My brother…and I…made a new friend. She's the first outsider I've told. And she's cool. She'll be teaching our art class after." Her eyes narrowed, then scanned around the circle. "And you all had better go."

Which was my cue to get ready. I glanced at my phone. *Fourteen minutes.*

"I'm still having problems at school…with other kids." At her words, a part of me wanted to stay. But she'd already asked me for advice about kids and school privately on that rooftop. Now was her time with her peer support group. And she'd asked me to help her in another way.

Nerves began to ping again as I crossed the hall and opened the door. But when I stepped through and walked farther in, I breathed a sigh of relief. The room was immaculate and bright; light radiated in from three big windows along the back wall. Long folding tables formed two rows five tables deep, a center aisle stretching down between them.

Supplies had already been set out, and I wondered who'd done that. Probably Logan. In front of each chair, items were arranged like place settings at a dinner table. Two brushes on the left, assorted watercolor tubes on the right, a white, round plastic palette in the center, and an empty mason jar in each upper right-hand corner.

"What do you think?"

I jumped at the bass-toned voice an instant before my heart warmed.

Darren.

He stood in the doorway, a forearm braced on each side of the doorframe. His damp gray shirt clung to his sculpted torso. Dark curls of hair stuck to his temples, glistening.

My breath caught at his raw beauty as I crossed the room toward him. "I think it's amazing. You did this?"

"Yeah. Figured you'd need a hand sorting it all out. There's other stuff in the boxes in the supply closet. Didn't know what paper to grab. There are different kinds, but not enough whole pads for everyone."

As I drew near, his delectable scent hit me—a mixture of his soap and his natural musk.

He took a step back. "Careful. I haven't showered yet. I'm all sweaty."

"I don't care." I fisted my hands into his shirt over his chest, then pulled him close, standing on tiptoe. He bent down and kissed me, tenderly.

Then I leaned against his side and glanced into the room. "And it's perfect."

He kissed my temple, then pushed me forward and swatted my ass. "Go. Help them find their inner artists. I'm heading to shower and then school. Last classes before finals."

"Really?" I turned as he began to disappear. "I hadn't

realized we were so close to the end of the school year."

He grabbed the doorframe, popping his head back into view. "Yep. After next Thursday, no more school."

The finality to his tone struck me. I thought he'd said he had another year. I wondered if his gig with Dino had changed that.

"Good luck, baby. You'll be awesome."

My heart warmed at the endearment, the first time he'd called me anything other than "Flash."

I smiled at him, all my anxiety forgotten. "Thanks."

He disappeared without another word.

But I felt him there—his support. It lay in plain view in the carefully arranged art supplies. And I was there to support Logan. I'd come today for them.

After assessing the paper situation in the supply closet, I chose a heavier weight better suited for watercolor. I tore off two sheets per student, placing them beside each setting of art supplies. Then I found a large pitcher and wandered the halls until I located a kitchen.

Minutes later, as I filled the last of the mason jars with a few inches of water, after already adding red Solo cups beside them for brush rinsing, my students began to file in. Only seven sat down, Logan at a front table with Carrie right beside her, big Ron across the aisle and a table back from them, and four others spread throughout the room.

After a brief fifteen-minute primer on how to use their palettes and experimenting on their first page with washes and color intensity, we were ready to begin.

"Okay. Now let's try our hand at painting. There are no

rules. Everyone has a different concept of what art is. Express yourself. But I do have a topic. Think of one memory filled with joy. Then paint a single image from it: a trigger for that memory."

My students nodded then their eyes grew unfocused in thought. Logan stuck the wood end of her paintbrush between her lips. Ron rinsed his brush, squeezed several paint colors into the divots of his palette, then began painting immediately.

At the empty front table, I sat down and stared at the blank page, joining them, imagining a happy moment. Images of Darren flooded my mind: us with our feet on the wall as we listened to drag rhythms, watching fireflies on a warm spring night with anticipation humming through us before our first time, the incredible awe-filled expression on his face as he made love to me…

Yet for some reason, the one moment that stuck in my mind more vivid than the rest was the first time we went on a trail run. At the top of the mountain, I'd raised my arms, energy buzzing through my veins, soul soaring with the wind, and shouted "be the tree" at Darren—at the world.

I'd let go—felt free.

Seconds later, the world showed me my mortality as I hung from a tree branch.

Then Darren saved me.

We'd laid on the ground, me draped over him, and experienced our first intimate moment together.

With a grateful sigh, I began painting that tree branch. I paid special note to its rough bark. With a light touch, I swept arcing lines to create the tufts of soft needles. The branch, true to its original form, remained slender and strong—full of life and lifesaving.

When I finished, I stared at it, remembering the moment with great clarity and fondness. That branch had literally saved me from a potentially fatal fall. Then it swung me into the waiting arms of someone who'd also saved me—who still fought hard to.

My phone buzzed in my back pocket. Unthinking, I pulled it out.

A text appeared. From Dino:

Where's my art?

The question slammed into my chest like a sucker punch. A second text came through.

Send pics of only your best pieces.

A handful of seconds. The blink of an eye. All it took for my mood to plummet.

"The best pieces are being held hostage," I growled under my breath.

Then a devious plan began to unfold.

Later that night, I sat in my car. Forced breaths filled my lungs.

Dark thoughts had overtaken my mind.

Breaking glass.

Alarm bells.

Cold cuffs biting into my wrists.

I gripped the steering wheel and glared at the innocent-seeming gallery.

It mocked me.

Plate glass stretched from wall to wall, showcasing beautiful pieces of art for onlookers to view. *My* art. Locked behind doors that had been sealed by the authority of the federal government. *Stolen* from me.

My phone buzzed from the center console. I picked it up. The screen lit with a text from Darren.

Watcha doin?

I sighed, both irritated and grateful for the intrusion.

Contemplating criminal activity.

A blue bubble appeared immediately.

Where?

Without thought, I answered.

Midnight Sky Gallery.

Then I tossed my phone back. It lit up again, but I ignored it.

Instead, I focused another scathing glare at the cause of my misery.

The gallery looked like every other storefront along the street: wall-to-wall windows, lights out inside, as if calmly closed for business for the night.

Yet the harmless, pristine picture it painted was all wrong.

No thick chain with a heavy-gauge lock hung from the chrome door handle. No yellow tape stretched across the threshold screaming that something had gone horribly awry inside—but it had.

It was bad enough my earned commissions had vanished, unpaid. To add insult to injury, that innocuous-looking storefront held my artwork hostage—some of my largest and best pieces. Wrongfully dragged into the undertow of someone else's crime, I was days away from being homeless. And the federal government felt comfortable in their authority to bind my hands.

I wasn't the only one. Besides eight of my sculptures, acrylic canvases by several in-demand painters hung on the walls. And near the front window, silver necklaces by a renowned jewelry artist sat quietly on display. All those pieces were held captive behind prison walls made of glass, erected by crooks and reinforced by power-entitled bureaucrats who were indifferent to the difficulties facing a starving artist.

I tightened my hands over the steering wheel, contemplating all kinds of nefariousness: driving my car through the glass, rescuing my artwork, spray painting my thoughts all over their pretty exposed brick wall.

A dark shadow crossed in front of my car. Then another.

In the space of a heartbeat, four large figures surrounded my front hood. They stared through my windshield.

The one directly in my line of sight cocked his head.

Darren.

A sudden knock at my window startled me. Cade wound his fist and index finger in a vertical, circular motion. When I rolled down my window, his brows raised. "Open up."

I unlocked the doors and those four big guys all began to load inside.

"No. I'm not sitting in the middle," Ben argued.

"No bitching. I drove." Mase shoved Ben forward.

The car rocked back and forth. I stared in the rearview mirror, mouth falling open, as three grown men squeezed into the back. Darren settled beside me in the front passenger seat.

"*Had* to be a Prius," Ben muttered.

"Shut it," Cade ordered.

"So. How we doing this?" Darren asked.

"Doing what?" My brain felt muddled from my earlier shady thoughts. And from too many mouth-breathers in the car. I tried to ignore the incredible presence of Darren sitting next to me, how my body pinged to life around him.

To distract myself, I glanced at the rearview mirror.

Ben stared back at me, with a look that said *duh.* "Breaking and entering."

Mase ripped open a Cheetos bag. "Pretty sure that's a felony."

"Only if we get caught." Cade reached into the open bag over Ben's lap. Crinkling ensued. Orange dust began to float around inside my car.

"No one's committing any felonies," I muttered. No way in hell I was risking orange jumpsuits on those pretty boys. Besides, that clusterfuck in the gallery was my mess. My cleanup.

Cade reached forward from behind me, resting his hands on my shoulders. "You could have told me, Keek. I can help."

Keek. The nickname he'd called me when we were kids. A memory flashed of when he had just learned to walk. I'd come home from my first day at kindergarten, one pigtail undone, dress torn from roughness on the playground. But when I'd walked up the driveway and the neighbor's three yipping Pomeranians growled and charged at me, Cade had tottered full speed between me and the fluffballs-with-teeth.

I let out a heavy sigh. "Thanks, Cade. But I don't want your money."

"We don't want you in jail," Mase mumbled around a mouthful of food.

"I'm not going to jail. I did imagine smashing that pretty plate glass window and taking my sculptures back."

"Totally blows they're locked up in there." Ben's brows furrowed.

"The damn IRS is holding them hostage," I snarled.

"Didn't those pieces sell at the exhibit in December?" Mase asked.

I took a deep breath, then let out a heavy sigh. "No. Others did."

The next seconds dragged by, silent. Like they'd all tucked deep into their minds, searching for the best way to tackle the problem. My thoughts swung back toward infiltration—Mission Impossible style. When images of me dropping from the ceiling in a ninja getup bordered on the ridiculous, I pinched my eyes shut.

"I'm just so—" Emotion clogged my throat. "A*aahhhrrr!*" I strangled the steering wheel.

"That a technical term?" Mase leveled a stare at me in the rearview.

"I know it well." A loud crinkle echoed in the car as Ben snagged the Cheetos bag. "Live it on a daily basis."

"You need to lighten up, Mr. Live and Breathe My Bar." Mase snatched the bag back.

The Cheetos dust swirled thicker in the air. A cheesy scent filled my nostrils.

"I know a great way to work out frustration." Cade put a hand on my shoulder as he leaned forward and planted the other on Darren's.

"Dude." Mase's tone dropped. "We are *not* talking about Kiki—*baby sister* Kiki—having sex with Darren."

"What?" Ben blinked, stared at me, then at Darren. "You two are…"

"Softball, *idiots.*" Cade reached over and punched them both at the same time.

More crinkling ensued, followed by grunts and car rocking, as the three of them wrestled—as best as three grown men could in the backseat of a Prius. My dark thoughts began to fade as I watched the comical scene unfold.

"Well, what d'ya think?" Darren, calm as ever, glanced at me.

"Softball?"

"Yep. Loading Zone's game is tomorrow afternoon. You know we always need more players."

I nodded absentmindedly. "Yeah. I'll go. It's for charity, after all. And I *really* need to whack something. Hard."

The ruckus settled down in the back.

The weight in the car shifted.

In the rearview, I caught Cade settling back into his seat, a thoughtful expression on his face. "Seriously, though. About the government-being-an-asshole issue. Let me make a few calls. Dad's got high-powered financial friends."

Ben turned toward him. "And our accountant used to work for the IRS."

Darren put his hand on my knee and squeezed it gently. "We're gonna keep you outta the slammer, Flash."

Warmth spread through my chest. That I hadn't asked for help, but my knights came to my rescue anyway. It all made me love these guys just a little bit more. One in particular.

I glanced at Darren and mouthed, "*Thank you.*"

He gave me a hard look. The kind filled with intensity and clear meaning. It said with its ground-shaking silence *There's nothing I wouldn't do for you.*

That warmth in my chest deepened, my heart melting for the man.

Then sudden fear settled in. What would happen if I cared too much, fell too hard?

The truth hit me like a bolt of lightning.

It's already too late.

32
IN PLAIN SIGHT

Darren…

The next morning, I balanced two coffee cups in a tray, gym bag hanging by a crooked finger, while I rapped on Kiki's metal warehouse door.

My knock echoed.

Then silence.

Her Prius was tucked into its space. So I knew she'd made it home safely.

And I'd driven by the gallery on my way. No busted glass. Artwork all in their same places. No felony committed.

A sudden thump hit the side of my calf, and I startled, nearly dropping our coffees. Big hazel eyes stared up at me. Front paws were propped on my leg. A faint meow squeaked out.

"Hey, Chipmunky. Where's Kiki?"

The kitten dropped down, threw his weight into a full-body rub against my jeans, then trotted off until he disappeared around the warehouse corner. I followed, passing under a rusted arbor that had steel vines snaking up and around through the arch.

Off in the far corner of a deep courtyard, Kiki sat on the edge of a raised planter with her back toward me. Sunlight glinted off her dark hair which fell in loose spirals over her shoulders. She hummed lightly, a thin white cord dangling from the ear I could see, while she snipped off the tops of plants with small scissors before dropping them into a napkin-lined basket.

A half dozen mismatched bistro sets were scattered over broken brick pavers along the perimeter, making the space look like a café graveyard. An old maple tree from a neighboring yard stretched its skeletal branches overhead, filtering the sun.

She turned slightly when she reached for another plant, showing her profile. Her lips were moving, and I could hear the faintest melody as she cradled various stems before selecting a few, then cutting them off.

A smile tugged at my lips. In the private time I'd stumbled into, she appeared peaceful. Happy, even.

No way in hell am I barging in on that. Didn't want to ruin it. Felt lucky to witness it.

Instead, I sat in the sturdiest-looking chair. I slid the drink tray on a nearby table and dropped my duffel bag on another chair as I surveyed the patio I hadn't realized existed.

It was sizable. The planter section where Kiki sat had

herbs growing in a bright patch where sunlight streamed through neighboring buildings, but the foot-and-a-half tall brick planter bordered the whole enclosure. The patio floor had missing bricks in many sections, but in between, the ground was level. Dark green tufts of grass and moss sprouted here and there. The maple branches overhead had new leaves pushing out.

My attention swung back to Kiki right as she turned toward me. Her eyes widened then a huge smile brightened her face. My heart thumped hard at seeing her light up, just for me.

I worked one of the cups free from its holder, then offered it up as she yanked her earbuds down by their cords. "Darren!"

"Thought I'd bring you some liquid fuel."

Her basket clattered onto the bricks before I finished my sentence. She rushed over and practically crashed onto my lap. Her coffee cup barely landed on the table with a clunk before I wrapped my arms around her.

"*Whoooa.*" She gripped my shoulders as we teetered on the back legs of the chair. The metal groaned out a low creak under our weight.

I spread my legs wider, preparing to lunge up with her in my arms if needed.

A second passed.

Another.

We didn't topple.

Warm minty breath fanned between our mouths; her lush parted lips were less than an inch from mine. Her chest heaved from her excited sprint, bared exquisitely by her low-cut pale blue sundress.

"What's with the gardening?" I wanted to kiss her. Bad. But the crackling tension, the anticipation between wanting and doing, made the drawn-out wait worthwhile.

"I was collecting parsley and chives. Thought I'd make us breakfast."

When she glanced at her abandoned basket and tensed her legs to move, I grabbed her hip, stilling her.

She turned back toward me, touched the tip of her nose to mine, then smiled. "Or we could do breakfast right here." Her lips hovered over mine again, teasing.

I growled and nipped her lower lip. Then I opened wider, kissing her more deeply. I loved her taste, a blend between mint and coffee. "You already brewed a pot?"

"You look surprised." She suppressed a smile.

"It's before noon."

She shoved lightly on my shoulder. "I'm in training. The best runs happen in the morning."

Gripping her hips harder, I positioned her right over my growing hard-on.

With a tiny gasp, she shifted her hand down between our legs, pressing firmly on the denim. Then she blinked on a heavy swallow. "Oh, my."

I groaned low as her hand skated over my rigid length then found and squeezed the tip. I dropped my head into the crook of her shoulder. "The best *everything* happens in the morning."

All of a sudden, a monumental idea hit me. My head

popped up and I narrowed my eyes, assessing her patio space. Keeping a tight hold of her, I twisted, taking in the bigger picture.

"What's the matter?" Her brow wrinkled in confusion.

Understandable. Since my excited mood-shift had nothing to do with the fact that sexy-as-hell Kiki sat on my lap.

And shocking—that so little blood left in my brain allowed me to connect obvious dots.

"This space." I glanced at the roofline.

"My courtyard?"

"Invitation Only." Thoughts raced faster than I could formulate words. I held on to her waist as I stood, then stepped away from her, pacing out the open area.

"Is this word association?" She planted her hands on her hips. "Belgian waffle."

"No." I shook my head. Then her reply registered in my sluggish brain. "Hungry?"

"Starved." She bit her lower lip.

"You need to have a party."

"What?" She grunted a disbelieving noise, then walked across the pavers before resting the back of her hand on my forehead. "You feeling okay? I'm about to be evicted. You throw a party when you *move in*, not when you're being tossed out."

I grasped her wrist, kissed her palm, then spun her around, tucking her against me. "Look at this amazing space. You already have artwork displayed: the walls of your outside maze. Invitation Only works like a well-oiled machine already. Use your sisters, your brother…me."

She glanced up at me with a dubious look.

I ignored it. "Our band will fit over there." I nodded toward a curve in the nearest maze wall. "Connect lights up there." I pointed to the top edge of the roof. "Maybe drape them down to connect to the fence."

"No, Darren." She shook her head, pushing out of my hold. "I don't want any handouts."

"It's *not* a handout. It's a party."

When she kept shaking her head and wrapped her arms around her middle, I glared at her, waiting until she stopped negating the damn idea.

"You ever have a housewarming party?"

She gave me another, smaller headshake. Good. She liked saying no? I'd work with that.

"Do you dislike parties?"

Another headshake, only this time her lips firmed into a line. She crossed her arms tighter and lowered her brows. Like she knew she was losing a battle, but wasn't going down easy.

Her face pinked in anger. Her chest heaved with shallow breaths. "I don't feel like partying."

"You will if you sell some of your pieces."

Her head tilted a little, her gaze settling on the ground. When my idea fully sank in, hope flickered across her face but disappeared just as fast. "It's too late. The landlord already served the notice of eviction."

"So give the landlord your 'notice of staying,' offer her an enticement."

"Like what?"

"Like making up back rent and a few months in advance."

She grunted in disapproval. "No way. I could never sell that many pieces at one event."

"Depends on what kind of buyers you have."

"I thought you said it was a party."

"What if it's a party…*and* an art showing?"

"But this isn't a gallery."

"Who said you have to have a gallery?"

Her expression clouded over. "All it's going to do is get my hopes up." Arms still folded over her chest, she drummed her fingers on her outer biceps.

I shrugged. "So don't expect anything."

"I only have six more days before the end of the month."

"Next Tuesday?"

She gave a short nod.

"Best get crackin', then. Lot to plan in three days—party's on Saturday."

When she didn't move—refused to agree—I lowered my head, keeping her in my sights. Then I began to stalk her, squaring my shoulders, spanning out my arms.

She blinked, her mouth falling open. "What are you doing?"

"Going to convince you."

Lifting her hands, she began backing toward her herb garden, shaking her damn head again. "You can't convince me."

"Wanna bet?"

The forgotten basket caught her back foot and she stumbled.

I lunged forward and grasped her forearms, staring hard at her. "Let me help you."

"Why?"

"Because I love you," I whispered.

Her breath caught.

The words silently echoed in my head. I hadn't meant to say them. Hadn't fully realized I'd felt them. But I'd blurted them out, straight from my heart. With zero regret.

Tears sprang into her eyes. Her lips parted.

I put my fingers over them. "Don't say anything."

She exhaled, her hot breath fogging over them. Then she began to bounce. When I removed my hand, she scowled. "You can't drop that…bomb…and expect me not to say anything."

"You're not ready." I sensed that much. "But if you care for me at all, let me help you."

Eyes sparkling with unshed tears, her shoulders slumped. Then she leaned into me.

I wrapped my arms around her, pulling her close as I pressed my lips to the top of her head. "What do you have to lose?"

Her entire body tensed at the question.

I held her tighter, wishing I could make all her fears go away.

"Let me try and fix this—for me." I closed my eyes, hoping she'd agree.

Because I couldn't sit back and do nothing.

33
FIGHTING HARDER

Kiki...

You. *I could lose* you.

When Darren had said it before, I'd been afraid, when the risk wasn't as great. It terrified me now.

On a shaky exhale, I clung tighter to him, gripping the back of his thin T-shirt.

He remained silent—simply held me close with his solid strength.

"Okay." I finally relented with the quiet word.

My greatest fear wasn't becoming homeless, although, no doubt, that would totally suck. It was anxiety about this unexpected hero of mine, a warrior for my cause, becoming larger in my life than I'd ever imagined. Then being stolen away.

Things that seemed too good to be true ended up being that way in my life.

But Darren was different, right? He would never betray me.

"I love you too." I whispered my confession into his chest.

He pulled away and stared down into my eyes. "It scares you."

"Yes."

Holding my gaze, he let out a gentle sigh. "Scares the fuck out of me."

"Good." A smiled tugged at my lips.

He huffed out a short laugh. "Well, great."

"Whenever I care too much about something" —I sucked in a shaky breath— "it gets ripped away."

"I know." His tone quieted. "Me too."

"So…how do we get past that?"

He trailed his fingers along my jaw, then cupped the side of my face with his hand. "We fight harder to keep what we want."

I closed my eyes, silently wishing it would be that simple: *Want it, fight for it, and it's ours.*

His breath fanned over my nose, my chin. A gentle touch brushed over my mouth, then a tiny kiss pressed to one corner. Slowly he swept all the way across before gifting me another. Then his lips molded with mine in an incredibly tender kiss.

When he pulled away, I let out a tiny moan and opened my eyes.

His lips quirked. "Hence the party."

I slapped his chest. "You're relentless."

"Always."

"How is this even going to work? Six days is nothing."

"We pull some strings. Remember how Dino kept asking you questions about your art?"

"Yeah." I took a deep breath. "That's how I ended up at the gallery contemplating the heist of my own sculptures. He bugged me to send him pictures of my best pieces."

Darren cast me an amused look. "Seems my *rich* new boss, Dino, is a major art collector. Art collectors have friends. Maybe the party can be to both celebrate my new job *and* showcase your art."

"Okay. I like that idea. Makes me seem like less of a charity case."

"You're *not* a charity case."

All the talk about my art and party planning made me restless. While clipping herbs earlier, I'd been zoned out listening to the playlist of drag-rhythm music he'd emailed me. I liked losing myself in uncomplicated stuff.

I picked up my herb-filled basket, looped an arm through the handle, then veered wide around him.

"Where are you going?" He blinked, turning as he watched me.

"Inside." After I rounded the corner, I spun and walked backward.

He edged into view, curiosity in his expression. "What about the party?"

"What about that *convincing* you threatened?" A corner of my mouth curled into a smirk.

His eyes narrowed a fraction. "It's not a threat if you're looking forward to it."

On the next step, I lunged toward the door. I barely had time to fling it open before his hand caught the edge with a deafening clang.

A stinging smack landed on my left butt cheek as I charged through the doorway.

Laughter rang out as we raced through the sculptures and into the living room. I darted toward my worktable, then rounded its far corner before facing him with the hefty piece of furniture between us. I flung my herb basket from my arm, and it spun across the table's surface. It teetered then toppled over, spilling out its loose stems.

Darren slowed as he approached, tilting his face downward as he smoldered at me from beneath those dark brows. His chest heaved with labored breaths. His hands clenched into fists held low at his sides.

I drew in a slow breath as delicious warmth sizzled over my skin and settled low, between my legs. My body pinged to life from that heated look—the promise hidden there.

A loud noise echoed between us. *From my stomach.*

I held my breath, blinking.

Had he stopped breathing too?

We both pressed our lips together, shoulders shaking with muffled laughter.

His expression gradually hardened. "You're hungry."

"Famished." But right now, not about food. *At all.*

"You're gonna eat first." He straightened, then walked around the other side of the table toward the pot of coffee.

"Won't we get a cramp?" I let out a slow breath, trying to calm my rioting pulse.

"That's swimming."

Annnd…a picture of us naked underwater flooded into my mind. I swallowed hard, imagining water flowing over my body, his warm, muscular frame holding me, caressing me, gripping my hips as he plunged…

"This almond butter fresh?" He glanced up at me from where he squatted in front of my open minifridge.

"Um, yeah." I blew out a hard breath, clearing out the unexpected fantasy. My mind rifled through mundane topics, trying to cool my overheated body. "You left your stuff outside. Coffees…and what's with the gym bag?"

"Softball later. Thought I'd change here." He pulled out the half-full container of almond butter and a jar of apricot preserves, then grabbed two spoons from a cup beside the coffeemaker.

"Oh." I stared as he unscrewed the lids to both jars. "What are we, prisoners?"

An amused expression flashed over his face before he arched a brow at me. "You want to make a full breakfast now?"

I glanced at the spilled herb basket, then bit my lip and shook my head. "No." Earlier, I'd wanted to make omelets. Upstairs. Too far away and too long from right now to contemplate.

"Good." He dunked a spoon into each jar resting on the table. "*Come here.*"

The command rang into my ears but coasted through me

like a whole-body caress. Without thought, I obeyed, closing the distance between us. The second I came within reach he grabbed my hips and lifted me.

I squealed as he plopped me onto the edge of the table.

"I like this," he growled, lifting my dress hem up my legs until the blue gingham bunched at my hips.

"My dress?"

"Yeah. First time I've seen you in one."

"I've been in skirts before."

"Not the same." He lifted a spoonful of nut butter.

"Hannah's wedding: I was in a ball gown. Other part—"

He gently pushed the spoon between my open lips. Sweet crunchy nut butter hit my tongue. When he released his hold on the spoon, I grabbed it and continued to lick it clean.

"Not the same," he repeated. "This" —he slid his index fingers under the shoulder straps and tugged, peeling the thin fabric down until my breasts were exposed— "you wore for you…for me."

I had, I thought as I leaned forward, sinking the cleaned-off spoon back into the nut butter jar. I'd awoken in an amazing mood, partly because of the late-night intervention he'd convened outside of the art gallery; my heart still melted at the gesture. And the morning had begun all warm and sunshiny. Such a glorious day demanded my favorite sundress.

Biting coldness shocked one nipple and I gasped.

When I pulled back to glance down, he dolloped a larger freezing spoonful of preserves higher up on my other breast and stared with fascination as it slid down toward the hardened peak.

My breaths shallowed, rising and falling as we both waited with heady anticipation.

A fierce throb began an insistent rhythm between my legs.

Finally, he lunged forward. Capturing my nipple into his warm mouth right as the ice-cold jam collided with it.

A low moan escaped my throat as he sucked. When he switched sides, laving the stickiness off my other nipple, I buried my hands into his hair, gripping the roots.

My breaths grew ragged.

My heart raced.

My head spun.

My entire body ached for him from my skin to my bones. And we hadn't even moved from second base yet.

He pulled back, gaze roving over my half-naked state, eyes wild. "You need more food?"

Biting my lip, I gave a slow headshake. "No."

I would've starved for days for a chance to devour him.

On a deep inhale, he bent an arm up and behind his back, gripped his T-shirt, and yanked it over his head before tossing it behind me. I leaned back on my arms, a slight smile curving my lips, as I watched his muscles bunch and flex while he shucked off his jeans.

When he fully straightened again, his erection bobbed between us, and my breath caught at the beauty of him.

He leaned his face down a little, into my line of sight.

"You sure?" His voice grew husky. "You look…hungry."

"*Ravenous.*" I pressed a hand to his warm chest, over his thundering heart. "For you."

I gripped his shoulders, pulling myself toward him and off the edge of the table, dress crumpling around my hips. Sliding down his body, I dotted the heated skin of his chest with tender kisses. Over his rock hard abs, I opened my mouth, drawing the taut skin between my lips with gentle suction.

His fingers speared into my hair when I nuzzled the faint line of hair leading down from his navel with my nose. His breathing shallowed as I knelt lower and inhaled leisurely up along the crease of his groin while trailing with a light lick of my broadened tongue. *Salty. Perfect.*

My hands curved around his thighs, upward, until I cupped the muscular globes of his ass. For a few seconds, I paused, turning my face toward his remarkable manhood. I closed my eyes, resting my cheek into the depression at his hip. As I held him in the intimate embrace, I inhaled his sexy musk, drawing it deep into my lungs. My body shuddered in recognition, craving him.

His legs began to tremble. His hands cupped the back of my head, holding me to him.

"*Kiki.*" My name rasped from his lips like the sweetest plea.

When I glanced up, my gaze locked to his. Incredible depth of emotion shone in his eyes: need, want, hope, gratitude…love—a million unnamable things, all fragile and priceless. The same emotions cascaded through me, for him. I exhaled, willing him to feel it from me too.

He sucked in a deep breath, eyes softening as he flexed his hands through my hair. He knew. *We* knew.

I blinked heavily, then leaned forward, running my lips along his length from base to tip. Hands still firmly planted on his backside, I touched a gentle kiss to the broad head, gave a tender lick to the underside, then pressed tight lips around the tip and sucked, pulling him deep inside my mouth.

His whole body shuddered on a low groan.

Exquisite ache snapped through me, from his response, at our poignant connection—at the total control I had of over his pleasure. And all I wanted was to offer him more, make him happy, give the generous man who trusted me— body, heart, and soul—what he'd denied himself for so long.

With a whimpering moan at the incredible desire building through me at the profound act, I eased back, darting my tongue out to lick as I went. When he nearly popped out, I paused to suck the flared head once, twice, then slowly surged forward once more.

By the time I drew back again, I'd grown breathless, from both lack of oxygen and electrifying arousal.

His choppy breaths huffed above me until he let out a loud growl and grasped my arms, tugging me upward.

My tightened lips released him with a loud pop.

"*Need*…you." His guttural words were rasped out, barely decipherable.

"I—" *need you too…*

His lips crushed down onto mine, silencing me with a fevered kiss. Then he gripped my hips through my crumpled dress and lifted me up. I clamped my legs around his waist, stabbed my fingers into his hair, and kissed him back with all the passion I felt for him.

The room suddenly spun as he whirled us around, bumping into the corner of the worktable then along its side edge. His rigid erection was trapped between us under my bunched-up dress, rubbing on my throbbing clit with every long stride he took.

Two faster steps, then the room tilted as we tumbled together onto a couch.

"Need…*all*…of you," he grumbled at my ear before nipping at the lobe.

Breaths reduced to shallow pants, vision hazing as blood rushed and pleasure ached, I watched him lean back and crouch over me. With impatient hands, he tugged my dress and panties off. The instant the material cleared my ankles, it disappeared behind him.

His body covered mine, heated skin and bunching muscles. Soft lips brushed my mouth, his next kiss filled with tenderness, as if he wanted to learn me all over again, as if he asked me to be his.

And I was.

"I'm yours," I murmured against his ear. "*All of me.*"

Another shudder racked through his body at my declaration, like he'd needed to hear me say the words to feel it, believe it.

With reverent deliberate motions, he took what I offered, nudging me open, then sliding powerfully inside with one smooth stroke. He brushed the hair out of my eyes and stared down at me, his darkened eyes sparkling. Our chests expanded and contracted as one, pressing our thumping hearts together. We belonged to each other. Had become one—in every way.

Then we began to move.

Breaths mingled between gasping kisses. Bodies arched in undulating rhythm. Hands gripped, hearts raced, pleasure burned and sizzled until on a cry, my orgasm exploded through me. He pressed his lips to my neck and let out a choked roar as his pulsed forth, seconds later.

Minutes passed in lazy time as we laid there, floating back down to earth from somewhere up in the stratosphere. He sucked in a slow, deep breath, then let out a contented sigh. When his muscles relaxed further, he moved slightly to the side, shifting his crushing weight. I gripped him tighter with my arms and legs, rolling with him.

No idea how long we laid like that. The dreamlike state we drifted into had warped time. And neither of us was in a hurry to go anywhere. Not to plan a party or worry about our complicated lives. Not even to make our long-forgotten breakfast.

Whenever he twitched, like he'd fallen asleep, I'd snuggle closer. Then he'd band his arms tighter around me. Nonsensical cozy images filtered into my mind: foamy ocean waves lapping a sugar-sand beach, the sound of the wind rushing through the needles of a pine forest, lying in cool grass while the sun warmed my legs. Gradually, I came back to reality. And my favorite thing of them all rested right there in my arms.

With a satisfied hum, I gripped him tighter once more, burrowing into his body heat.

"Mmm. You smell so good."

"Hhhmmmph," he grunted.

"No, you do." I pressed my nose to his hairline, above his temple. On a slow inhale, I drew in more of his delicious scent. "Smoky sweet, like toasted marshmallow. With a hint of spicy earth."

His chuckle rumbled out. "Thanks. I smell like a dirty marshmallow."

I smacked his stomach lightly. "Not *at all* what I meant."

He let out a snort. "You described a gooey burnt blob dropped into the dirt."

I skimmed my hand over his taut abs, sliding down along his side and tucking closer until I curved a hand possessively around his far hip and hooked a bent leg over his thigh. "Not a chance." I pressed a gentle kiss to his chest. "I take great care of my smoking marshmallows. My hand would cradle below. Mouth watering, I'd want to taste. But not yet." I brushed my lips over his skin. "Too hot." I exhaled a slow sigh, leaning into his solid body. "*Sex-on-a-stick* hot."

His hand covered mine, fingers curling around to grasp it. Then he moved my hand toward me, lower, until he pressed my palm firmly over his rigid length. "I'll show you sex" —he arched his pelvis into our hands— "on a stick."

Heat coiled through me, low and demanding. Even as humor teased my brain. "No. *That* is no stick." I wrapped my hand around his impressive girth, fingertips not quite touching. "It's a thick branch."

All of a sudden, the world flipped. His weight pressed over me. My body sank into the couch. "Not a branch." The argument was growled against the column of my neck.

I swallowed hard, wrapping my body around him. "No."

No description encompassed all that he was. He was the trunk, the tree, the whole damn forest, the continent below and the sky above. When he slid inside, inch by inch, all thoughts of comparison melted away.

He became my whole world once again.

34
WHO'S ON FIRST?

Darren…

Kiki backed into her bathroom, eyes widening. "Shouldn't we start making calls for the party?"

"Later," I murmured, taking another step toward her.

Steam fogged the mirrors.

Water spattered the tiles.

But the second Kiki stepped under the spray?

Nothing else existed.

I couldn't get enough of her. Had denied what I'd needed for too long.

And I now knew, I needed *her*.

My brain short-circuited for further coherent thought. Dark glossy hair. Bright blue eyes. Pink smiling cheeks. Wet and naked…*miles and miles* of wet and naked.

I crowded her through the spray, then pressed her against the tiles.

Her smile drew together into a luscious purse of her lips as she blew out a breath.

"Whatcha doin', Darren? Hard to get clean this way."

"Dirty," I growled, sliding my hands up her slick skin. "Always *dirty* first."

Her soft laughter was muffled by my hard kiss. Seconds later, her low moan vibrated.

When I hoisted her up, she wrapped her legs around me, arching to trap my erection right where she needed it between our bodies. We kissed, exploring our mouths with hungry strokes as she slid her clit up and down my length.

Her hands gripped fistfuls of hair at my scalp. Her bare heels dug in over my ass.

When her breaths began to catch, her tiny whimpers growing louder, I gave her several hard, fast hip thrusts. On a held breath, her entire body froze, rigid. Then she orgasmed on an ear-splitting scream, echoes bouncing off the tiles.

Before she could catch her next breath, I finally plunged deep inside her. She clung to me, her small hands nearly pulling my hair out, her tight body gripping my cock with hot spasms, until, on a deafening growl, I came.

We stayed like that, pressed together as one against the cool tiles, hot water streaming down my back, steam billowing around us. Neither of us moved to break our tight hold. The intimacy we shared seemed so vital to my existence, I wanted to breathe it in and never exhale.

But eventually, we let go. My body began the reluctant

separation, slipping from hers. She released her grip on my hair and relaxed her legs down mine until she stood before me. And yet, we both kept a loose hold on one another, bodies trembling.

Our breaths were labored, hearts still pounding.

On a growl, I stole one last kiss, before reality fully set in.

Clean first. Softball next.

Then? We had a party to plan.

Kiki…

"**D**id you just shake your ass?" Darren slapped the softball into his glove again.

I adjusted my grip on the bat, forcing my twitching lips to stay relaxed, feigning neutrality. After a deep inhale and slow exhale, I bent one knee then the other…again…knowing my short polka dot skirt flounced a little with each hip sway.

My black cotton bikini-brief underwear were innocent. My intentions were not.

"Did it distract you?" I called out, not caring who overheard.

"No," he scoffed.

I finally let my lips curve into a smile and slowly arced the bat around until the tip pointed toward the outfield, exactly where I planned to launch that ball.

"Liar," I muttered so no one could hear, but mouthed big

enough for him to know exactly what I'd said.

He reached up, pinched the bill of his baseball cap, then lowered it to hide his eyes.

I grinned wider, stretched out a couple more practice arcs of the bat, then waited, coiled and ready to strike.

Cheers came from the stands where spectators had gathered: neighbors, friends, family, customers of Loading Zone, and supporters of The Unity Foundation, our charity.

"Bring it home, Kiki!" The clear shout came from Logan.

She'd already rounded the bases.

We'd decided to be on the same team. Against Cade's team. *Darren's team.*

But we had a few ringers: aka Cade's entire security staff. Even though they were more muscle than speed. No matter. *We girls have cunning.*

With all the waiting, I stepped back from the plate, stretched my face up to the sky, shoulders back, chest out. After a deep breath, I tilted my head from side to side.

"What is this? A Victoria's Secret ad?" Cade snapped his gloved hand out and gave an impatient shrug from where he stood behind first base. "Quit flashing your goods at the world. Let's play ball already!"

Darren hunkered into position, hands curled into his chest, eyes hidden in the shadow of his hat.

His breathing changed.

Deep in, in, in…

Slow out, out, out.

Measured. Controlled.

Barely…

Okay. I'd done my obligatory duty. Gotten into Darren's head.

I stepped to the plate again, choked up on the bat, kicked my toe into the dirt, then coiled my arms up and over until the wide stretch of wood hovered behind my ear once again.

The truth was, *he'd* gotten into *my* head, bad. Under my skin. Into my heart.

We'd be returning to the harsh reality of my life soon enough. After the game, we planned to enact his strategy to save me from homelessness.

But for now?

I intended to stay in our blissful honeymoon-fantasy bubble for as long as humanly possible.

Darren…

"Don't you want something to eat?" Cade watched as Hannah put down her menu.

"You know what I want." Hannah closed her eyes and took a deep breath.

Cade gathered her into his arms and murmured, "I'm beginning to think you have a cinnamon bun in that oven instead of our baby."

My gaze shot to Kiki.

She gave a slight nod. Clearly she'd overheard it too.

As always after the game, most of us ended up at Lila's. The neighborhood café was built into the lower level of a century-old house. The furnishings were quaint and unassuming. But the food came straight from heaven.

The screen door slammed shut behind Lila. She had a fierce expression on her face and brandished a broom like a weapon. The curvy woman reminded me of a Southern grandmother: ruddy cheeks, snow-white hair pulled into a loose bun, often smiling, regularly gossiping.

"What's all the racket?" Lila's brother called from the kitchen through the open counter.

"Nothin', Willard." She leaned the broom into a corner near the bathroom. "Jus' the IRS decidin' they wanted to stalk one of our own." When she walked by, she gave a pat to Kiki's shoulder. "Don't you fret none, dear. I chased him off right good."

Kiki blinked. "Hold up…what?"

"The I. R. S." She punctuated each letter with disdain as she rolled her eyes toward the ceiling then Willard. "It gripes my gut them thinkin' they can come anywhere and do anything. We pay our taxes, so leave us alone."

Kiki darted from our corner table and pressed her hands to the café's front window. "The car's pulling away!" She spun back around. "Did he mention his name, leave a business card?"

"Sure did." Lila plucked a card from her apron pocket. "He tossed this at me—right before my broom made contact." She gave an emphatic nod. "I might should give his boss a call. Give'm a piece of my mind."

Kiki reached out, hand trembling slightly. "May I have the card?"

"Suit yourself." Lila handed it to her with a stern look. "Don't let 'em bully you around."

Cade scowled. "How the hell did he find Kiki here?"

"My phone calls." Kiki muttered absently while she sat beside me again, staring at the card. "Timothy Williams," she whispered.

After a beat of silence, I put a hand over hers. "Know him?"

"Yeah." Her gaze met mine. "He's the agent assigned to my case. I gave him a few places to track me down if he couldn't find me at the warehouse."

She took a deep breath, eyes lighting up as the corners of her lips twitched.

I gripped her hand. "You thinking what I'm thinking?"

"Damn, I hope so." She finally broke into a smile.

"Well?" I nodded at the card. "What are you waiting for? Call the man."

I pounded a flattened hand on the table a few times and stood. "Listen up!" I scanned the room to make sure her brother and sisters were paying attention.

"We've got a party to plan."

Kiki...

By midday Thursday, chaos had officially erupted.

A landscape architect surveyed the space.

Electricians stood on ladders, splicing wires.

The caterer unloaded samples of hors d'oeuvres.

"Dino's a go!" Darren collided into my side then pulled me into his arms.

"He's coming? That's wonderful!" I kissed him, but my gaze locked on to the newest guy to invade my private space. Wearing a vintage Orange Crush T-shirt and tattered jeans, he methodically tested each chair and table in my courtyard for stability.

"Hey!" I shouted as he carried away two chairs from different sets. "Those are staying!"

Kristen appeared by my side. "They're going. We'll put them in storage until after."

"No." I pushed out of Darren's hold and followed my chairs. "They're not leaving." All I could imagine was my prized garage-sale finds suddenly disappearing.

"We can't have guests sit on collapsing rust-buckets." Kristen jogged ahead, then stood in my path with a held-up hand. "In the back of your warehouse, then?"

"I don't want strangers traipsing through my house."

She arched a brow. "In two days, guests will be traipsing through your house…to use your bathroom."

I let out a frustrated sigh, blowing a stray piece of hair away from my lips. "Fine. Have him leave the discards by the front door. I'll put them back there."

"Done." Kristen ran after Orange Crush Guy to retrieve my confiscated chairs.

Darren's scent and warmth wrapped around me an instant later. His arms slid around my hips, then my belly. He rested his chin on my shoulder. "You okay?"

I let out a slow breath. "Yeah." *No.*

All the buzzing activity in my quiet world stressed me out. But I'd deal.

"And Dino's not just coming, he's playing. *We* are."

"Really?" I spun in his arms. "You, Dino, and Gordie?"

"Yep." Happiness sparkled in his eyes. "And right now, he's spreading the word to his closest friends and connections in the industry."

"Wow." I blinked, then stared at the intimate space. "That sounds like a lot of people."

He dropped a gentle kiss on my nose. "He's only inviting art lovers who are serious collectors."

"Oh." I nodded and swallowed hard, hoping the party stayed under control like he imagined.

The rest of the day and Friday passed in more of the same frenzied blur.

I survived the ordeal by running. *A lot.*

By Friday night—T minus twenty-four hours—my modest courtyard had been shaped into a wonderland. Blooming plants with delicate foliage had been added to my raised planters. Pretty bistro sets awaited guests with white tablecloths and rose-shaped crystal tea light holders. Strands of round, clear party lights stretched above us, swaying in the slight breeze.

"It's beautiful," I whispered, leaning my head against Darren's chest.

He squeezed my shoulder and pressed a kiss to the top of my head. "Beautiful party for a beautiful girl."

Kendall's voice murmured in the background as she

confirmed arrangements with the caterers. Kristen sat at a far table, clicking away on her tablet's to-do list.

Cade was down at Midnight Sky Gallery with Ben, Mase, and a fifteen-foot U-Haul truck—along with IRS Agent Timothy Williams, who'd finally agreed to release my sculptures upon my providing him satisfactory ownership documentation.

All my artwork will be here.

"So…" Logan snuck between us from behind, and we widened our embrace into the three of us. "Kiki says it's okay if I miss the party. You cool with that, D?"

He frowned down at her. "Why would you miss it?"

"It's okay," I assured him. Logan had privately enlisted my help a few minutes ago. "She's got her own party to go to. One where a certain guy will be there."

"*Please*, D? I haven't ever been to a party before. Or asked you to go anywhere."

Darren stared at me for a beat, then glanced back at Logan. On a heavy sigh, he gave a nod. "But be careful. And be home by midnight. And no drinking. And for fuck's sake, no—"

"—condoms," she finished for him with a soft laugh. "No sex. Got it. And not planning to."

"Good."

I grinned, wrapping my free arm around Logan and squeezing them both. We'd become a family of sorts, looking out for each other—loving each other.

I stared at the evidence of how much Darren loved me, the transformation of my courtyard from dull charcoal into sparkling diamond. And I relaxed on a slow exhale, warmth spreading through my chest, as I realized I'd transformed too…we all had.

Then a greater understanding hit me…

The best miracles happen when we least expect them—when we finally let our guard down.

35
CLOSE CALL

Darren…

"It's working." Kiki's amazed whisper brushed over my ear from behind.

I smiled as her hands touched my shoulders, slid forward, and wrapped around my neck. The band was on a break between sets, and I sat at an unoccupied table near the sculpture maze, observing the party.

Her lips pressed to my earlobe with a soft kiss. "Thank you. You were right."

"Just a hunch." An educated one. But Dino's connections had paid off. Bigtime. I put my hands over hers, then pulled her around, tugging her into my lap. "Glad you caved?"

She nodded. "Thank you for being persistent. I'm truly grateful." She held her hand up, then fanned her face with a half dozen checks. "These babies will pay the rent for the rest of the year."

"That's what I'm talkin' about." I'd hoped. But art, like music, was subjective.

She beamed with happiness. Then her eyes softened. "Really, Darren. Thank you. For caring enough to know when I needed help. Even when I was too stupid to realize it."

"Not stupid. Stubborn."

"That, I am."

"And I won on oral arguments. Didn't even have to pull out the big guns."

Her breath hitched and her gaze lowered to my crotch. "And yet you did anyway…"

My lips quirked into a smug grin. "Had to seal the deal with something memorable."

She blew out a slow breath, lips brushing over mine. "*Definitely* memorable."

My phone vibrated in my back jeans pocket. I shifted her weight, then pulled it out and pressed the control button to light up the screen.

I frowned; I didn't recognize the missed number. The phone chimed, the screen showing a new voicemail message. The phone vibrated again an instant later with another call: same number.

Curious, I answered. "Hello?"

"Is this Mr. Darren Cole?" A woman's unfamiliar deep voice sounded over the phone.

"Yes. Who's this?"

Kiki moved off my lap, but turned to face me, brows drawn in question.

"I'm Nurse Langston from Riverview Hospital. We need you to come down here right away."

My heart jammed into my throat and I stood. "Logan?" I croaked out. "Is she…okay?"

The too-long pause that followed nearly brought me to my knees.

"Tell me!" Partygoer faces popped up, swiveling my way. I turned toward the warehouse, hand shaking as I crushed a fist around the phone. I lowered my voice. "You have to tell me."

"Yes, sir. She's alive and stable now. Please drive carefully."

My breath shot out, temporary relief coursing through me. "I'm on my way." I yanked my keys out of my front pocket.

In the next instant, the world spun, everything in it wrong. Dino and Gordie were gathering their instruments, prepping for the next set. People milled about. Glasses clinked. Laughter rang out.

Kiki stepped in front of me. "What's wrong?"

"Logan. Hospital." All I could manage to spit out.

She took the keys from my hand. "I'm driving."

"No." I snatched them back. "I need to drive."

"Do you even know where you're going?"

"No." I tossed her my phone. "Riverview Hospital."

I began weaving through the crowd, Kiki right on my heels.

As we passed Cade, she stuffed the wad of checks into his hand. "We have to go. Logan's at the hospital. Will you—"

"Dino—" My gut clenched. I'd convinced my new boss to come.

"Go!" Cade barked. "We got this."

We raced to my truck. Seatbelts clicked as we jammed them shut. I had to wait for several people to move out of the way as I inched the truck backward. As soon as we were clear, I threw it into drive and squealed onto pavement. Three quick neighborhood turns, left, left, right, and we were on the highway.

Kiki gripped the overhead grab bar with one hand as she scrolled through my phone with the other. "There it is. Two more freeway exits."

I floored it. We both leaned to one side, then the other, as I weaved through light traffic.

"No accidents would be good." Kiki's nervous tone broke through my mental haze.

I glanced at the speedometer.

Eighty.

Eighty-five.

Ninety.

Common sense screamed to slow down.

It took Kiki smacking a palm on the dash for my foot to finally ease off the gas.

By the time I glanced at her, she had braced her hands and feet against every available point in her corner.

"Sorry."

"It's okay." She let out a gradual breath. "I get it."

My heart raced so damn hard, I could barely hear her past the rushing of blood in my ears.

She removed her hand from the dash once our speed dipped below seventy-five. "It's the only control you have."

Didn't feel like control to me. Logan was hurt. *Stable now.*

Panic flooded my mind as memories of past and present blurred together: racing to the hospital on another phone call, no one bothering to tell me it had been too late. The trip to that hospital had been a formality: a way to break the horrific news.

She's alive. I just needed to get there. Hold her hand. Assure her it would be okay.

The rest all happened in a daze. Kiki led me to the right, quickly finding a parking space. Then she told me which doors to go through. She stood by my side when the intake nurse handed me a clipboard. She held it tight when I almost flung it back at the nurse.

"I need to see her!" I shouted, desperation in my voice.

My muscles shook. Air came in short gasps. My whole body felt like it was about to implode.

When a warm hand touched my cheek, I looked down.

Kiki stared up at me, her big blue eyes reassuring. "We got this."

I blinked heavily, not understanding. She'd repeated her brother's words.

She gave me a light smile. "They'll only let us back there if we're calm."

Calm. Nothing close to calm was even possible. But I stared at Kiki and took a slow, deep breath—let her quiet the racket in my head. Miraculously, she also slowed my rioting pulse.

When I inhaled a second time, she glanced over her

shoulder at the nurse. "I'll fill out the forms."

The nurse arched her brows. "And you are?"

"Their sister."

My sluggish brain processed Kiki's lie through my fog of panic. "Sister," I repeated.

"How they'll let me back with you. That okay?"

I gave an absent nod and stared at the nurse, who stared at Kiki, then me.

"Please." The one quiet word I spoke sounded exactly like the desperate plea that it was.

The nurse let out a surrendering sigh and gave us a brief nod. "Follow me."

Automatic doors whooshed open after she punched the wall on her side of the barrier made of low desks and plexiglass windows. Sterile smells punched me in the face, bleach and antiseptic, as we walked down a white-tiled corridor. Two paramedics in navy T-shirts rushed a gurney in from a side door and chaos exploded around them, two orderlies and a doctor shouting orders and pointing toward a curtained room.

"This way." With an arm sweep, our nurse gestured in the opposite direction of the commotion. We rounded a wide nurses' station and passed two "rooms" before she pulled back the pale green curtain-wall of a third.

Logan.

I lunged to her side. Touched her exposed arm. Warm. She was alive. Though she didn't look very: pallid skin, head tilted to the side, eyes shut, lips gray, plastic tube clipped into her nose.

"They're admitting her," the nurse commented.

"Admitting her." Nothing made sense. I scanned Logan's body from head to toe. Didn't see any scrapes or bruises.

The nurse pulled the clipboard from a plastic pocket bolted to the wall, scanned the chart, then slid it back in. "She'll be in psyche for observation."

"Psyche?" Did they know about her depression? I struggled to connect the dots.

"Alcohol. Drugs. Then an OD on pills. They need to make sure she remains stable. Not a danger to herself."

"What happened?" I had to know. Thank fuck she hadn't jumped or fallen from that roof. But drugs? Pills? None of that was Logan.

"Look" —the nurse stepped between Kiki and me, lowering her voice— "I'm not even supposed to let you back here, let alone tell you all of that. The doctor's in emergency surgery and won't be able to talk to you until much later."

Translation: no info.

"Her vitals are stable. She's been given a sedative to help her sleep, and she'll probably be out for the night. Why don't you two fill out the forms, then go home. Get some rest. Come back in the morning."

"No fucking way," I growled at the nurse.

"Darren." Kiki put her hand on my forearm.

I unclenched my fist. Then I exhaled a sharp breath and glanced at Kiki. "I'm not leaving her."

"Then we'll stay." Kiki nodded to a lone blue plastic chair off to the side.

I planted my ass in it. Crossed my arms. I'd chain myself

to the metal guard rail of Logan's bed if need be.

The nurse gave a relenting nod. "Make sure I have those forms in the next thirty minutes."

Then she left. And the general buzzing in my head faded. Sounds began to filter in from the partitioned rooms beside us.

Off in a distant part of the floor, a woman wailed. Her agonizing howls continued, making the layers of other sounds—metal clanging, wheels squeaking, automatic doors whooshing, phones ringing, dozens of conversations—background noise.

The woman's pain was unnerving. And familiar. My mind flashed to a time when I'd been in a hospital just like this with Logan. Only then, Logan was the one crying out her pain, inconsolable. I'd held her through it. Heart shredded too at the loss of our mom, I'd stuffed down my suffering and had become the rock that Logan needed.

It all rushed back to me now. The shock of it hit me like a ton of bricks, crushing my chest, making it difficult to suck in air.

In a sudden panic, I launched up from the chair and went to her bedside. I clasped her limp hand into mine. A cord prevented me from pulling it too far from the bed.

"What is this?" I snarled, angry at the fucking world.

Kiki appeared at my side and followed my gaze to Logan's hand. "It's an oxygen sensor, I think."

Looked like a white plastic clothes pin had been clipped to her finger. "How does it work?" Didn't really give a damn, but it distracted me out of my head. And I *needed* out of my head.

Kiki shrugged. "Not sure."

I stared at the red light glowing faintly around Logan's finger and began to hate it a little less. The tubes, the monitors, they were there to keep her safe. Keep her alive.

I'd failed her. Failed Logan. I was supposed to protect one person—and hadn't.

My breaths grew shallow. One caught, but I forced past it, sucking in a heaving lungful of air as I stared at my baby sister's sleeping face. *I failed Mom and now Logan.*

What if she doesn't wake up? What if she can't live a normal life? What if she's never happy? What if she tries again? And succeeds?

"Darren." Kiki roped an arm into the crook of my elbow.

It took several seconds for me to come back out of my head again.

"Sit." She tugged gently on my arm. "Help me fill out this form."

On a hard swallow, I nodded. Then I realized my face was wet. I wiped my cheeks and licked my lips. Salty.

"Fuck." It pissed me off that I'd been crying. And in front of Kiki. "Sorry." I sat and buried my head into my hands.

I felt her hair brush over my arms as she squatted in front of me. I didn't move.

"It's okay, Darren. You're human. You love her."

All I could manage was a weak nod.

"Now," she continued, "Logan's full name."

I exhaled a long breath. "Logan Amelia Cole."

"Date of birth."

I rattled it off.

"Social security number."

I leaned forward, digging my wallet out of my pocket, grateful for the mind-numbing task. And thankful as fuck Kiki was here to steer me toward it.

After we finished the forms, me answering Kiki's questions as she jotted down answers, I signed the handful of pages and Kiki disappeared down the hall. For about ten minutes, I stayed alone with Logan, machine beeping, me breathing, our curtained room's stable sounds what I willed myself to focus on.

When Kiki returned, she handed me a paper coffee cup while dragging in a second blue chair. Without a word, she positioned the chair beside mine, then sat with me, shoulder to shoulder.

After a while, she broke the silence, "It's not your fault."

"Don't be so sure."

She laced her fingers together with mine, then squeezed.

Odd what a powerful effect that action had. Her tiny hand. A reassuring grip with hardly any physical force. But I felt it to my bones.

After she relaxed her grip, but kept her hand securely clasped with mine, she nudged my shoulder. "You didn't give her any of it."

"Didn't I?" I glanced down at her. "Isn't my absence in her life acceptance of it?"

"You don't know why she did it."

"Sure I do." I growled and stared up at the ceiling. "Life sucks. Why my mom ended hers. Maybe if Logan's didn't suck so bad, she'd have a reason to live it."

Kiki made a frustrated noise and yanked hard on my arm.

I blinked and turned toward her.

Anger sparked in her eyes. "No. You don't get to take blame for what someone else does. Not your mom. Not your sister. You can't control the world. All you can do is survive in it."

"Ain't that the truth," I muttered.

Guess everyone had a different definition of survival.

Hours later, Logan was admitted and moved to a private room. At her new nurse's insistence, with visiting hours not until 8:00 a.m. and her only willing to bend the rules for one of us, I stayed behind and Kiki went home.

After she left, I dimmed the room lights and pulled out my phone. It was just past midnight.

Planting my ass on a pleather recliner in the corner, a huge improvement over the rigid plastic thing in the ER, I leaned back and closed my eyes. Exhaustion sucked me down into the cushions, and I let it pull me under.

A light knock startled me awake, and I jolted upright. The recliner's footrest snapped down with a click.

Another double-rap sounded. "Mr. Cole?"

I rubbed my eyes, adjusting to brighter room lights than I'd remembered. "Yeah."

A quick glance at the bed confirmed Logan was still out cold.

A uniformed police officer stepped through the opening door. Then a second followed. They took up all the empty space in the entryway near the open bathroom: bulky vests under the dark blue, black leather belts holding their guns, batons, pepper spray.

My brows furrowed. "Can I help you?"

Since when is a suicide attempt criminal?

Sudden anxiety spiked through me. What if they deemed me an unfit guardian? Would they file a complaint with social services? Could Logan get shipped off to a foster home?

I shot out of the chair so fast, the officers alerted, bodies tensing. The lead officer raised his hands. "It's okay, Mr. Cole. I'm Officer Day. This is Officer Blanchard. We just need to follow up on a complaint Logan made."

"My sister?" Now I was really confused. "She made a complaint?"

They both gave a nod. The lead officer gestured an arm toward the hall. "Mind if we talk outside?"

I glanced back at the bed, then checked the time on my phone: 1:42 a.m. Logan wouldn't be waking anytime soon, according to the nurse. But whatever we had to discuss was probably better said outside of her earshot. "Yeah."

When we entered the hall, they kept walking and I followed. They stepped into a waiting room just before a set of double doors. Once inside, surprising scents hit me: brewing coffee, fresh-baked muffins.

My stomach growled and mouth watered as I passed a table covered with platters of cookies, snack bars, bagels, and muffins. A large bowl held bananas and apples. I poured a cup of coffee, grabbed a blueberry muffin and a banana, then took a seat in the corner that the officers had claimed.

After testing the coffee and finding it hot but not scalding, I took several gulps then tore into the muffin with a large bite. While I munched, I stared at them, waiting.

"Did your sister call you at any point last night?" Officer Day asked.

I swallowed the enormous mouthful, almost lodging it in my throat. "No."

"Well, it seems your sister was at a high school party. No adults present. Underage drinking."

Sounded typical. Like parties I'd gone to a few years back.

"A girl at the party called 9-1-1." He glanced down at a clipboard he held. "Monica Schafer. Do you know her?"

I shook my head. "Logan doesn't talk much about her friends." I wasn't sure she'd had any in the past couple of years.

"Does Trevor Donaldson ring any bells?"

"Yeah. She mentioned him a couple of times." And speaking of the fucker, *the guy who was* supposedly *interested in her*, why wasn't he here with her?

Officer Blanchard leaned forward, bracing his forearms on his thighs as he glanced over at Day's clipboard. "According to the girl who made the 9-1-1 call, and several other witnesses at the party, Trevor burst out of the upstairs bedroom he and Logan were in. He allegedly shouted 'Logan is as crazy as we thought. Bitch just downed a whole bottle of pills.' as he ran down the stairs."

My chest grew heavy as I struggled to listen.

Officer Day nodded. "Thankfully, that girl called for help right away. Paramedics found Logan unconscious at the scene."

I scrubbed my hands over my face. "There's got to be more. Logan told me she'd never kill herself." Truth. And if the officers didn't already know about our mom's and Logan's rooftop visits, they weren't going to.

"There is," Blanchard replied.

My paper coffee cup gave a loud crinkle, and I looked down to find it warped in my hand. I downed the rest of it, even though it nearly scalded my throat, then crumpled it the remainder of the way before tossing it onto a side table.

"We followed the ambulance to the hospital," Day said. "She regained consciousness shortly after they stabilized her. When we asked for her side of the story" —he flipped a couple of pages over on the clipboard, scanned down the page— "she said Trevor gave her a red plastic cup of beer that she drank from before he led her to the upstairs bedroom. When she pulled away from his hold and said she still wasn't ready to have sex with him, he locked the door, turned around, and told her that he'd 'roofied' her drink and she would do everything he wanted her to."

"Roofied," I repeated, breaths suddenly coming in short bursts.

"Rohypnol," Blanchard clarified. "The date-rape drug."

I knew what it was. Rapists used it. Trevor was a rapist.

The world began to tilt. I gripped the wooden chair arm. "Was she raped?" My voice cracked on the last word.

"No, not according to your sister," Day replied.

"Have you arrested him? Is he in custody?"

"Not yet," Blanchard said. "We've contacted his parents, but he hasn't returned home."

A buzzing sound filled my ears and the room fuzzed out, turning a reddish color.

Another cup of coffee appeared in front of my face. I hadn't realized Officer Day had gotten up. "Here. Drink. There's more."

"More?"

"Turns out your sister did swallow pills. She'd only started feeling woozy when he admitted what he'd just done to her, but she panicked, grabbed her purse, and downed the whole bottle of pills."

"Which pills?" For some reason, I needed more information. Every little detail. Because if I didn't distract my mind with something, I'd be hunting down some fucker who liked to drug then rape girls.

Day flipped another page. "Ascendipam. It was the empty medication bottle in her purse."

The drug she stopped taking after only two pills. So the bottle had twenty-eight pills left.

"Toxicology report confirmed alcohol, Ascendipam, and Rohypnol."

"Will she be okay?" Sounded like a lot. Organ failure popped to my mind. And I hadn't seen the doctor yet.

"We've been told she should make a full recovery. They pumped her stomach in time."

"*Thank fuck.*" I blew out a hard breath.

"If you see or hear from Trevor, be sure to call us

immediately." Day opened the bottom of the clipboard, pulled out a card, and handed it to me.

I stared at the damn thing, imagining how that meeting would go if Trevor showed his sorry-ass face to me. Sure. I would call them 'immediately'…right after I beat the shit out of the punk.

"We've got the hospital staff monitoring her room," he continued. "She's to have no visitors other than you."

The rest of the time, however many minutes it was, went by in a blur. They didn't need me to press charges; it was automatic for attempted rape of a minor. But I signed their forms anyway, pressing formal charges. The rage that welled up within me wanted to do so much more than sign pieces of paper.

By the time the officers left the waiting room, two other families had come in. One had a toddler who ran around the room, bumping into everything, my legs included.

I didn't care. The jolt of the kid pulled me out of a numb haze I'd fallen into.

Exhausted, I got up and went back down the hall. I stood silently in her doorway. Her sleeping body lay in the same position it had when I'd left with the officers. She looked so innocent. She'd almost had that innocence ripped away— nearly her very life.

A heavy pulse beat in my head. Her being there in that bed was my fault. She was my responsibility. While she'd been assaulted, fought for her life, I'd been at some party.

Not just some *party.* I'd been trying to save Kiki from homelessness.

But I should have been saving my sister from a rapist.

Life wasn't fair. At times, I felt like a kid myself—with dreams and college—but I'd been shoved into the role of parent. Guess I didn't get to choose. I'd taken a shot at happiness with all the responsibilities I had and got smacked hard.

Could have been worse. The beeping monitors meant Logan was still alive. She needed me. Now more than ever.

My happiness?

Would have to wait.

A vibration in my back pocket pulled me from my thoughts. I tugged my phone free.

One line from Kiki flashed up on the screen. Six little words came out as an order my exhausted body didn't think to disobey:

Come over. No matter how late.

36
FOREVER AWAY

Kiki…

"**C**ome on *in*?" Darren's voice boomed as he slapped my note onto the worktable.

Anger rolled off him. It snuffed out the cute smartass retort I nearly lobbed back before glancing up. He was in no mood to play.

"I didn't know what time you'd come by."

"So you left the door unlocked."

"You don't have a key."

"And you taped an open invitation to every asshole guy walking down your alley to come in and rape you."

I swallowed hard, pulse beginning to race. I'd never seen him angry. And he was *furious*. At me.

Arguing with him seemed asinine. I had no idea what news he'd gotten. And I wanted to support him. Help him any way I could. Which meant taking the force of his anger. We could deal with tiny issues like home security later.

"How's Logan?"

He whooshed out a harsh breath. "They say she's going to be okay. She's out for the night."

What happened? What I wanted to say, but was afraid to ask.

A small meow sounded from below the worktable. *Chipmunky.* He'd sensed something was wrong.

Darren stared straight down, presumably at the kitten. But he didn't move. Didn't react. Like his ability to respond to any stimulus had gone haywire. Like thinking a note taped to my front door had been a beacon to thugs and rapists.

Then he slumped onto a barstool. His face dropped into his hands.

"She's going to be okay." I repeated his news with a soft tone, in case it hadn't sunk in when he'd uttered it.

Silence followed. The eerie kind when you're sitting in an enormous warehouse and not even the wind dares vibrate a window.

"She almost killed herself," he whispered.

Killed herself. The impact of those words hit my chest like a sledgehammer. Had to have crushed him like a wrecking ball.

"Because that *asshole* Trevor was going to rape her."

"Oh my God," I whispered, shocked. Suddenly the horrendous images of assholes and rapists had an explanation. He'd been thrust into the middle of that nightmare.

Fury welled up from my gut too. That Logan had her

heart into that *asshole* guy. And he'd wanted to use her—to hurt her. So much worse than what I'd gone through. At least mine had been consensual sex.

Darren just sat there, defeated. I got the sense he wanted to stay there—punish himself.

Before he had a chance to move or reject me, I rounded the table and wrapped my arms around him. He didn't fight my hold. Instead, he let out a long exhale.

"I'm so sorry, Darren."

In my embrace, his breaths grew deeper. My arms expanded, then contracted, in ever-widening circles.

"I can't do this." His voice had gone so quiet, I almost didn't hear him.

"Yeah, you can." I squeezed him harder, hoping my strength would seep through. "We can."

With a headshake that filtered down to his shoulders, he broke out of my hold. "No, I can't." He stumbled off the barstool, distancing himself a good couple of feet from me before he looked up. His expression twisted into something tortured by the time his eyes met mine.

"I can't do…*us*." The barest whisper made it from his lips.

My heart slammed into my throat. I couldn't find my next breath as tears welled in my eyes.

His teared up too. He pinched his shut and turned away from me, griping the edge of the worktable. "I let her down, Kiki. I wasn't there for her."

He'd been at my party. That he'd thrown for me. To save me—and he'd almost lost her.

The world spun off its axis. I gripped my section of the

table edge trying to hold on. Finally, I sucked in a breath to keep from passing out. But the air burned going in.

Everything from my skin to my soul ached.

"She almost died." His tone held somber finality. Like that horrifying truth had become his death sentence.

"You couldn't have prevented what happened to her tonight."

"You don't know that."

I didn't. And I wasn't selfish enough to kid myself that I knew best in their circumstances.

"So you're just going to shut me out?" My voice sounded thready.

"I never had any right to let you in."

"But you did!" The anguished roar bounced off the concrete floors, echoed from the walls. A sob tore free as I tried to hold it together. Tears streamed down my face. "You were—" The words got stuck in my throat. "You were only supposed to be a one-night stand."

"I'm sorry, Kiki. I didn't mean for any of this to happen." He didn't move. Just stared at the table.

"But it did." I closed my eyes, unable to believe what was happening.

"It was my worst nightmare. Taking something for myself…then having it cost Logan."

"You didn't take 'something.' You took some*one*. You took me." I opened my eyes and glared at him.

Finally, after a long shaky inhale, he glanced at me. "The last thing I wanted to do was hurt you."

"You didn't hurt me. You *are* hurting me. *Right now*." I

wrapped my arms around myself, pinching my eyes shut as I tried to fend off the pain.

Heart shredding, I curled up into the chilling emptiness of my mind, even as I willed him to see that I was worth it. Just as much as Logan was worth protecting and fighting for, so was I.

Warmth wrapped around me, his powerful arms banding around my body. And in that heartfelt gesture, I lost it. My head fell against his chest and my shoulders shuddered as gut-wrenching sobs racked my body.

Long seconds later, when it began to subside, I gasped for breath, only to have it all crash into me again.

My lips started to tingle from hyperventilating.

His measured breaths were labored, forced. "Please, baby. I'm so sorry."

I hiccupped. "Stop saying that."

"But I am."

"Doesn't change anything." Bitterness clipped my accusation.

He let out a heavy sigh. "No."

"You said we could only be *just friends*."

He let out a sardonic laugh. "We should have listened to me."

I pressed my palms to his chest, pushing away from him to meet his gaze.

Unshed tears glittered in his eyes.

Mine filled anew as my voice fell to a whisper. "You made me fall in love with you."

He stared down at me, brushed a tear from my cheek as

one of his finally broke free. Then he sucked in a deep breath. "I know, baby. I know. Me too."

My next breath kept catching as I battled to fill my lungs. "Great. So now what? You saved me from homelessness. Now you're abandoning me."

"Not abandoning. Just…I can't do us right now. It's…it's too much. For now."

After the crushing shock of it all, I gradually began to see his side. I got it. He'd said from the beginning that we couldn't be together. His reason had been that it was complicated.

It was now more complicated than ever.

I clung to him, fisted my hands into his shirt at his lower back. I didn't want to let go. After an unsteady breath, I sighed. "Not sure I can be 'just friends' with you."

I felt a slight pressure on the top of my head. Like he'd rested his chin there. "Me either."

So there it was. We were nothing.

For now. Those temporary hope-filled words finally filtered into my brain.

"You need to sort things out." Maybe he only needed a few days to get a grip on things.

I felt him nod gently over me. "I need to make sure Logan is okay. That she's stable. We've got to make it two more years before the state can't take her away from me—from the only family she's got."

Of course. In my selfishness, I hadn't realized how precarious they had it. And what an enormous responsibility he had. I knew they loved each other deeply. They just struggled how to right themselves in the aftermath of tragedy.

He didn't need a few days. He needed years.

Could we survive that?

"Will you wait for me?" His voice trembled.

My insides caved at his uncertainty. Hope had tinged his plea.

I squeezed him tight as tears began flow again. "Yes." I swallowed past the giant knot in my throat. "Yes. I will wait for you."

He was our hero. *My* hero.

I'd been waiting my whole life for him. *What's a couple of years more?*

Yet…fear gripped me at my core. Tonight sounded too much like good-bye.

And for two people who'd only had a handful of days to love each other…

A couple of years? Seemed like forever away.

37

THE RESPONSIBLE THING

Darren…

"**Y**ou look like shit." Logan accused from nearby, tone matter-of-fact.

I scrubbed my face. Bone-deep sleep fuzzed my brain as I blinked my eyes open.

She stared at me from her hospital bed.

"You're up." Adrenaline flashed through my veins. I launched from the recliner and rushed to her side. "Need water? I think they allow ice chips." I grabbed the bed controls, went to press the nurse's button.

Logan stabbed her hand between mine and the electronics. "Calm down. I'm fine." Although her voice came out gravelly, her skin had better color.

Still, I narrowed my eyes at her. "You are not fine."

"I'm better than you. You look like a freakin' zombie."

She cocked her head. "Pasty skin. Red-rimmed eyes. Well-nourished, but still the living dead."

"Not funny."

"Have you been crying?"

"Not over you."

"Gee, thanks." She folded her sheet down, then smoothed the blanket. "Trying not to be insulted."

"You" —I pointed an accusing finger at her— "scared the ever-loving fuck out of me. Hard to cry when you can't breathe."

"Sorry."

The quiet word stung. Then I heard myself saying it to Kiki. Total loser-word. Didn't begin to cover the damaging heartache. Not even close.

"It's okay." It wasn't. But it would be. Had to be.

"So if you didn't cry over me, who got the lucky honors."

"Kiki."

"Kiki?" Her furrowed brow lasted only a split second. Then her eyes widened. "Oh my God. What happened? Is Kiki okay?"

I snorted. "You almost kill yourself, and you're worried about Kiki?"

"I did *not* almost kill myself," she growled, eyes narrowing. "Answer the question."

"Kiki's fine. Or she will be." I hoped. "I broke up with her."

"You did what?"

"I broke up with her." I said it more forcefully, swallowing down my punishment.

"You're an idiot."

"This idiot plans on keeping us together."

"At what cost?"

"You weren't there in the waiting room, Lo. Police officers were there. Scared the fuck out of me. If they thought we weren't holding it together, the next government officials sitting me down will be case workers."

On a deep exhalation, she leveled a hard look at me. "You're not listening to me, D. Did you *not* notice that we weren't living? I was holed up in my room, depressed as hell. You were a zombie, going through the motions of work and school. Keeping food on our table isn't living, it's slaving."

"What do you want me to do, Lo?" I backed up and sat down on the small couch beside the recliner.

"Live."

The powerful word echoed between us.

We'd only been surviving, making it from one day to the next. "I wasn't *always* a zombie."

She crossed her arms, gaze still pegged to me. "Not in the last few weeks, you weren't."

Right. Because of Kiki.

I sighed and shook my head. "It's too much, Logan. Kiki deserves more than the time I can give her. You're my family, and I'm not risking something happening to you again."

"You aren't in charge of my every move." Her voice quieted and she looked away, picking at a thread on the tan woven blanket. "I only took the pills to save myself."

"How ridiculously ironic."

"Didn't know what else to do. Trevor scared me. And I

panicked." She gave a half-hearted shrug. "Downing the pills right in front of him was the only thing I could think of. I knew it would make him freak."

Couldn't fault her for using a last-ditch effort when she only had seconds to defend herself. "Well, thank fuck it worked."

Her lips tilted up a little into a lopsided smile and her brows raised slightly. "Still glad you're stuck with me?"

I blew out a lungful of air, then crossed the room and tugged her into my arms. "More than you'll ever know."

She squeaked and shoved against my chest. "Patient needing oxygen here."

After a few quiet seconds, both of us clinging to one another, glad to be alive and kicking, I released my hold and stared toward the medical file tucked into the plastic holder on her open door. "The doctor's supposed to be coming by around lunchtime to give us a report."

"How long do I have to stay?"

"Nurse said a few days. Think they're required by law, whenever it's…"

I struggled to say the devastating word.

Her hand gripped my forearm. "Don't say it."

"Okay. I…okay." A cramp choked my throat. Over how much I'd lost…and almost lost.

"Can we break out?"

I snorted out a short laugh. "Only if we want social services hunting us down."

A nurse filed in. "Oh, you're up. How are you feeling?"

Logan blinked in surprise at her. "I'm okay. Could I get some water?"

When the nurse nodded and disappeared, Logan glanced back at me. "So…now what? Back to the zombie slaving?"

"Very funny."

My heart sank at her point.

But it had to be done. My number one priority was to keep her safe and provided for. And I needed to be involved in her life, make the time to be a more active participant.

Logan had to come before everyone else, including me.

Without being able to stop it, my thoughts drifted to my last image of Kiki: her staring up at me with tears in her eyes.

I did that.

A burning sensation ignited in the center of my chest. After several deep breaths, I rubbed my sternum in a weak attempt to ease the pressure.

A flash of movement tore me out of my thoughts, then a small tissue box smacked the spot where I'd been rubbing. It tumbled into my hand.

Logan's face twisted into a deep scowl. "You're an idiot."

38
AMPLIFIED SILENCE

Kiki…

Silence echoes the loudest when you listen to it.

I'd cried myself to sleep the last few nights, but I felt like I had nothing left inside me to sob out. Numbness had taken over.

Home saved—by a hero who'd won over the girl, then vanished—I wandered through my empty warehouse, struck by the intense quiet.

After I sat at my worktable for a few minutes, Chipmunky jumped up and sideswiped the arms I'd propped under my chin, as if sensing I needed some TLC. His loud purr broke into the deafening silence in the best kind of way.

"Hey, munchkin." As I ran my fingers over his sleek multicolored coat, a memory flashed: *At least one guy wants what I'm offering.*

My fingers froze midstroke. I'd said that to Chipmunky the morning after Darren had dropped me off and then found me in the alley. My last attempt at a one-night stand had turned into the beginning of Darren and me.

And mere feet away from where I sat had been the end.

My chest burned, unable to take a next breath.

My eyes ached, welling with tears.

Then big, fat drops streaked down my face, and I started sobbing all over again.

Tuesday's art class came and went. I forced myself to go. Logan didn't show.

No calls. No texts. Not from her. Not from Darren. *Utter silence.*

And although I worried about them—hoped Logan was doing okay, missed Darren to a level I couldn't describe—I kept my distance and didn't make contact.

After all, we weren't friends anymore.

Wednesday, I woke up and went running for the first time in three days.

It felt good to get out into the fresh air and sunshine again. I tested out a new trail, upping my distance to almost five miles. For the first time, I ran the downhills, careful to step with precision while keeping a steady pace.

Every time my thoughts drifted to Darren?

I pushed myself harder.

Happened a lot.

But the mental anguish translated into physical pain, which only fueled my determination to keep my focus on the trail—nothing else.

And in the vast wide open space, in the middle of wilderness, I found a different kind of silence: A peace in my head and heart. It had become a compromise between what my body could endure if I punished it and what my brain was willing to let go of in order to ease the pain.

When I got home that afternoon? I made it official: I registered for the race.

Then I downloaded the race map of a park I hadn't yet visited. I made a mental note to begin training on the race trail starting tomorrow. The website described the trail as a lollypop loop: the same straightaway start and finish with a four-mile circle at the top, five miles total.

The rest of the afternoon I kept busy, packing boxes of sold artwork to ship to buyers.

And I did *not* think of Darren while I did so. *Much.*

Thursday afternoon, I went to art class stemming a bit of an attitude.

Because…really? Darren inserts himself into my life, then just pulls the plug?

And then…not one text or phone call?

Doesn't he want to know if I'm okay?

At the last thought, a twinge of guilt speared through me. He needed to focus on his sister—who almost *hadn't* been okay.

Then I sighed, giving him a break.

His love for me had been real. *Incredibly* real.

No matter what happened, even if we never found our way back to each other again, my life had been irrevocably altered by him.

I've been truly loved.

The door opened, startling me out of my thoughts. Logan stepped through. So did ten other students.

Her gaze caught mine, and she beelined straight for me. "Hey."

I blew out a shaky breath. "Hey. You okay?"

"Yeah. Got out of the hospital yesterday. They had to keep me until then." Legs bouncing nervously, she glanced at the others as they took their seats.

"I'm glad." I nodded, giving her a warm smile. "Was really worried about you."

She tilted her face slightly downward, staring at me from under the brim of her black newsboy hat. "*We* are still friends. I…he…" She huffed out a frustrated sigh. "Just wanted to say that."

"Thanks. That means a lot."

I glanced at the class, who one by one had begun to stare at us as we talked softly at the front, then back at her. "Does he…"

What? Think about me? Miss me as much as I miss him?

Instead of sounding lame and desperate, I kept it neutral. "Is he okay?"

She dropped me a deadpan look. "*Define* okay."

39
UNEXPECTED LESSON

Darren…

"**W**hat?" I snarled at my bandmates. "Waiting for an invitation?"

Nick clenched his jaw.

Trey narrowed his eyes.

Skinny JJ just shook his bleach-tipped head, then hit the first note on his keyboard—and dragged it out, letting the note die when Nick and Trey didn't join in.

They kept staring at me.

I wasn't in the mood. Couldn't breathe. Hadn't been able to sleep. For the last few days—since Sunday—I'd been doing all the right things. Yet the world felt wrong.

"What's with him?" Nick shot a glance at Logan, shaggy red bangs falling over his brow.

"He's being an idiot," she muttered.

"An idiot who went to your high school rock concert last night." I'd kept the promise I made to her weeks ago when weaving through traffic, late to my studio audition. "You were awesome, by the way."

Murmurs of agreement echoed into the garage. Nick nodded and gave her a half-hug. "You done good, kid."

"So, we playin', or what?" My knee bounced as I let out a hard sigh. If the fuckers didn't start in the next few seconds, I'd rip out a rhythm without 'em.

I'd been agitated all week, bouncing off the walls with not enough to keep me out of my head.

School was out.

Studio work didn't start till next Wednesday.

And the insane amount of money I now made with Dino justified lightening my load. I'd handed over my DJ gig to my boy, Rick, who'd already been helping out at Loading Zone and events. Cade had agreed to have me work Invitation Only parties on a case-by-case basis. I'd handle the ones I could and delegate the rest to Rick.

"Not until you unload, dude." Nick yanked off his guitar.

Trey did the same. JJ sat on his stool with an emphatic nod.

"He fell in love." Logan remained where she stood, hands resting on her guitar. Her charcoaled eyes narrowed at me. "Then the idiot dumped her—for me."

My gut clenched at the truth in her words.

An ache burned, deep in my chest. *Again.*

Been going on for days. Couldn't stop thinking about Kiki no matter where I went or what I did. And my heart kept shredding over and over, each and every damn time.

Fucking drove me crazy, wanting…*needing*…what I couldn't have.

"I'm not listening to this." I stowed my sticks in their case. "Thought maybe we'd play one last time. But if you guys don't want to, I'm out."

"Saw her at art class today." Her voice softened.

My legs tensed. My breath caught. I'd been about to stand, but stayed right where I sat. "Yeah?"

Don't ask.

Do not *ask.*

I stared at a piece of lint on the cement by the minifridge. If I didn't look at Logan, maybe I wouldn't fucking lose it.

"Yeah." All she said.

Silence followed. Except for my pulse that hammered a wicked beat in my ear.

"*Annnd*?" Trey arched his brows.

"She looks like crap, D, just like you. Barely held together on the outside, eyes full of pain."

Nick gave a solid nod. "You're a fucking mess."

I leaned back on my stool and crossed my arms. "Didn't realize this was gonna be an intervention."

"It is what it is." JJ leaned an arm on the steel shelving unit against the wall. "Whatever you need."

Nods followed around the room.

Great.

I let out an exhausted sigh, ready to bolt. I did *not* need to get in touch with my feelings. Been down in that dark hole all week. *I came here to get* out *of my head.*

"Hey." Logan's face lit up. "*That's it.* You need to come to our next SSL meeting."

I snorted. "Like hell I do."

"No. Really, D." She stepped closer, voice lowering. "You do."

Our gazes locked. Brother to sister. Guardian to charge. *Family.*

As I stared into expressive eyes that held experience beyond their years, I let out a slow breath. "You need this."

"I do." She put her hand on my forearm. "You need this too. I need you to be whole for me. You need to realize that you can't stop living to take care of me. You have to live for you first."

"I will, Lo. Just not yet."

"Now, D. You have to live for you now. We don't get chances at happiness often. You need to take yours."

"We've been over this. I…I can't do both." I pinched my eyes shut for a beat. "Not well, anyway. Look what happened."

"Shit happens, D. *We* know this. But you can't control everything, so stop trying." She squeezed my arm. "Come to Tuesday's meeting. Promise me you'll be there. You'll see that you *can* do both."

I had no idea how she had all that confidence about something I couldn't see past. All I knew was Logan needed me—all of me. I thought that meant centering all of my focus only on her. She insisted there was more to it than that.

And I would do anything for her—especially when she looked up at me with that pleading look in her eyes.

"All right. I'll be there."

But I'm not promising anything.

'd never been to one of Logan's SSL meetings. Not as a participant. Sure, I'd watched a couple of times for a few minutes from the back. Had walked by the door once or twice, glanced in the windows. But I'd never actually attended from the beginning, become a part of the group.

The room felt hot and I plucked my T-shirt from my chest for a split second as I took a seat in the chair nearest the door. My heart thumped faster than made sense while I glanced at the other fourteen people as, one by one, they each claimed a seat in the circle.

I took a deep breath, trying to calm the fuck down.

It's just a harmless meeting, D. Get your shit together.

I'd come for Logan. Not for me.

Near a dry-erase board at the front, Logan spoke in hushed tones with a large middle-aged man who glanced toward me. Then he gave Logan a nod and a pat on her shoulder before she sat in the empty seat beside me.

The man she'd talked with addressed the group once the last person was seated. "Hi, I'm Ron."

"Hi, Ron," the group replied, me included.

"Some of you have heard my story, others haven't. Helps me to share it once in a while. Because, when I lost my baby girl, Denise—just fourteen with everything to live for, gone in an instant—I shut down for a few weeks. Then? I centered all my focus on my boy, Dillon, a senior in high school.

"Drove that poor boy nuts. I was all up in his business and worried about everything: his friends, what he did at night, how his grades were, if he drank or doped. Whenever he went out, I agonized about him coming home. Even tailed him a couple of times."

Ron shook his head. "Crazy, I know. But I" —his voice cracked— "felt like I'd failed my daughter. I refused to fail my son. Except…I was doing just that when I began to smother him. We started fighting, bad."

His voice lowered. "And I put all that focus on my son at the expense of my wife—our marriage. She kept quiet the whole time. Suffered in silence at the loss of our girl even though she needed me.

"One day? I just stopped. Stopped trying. Stopped overmanaging my son. I just let go. Once I did, an enormous weight lifted. Took a while, couple of weeks maybe, but eventually, my son started smiling again. So did my wife. Because I made time for her too—for us."

He pegged a hard look at the woman directly across from him, then scanned his gaze across the circle until it landed on me. "Took a lot of heartache to realize the best gift we can give those we love is ourselves—whole and happy. We have to let them breathe, let them live and make mistakes. And we need to live too. We owe it to ourselves and to them."

My head buzzed at Ron's story. The parallels…the lesson…hit me hard.

When I glanced left, Logan stared at me with a soft expression. Then determination flashed across her face. She grabbed my hand and tugged me out of my seat and toward the corner of the room while the group continued, murmuring in the background.

She stared up at me, compassion in her eyes. "You said you can't do both. *You* don't have to. *We* will. I'm not thirteen anymore. You don't have to handle everything alone. We do this together. I need you to *live for you.*"

I gave a weak nod, unable to speak with the cramp locking up my throat.

Logan needs me to be whole…and happy.

And fuck, I needed Kiki for that.

But first, I had to get my head screwed on straight.

40
THE FINISH LINE

Kiki...

Race day came without any fanfare.

And yet, I'd hit a major achievement before I'd ever stepped foot on the trail.

I'd finally begun to stop mourning the devastating loss of Darren; self-preservation demanded it.

In small increments, while pushing my limits with daily trail running and immersing myself in several new sculptures, I'd painstakingly stripped the "we" out of my head—and heart—and had slowly become a "me" again.

But the new me turned out to be profoundly different. I'd become a better version of independent me: brighter on the inside, ready to face whatever challenges awaited me on the outside. All because I'd loved and been loved. *Because of Darren.*

I'd even begun to trust with my art again: I approached the owner of Eiselmann's Gallery, where we'd held the Industrial Grunge party, and made arrangements to create a few pieces to sell there.

But when I touched my Vibrams to the dirt, adhesive racing number affixed to my shirt and baseball cap tugged down low, I missed him. A huge part of me wanted to share the incredible experience of the race with him, show him how far I'd come.

The starting gun fired, its shot echoing off the rock walls of the mountain to my left, scattering my thoughts. Our pack of men and women took off together, one hundred and thirty-seven in total, according to the race official who'd checked me in at the starting area.

Not having raced before, I kept toward the back to begin, wanting to make sure all the extremists had full command of the trail at their breakneck pace. Runners had varying options to race: five miles (once around the four-mile lollypop loop and back to the finish line) or nine miles (taking a second turn around the loop). I went for the five-mile race.

Before long, I passed several runners, both women and men. A few bottlenecks occurred at boulder outcroppings, forcing me to scrabble up the steeper outside so I didn't have to slow down.

In the last mile of the loop, while negotiating a downhill filled with loose granite and ducking under pine branches, my shoulder got jostled, a rude female competitor shoving her own path through. I stumbled, causing a slide of loose rock, then fell into a tumbling roll over jagged riprap along the edge of the trail.

Pain flashed into my head, my knees, and my hands as the world spun wildly. And then I finally skidded to a stop on softer dirt. On a dragged-out groan, I slowly rolled onto my back. I had a sudden splitting headache while I sucked in deep breaths, beginning to take stock of my injuries. I could breathe without pain. *Always a good sign.*

"You okay?" A deep voice rumbled above me.

I blinked open my eyes to see a dark-haired stranger staring down at me.

"Think so." My mind flashed to another fall, another trail, and Darren's concerned words: *Shit. Kiki, you okay?*

"Let's make sure everything's working." The man assisted me up, then handed me my dusty baseball cap that had been knocked off my head. After a few seconds of arm and leg bending, and his quick check of my pupils, we verified I didn't need immediate medical attention.

His thigh muscles twitched, and he shifted his weight from one leg to the other. I glanced at the race-number bib on his shirt. He wasn't a racing official; he was a runner.

"Go!" I laughed, pointing down the trail. "Kick some ass for me!"

After he tore off, two other kamikaze runners whizzed by, bounding down the rocky incline at insane speeds. Once I sensed a safe opening, I walked onto the trail. Other than a headache which had dulled, scrapes and bruises that stung, and general soreness, everything seemed to be functioning properly for me to continue the race.

I took a couple of tentative skips, then settled into an easy jog down the incline, planting careful footfalls on packed earth. When nothing sparked with pain, I picked up the pace until I returned to my former racing speed.

From practice runs, I knew less than half a mile remained of the loop and half a mile of return straightaway, which led toward the finish line. My guard was up, every sense heightened after the fall. I actively listened for footfalls behind me, shoulders tensed, prepared to body check any other runner who felt trail running was a contact sport.

But the remainder of the race passed without incident. Four runners sprinted by in the last hundred yards. I increased my speed, nice and steady, until the finish line blurred by.

Cheers and shouts rang out from spectators, officials, and other race finishers.

But no one for me specifically.

Because I hadn't invited anyone.

A tiny romantic part of me hoped Darren would be there. But logic told me he couldn't be. He needed to be strong for his sister. We couldn't be "just friends." And not once had he ever sent mixed signals.

Gasping for air, I jogged a few more strides, then slowed to a brisk walk, raising my arms over my head as I spotted the aid station. After my breaths slowed enough, I slammed a few small cups of their electrolyte drink.

Two medics sat behind a table on the end. One of them raised his brows at me and stood. But I felt fine, so waved him off and wandered past, planning to check out the two rows of vendor tents at the near end of the parking lot.

"Congratulations, Flash."

My heart stuttered. The deep familiar voice slid over my skin like a sensual caress.

This isn't really happening. I kept walking and lifted a hand to rub my fingers over my scalp through the canvas baseball cap. *Must've hit my head harder than I thought.*

"Flash?"

Darren.

I froze in place. "You're real," I whispered, unable to believe it.

My knees began to shake, and I spun around slowly so I didn't crumple onto my ass.

There he stood. That shaggy black hair I loved so much framed his face. Those deep green eyes sparkled in the direct sunlight. A thin black T-shirt hugged his muscular frame, draped over faded jeans.

Beautiful.

Here.

His eyes suddenly widened and he rushed over, closing the seven-foot distance between us. "Oh, shit. Kiki..." His voice softened at my name and his hand raised, hovering over my left cheek. But he didn't touch me. "*Damn*, baby, are you okay?"

I blinked. Nothing made sense. Clearly I suffered from a concussion. Because my gorgeous, sunshine-haloed hallucination of Darren had called me "baby."

When I grinned at the vividness of the dreamlike experience, ready to touch my apparition to see if he burst into glittery golden dust with the slightest poke of my finger, my lip hurt.

"Ow." I winced at the sudden stab of pain.

He frowned. Deeply. "Kiki?"

His gaze roved down my body.

I followed it, glancing at the dirt caked on my shirt, the jagged rips in the knees of my pants, and spots of dark crimson spattered all over the fabric of both.

I sucked in a shaky breath, unsure about what was happening. "Why are you looking at me like that?"

He swallowed hard, then let out a measured breath. "You have blood dripping down the left side of your face."

"Oh." I touched a finger to my cheek. Sticky...wet. *Real.*

Then I reached out, staring at my hand until it made contact with his forearm. Warm. Solid. *Very real.*

"*You're here,*" I breathed out, amazed. And more than a little stunned over the fact.

"I am. Hope that's okay." He reached up for my sunglasses. "May I?"

When I nodded absently, he removed them. Then he squinted at my face, above my left eye. "It's a clean cut about an inch long, just under your eyebrow. Bleeding seems to be slowing."

The clinical words blurred, my injury inconsequential. After all, I had finished the race.

But he *is standing right...*

"What are you doing here?"

"*We* are here." He nodded back over his shoulder. Logan stood beside the nearest booth. She waved excitedly, a huge grin on her face.

I lifted a hand and gave her a half-wave as a tentative

smile began to form, but the pain in my lip stopped me again. So did my confusion.

"But…*why?*"

"Logan got me to see that I didn't have to control everything. She helped me realize what was important."

My heart began to thump harder. But I took a deep breath, refusing to jump to conclusions.

"Logan needs me whole," he continued. "For her."

He searched my eyes for long seconds. "For me to be whole—I need you."

Overwhelmed, tears welled, threatening to spill over. "Us...couple...together?" My words sounded nearly incoherent through gasped breaths.

With care, he wrapped his arms around me in a tender embrace and gazed into my eyes. "Only if you'll have me, Flash. Only if I'm lucky enough..." His tone lowered to a whisper. "Only if you need me too."

Heart thundering, my body trembled. I slid my arms around his waist, then clung to him, reveling in what he'd said—what his weighted words meant. Because although I could trudge through life without him, if forced to, my humble, artistic, trail-running world was *complete* with him in it.

I let out a grateful sigh and tightened my hold, determined to never again let go.

"I do." I rested my right cheek on his chest, closing my eyes. "I need you too."

EPILOGUE

Darren…

The following night, Kiki and I had our first date—post reunion.

Actually, our first real planned date ever.

Before we'd left the race, she'd gotten medical attention, at my insistence. Then after we'd parted ways—Logan and me to our house, Kiki to hers—we'd texted almost nonstop. And had three lengthy phone conversations, the last of which continued late into the night until we'd started to nod off. Two weeks of zero communication had demanded it.

Now we stood in her courtyard in the cool night air, her hand clasped tightly in mine.

We stared out at the quiet patio space that seemed more alive from the party we'd held there. All of her cherished mismatched bistro sets had been returned to their places. Strands of clear party lights remained above us, swaying in the breeze. The brick planter, once sparse with only a few herbs, now overflowed with blooming plants.

Over the last hour, we'd fed each other Chinese takeout—one chosen entrée each instead of the whole buffet. Minutes ago, we'd tossed the demolished cartons into her trash can.

"Thank you. For everything." She leaned against my side as her voice lowered to a whisper. "For loving me."

"Thank you for letting me… for waiting."

She gave a silent nod. Then she spun in front of me, grasped two fistfuls of my shirt, and tugged me down until my lips gently crashed into hers.

Gratitude filled my heart as I wrapped my arms around her, sighing into our kiss.

She abruptly pulled back, then grabbed my hand and tugged me toward her front door. "C'mere. I have something I want to show you."

My chuckle echoed out as we entered her warehouse. "I have something I want to show you too."

"Not *that*." She smacked my hand away when I curved it around her hip. "I want to show you something I made for you."

"Not *yet*," I growled out the correction, crowding her into my arms when we reached the stairs that led to her loft.

As we climbed, I kept her in my hold and nuzzled her neck. Every shudder and tiny moan she made imprinted into my brain, etched into my heart.

"Stop." Her eyes lit with mischief when she opened the

door, spun around, and put a hand up between us. "*Wait*. For just two minutes."

On a steadying breath, face tilting down, I tracked her every move while counting down the seconds. "One nineteen, one eighteen, seventeen…"

Pressing her lips into a firm line, trying to fight her smile, she went into her kitchen and pulled open the nearest drawer under the counter. Then she carefully removed something wide and flat. She held the edges with care before resting it on her dining table.

"Ninety-eight, ninety-seven," I teased, drawing closer to have a look at what she'd made.

My counting stopped as my jaw dropped open. "Animal," I whispered.

The beloved Muppet character had been sketched in bold black lines on heavy white paper.

She touched my arm with a nod. "After teaching a few classes, I dug out my charcoals. And…even though we weren't together, I just…" She took a deep breath. "Drawing him made me feel close to you."

"I love it," I rasped out. "Made something for you too."

I caught the confusion furrowing her brow right before I turned and stepped away from her, facing her bed. I lowered my head, reached a hand over and between my shoulder blades, then grabbed my T-shirt and pulled it off.

Leaving one arm bent up, I rotated back toward her.

She gasped, then came closer. "It's beautiful."

"It's you."

Her fingers traced along the new crescent of ink, as thick

as my crescent. It curved forward over my chest, its point culminating over my heart.

"When?"

"Days ago. Once I believed I could have" —I got choked up with all the things that flashed into my mind: love, happiness…her— "and hoped you would have me."

She swallowed hard. "I love it," she whispered.

All of a sudden, a devilish look crossed over her face. She planted both hands on my chest, then shoved hard. I landed flat on my back on her bed seconds before she pounced on me, straddling my body.

She searched my eyes for a moment and hers softened with emotion. Then her lips brushed across mine, once, twice, before they opened further.

I wrapped my arms around her and sighed into our extraordinary kiss, so damn glad I'd chased after the girl who thought she could only handle a one-night stand.

Then I tightened my hold, warmth filling my heart when she murmured against my lips, "Let's stay here forever."

Please read on for an author's note from Stone
Note from Author Stone Bastion

Enjoy your sneak peek of *Rule Breaker*, the next novel in
The Unbreakable Series
Rule Breaker

NOTE FROM AUTHOR
STONE BASTION...

I'm a drummer.

Why drumming?

It's the core—the driving force—of every song.

Awestruck by blues and rock greats who gathered at my house when I was a kid for jam sessions, I picked up my first sticks before kindergarten…and never looked back.

Rhythm took root in my veins and underlaid my whole perception of the world. It pulsed a constant soundtrack in my head and still does to this day.

One moment that resonates with me?

My high school's first ever drum-off.

There were two of us. We were known as the jazz drummer—that was me—and the rock drummer. Everyone knew his strength was power, mine was speed. Over the years, students and teachers alike debated who was the *better* drummer. The week before graduation, we decided to put the matter to rest once and for all.

A hush fell over the audience before we began.

One of us laid down a short burst of rhythm.

The other matched it perfectly, paused, then volleyed back something new.

He mimicked my jazz.

I mirrored his hard rock.

Each changeup passed with longer and more complicated patterns. The performance continued for a sweat-inducing fifteen minutes, back and forth, tension building to a crescendo.

Until a heavier pause followed our last matched set.

Breaths ragged, hearts pounding, muscles burning, we gave each other a nod. Then we began a rehearsed extended sequence as a finale, commanding every piece on our drum kits.

After the final bass tone echoed into the auditorium, utter silence followed for a few seconds. Then thunderous applause erupted, everyone jumping to their feet.

That day, we proved either of us could hold our own against the other—there was no better.

Life is filled with special moments. That was a good one.

As authors, we weave glimpses of our reality into the stories we write and greatly enjoyed doing so with *Heartbreaker*. Like Darren, I loved Animal as a kid, drummed on my girl's (Kat's) back to rock music, even considered a career in sound engineering…

My wish? That you enjoyed Darren and Kiki's story and experienced a taste of the passion of drumming in *Heartbreaker*.

If you did enjoy it, please consider leaving a review for the book. Your thoughtful feedback is greatly appreciated by both us and future readers.

Thank you for reading and sharing *Heartbreaker*.

~ Stone

RULE BREAKER
SNEAK PEEK

Mase…

The wave can kill…or save.

Its staggering force humbled—kicked my ass often.

But when I pointed toward the curling crest, shot up from its thundering energy, then caught perfect air…the rest of the world faded.

Breath.

Pulse.

Wind.

Spray.

Gravity…ruler of all.

I dropped in on a one-eighty spin. Tail skimmed down the face of the wave. The collapsing barrel roared with fury behind me. And through a salty cloud of mist, I glided out, riding the exhilarating power of nature.

But once I hit sand, the peace I'd sought ended. A lone girl stood by my gear.

I heaved out a sigh and tucked my board under my arm, preparing to face yet another one.

"Are you Mason Price?"

"Mase." I dropped my board, then grabbed my towel. Had to tug the corner out from under her bare foot.

"Mase, for sure." She gave a nod.

Pretty thing, but then they all were. Want to bait the fish? Need a tempting lure.

"I'm Leilani Kealo—"

"*I'm* not interested," I grumped. My stomach growled; even my body hated her intrusion.

Her expression darkened. "You don't even know what I want."

"Not interested in a sponsorship." I did my best to ignore her exotic beauty and enticing curves when I uttered the rest with a poker face, "Not interested in a beach-bunny fuck."

Her eyes narrowed, gaze locked to mine. Unlike all the others, she didn't notice my body. They'd always swept hungry gazes over me like I was a mouthwatering cut of steak. But not her.

"*I'm* not interested in either."

I snorted. "On an isolated beach that took me days to find, on a tiny island in the middle of the South Pacific, you show up with your very *Hawaiian* sounding name" —I arched my brows on a questioning pause— "standing by my stuff. What do you want, then?"

Fists clenching tight, she rose to her full height—all five-foot-nothing of her—pulled back her slim shoulders, and lifted her chin. "*Not* a *damn* thing."

She scowled then stormed off in a huff.

I grinned, entertained by the drama.

But a frown pulled at my mouth as I watched her.

She plucked a stubbed-antenna satellite phone from a front pocket of her short flowery dress and crossed the single-lane dirt road. A horn blared from the one moving car on the roadway as she stepped in front of its bumper without looking up. Hand still on her phone, she held the other up and gave a slight apologetic headshake to the driver. After jogging out of harm's way, she stopped a short distance down an alley beside the only restaurant on our windward side of the island, then dropped her head, talking into the phone.

Curious, I grabbed my gear and followed.

"…don't know why. Yeah, probably every other idiot after a money grab. No, I know that's not what we're—" She paused, as if cut off. "I'm here aren't I? N'kay, fine. I will. *I will try.* Yeah, Makani, 'ohana. I know. How can I forget? You keep reminding me."

"Trouble in paradise?"

"Gotta go," she murmured into the phone before dropping it back into her pocket.

Coffee-brown eyes pegged me with a penetrating gaze. On a slow breath, her expression softened and she gave me an assessing once-over. "Could we—"

"Look I was—" I ran a hand through my hair.

"—start over? I didn't mean to stomp off…"

"—rude back there…" We paused, processing what we'd said while talking over each other.

She let out a defeated sigh. "Could I buy you lunch?"

"Now *that* I'm interested in." I leaned my board against the faded red wall beside the door.

When I gestured an arm ahead for her to take the lead, she paused in the doorway and stared at my beat-up surfboard. "Not windsurfing?"

"Not always." *Obviously.*

"But you do windsurf…competitively?"

"Plan to."

Also obvious? Her line of questioning. It smacked of sponsorship.

I held up two fingers to my man Rico behind the bar and he nodded. By the time I glanced back, she'd already grabbed a table by the window, one apparently she'd claimed before: Pale green sandals hung from a corner of her wood chair, a Tommy Bahama beach bag slumped on another chair nearest the cement wall, right under a framed and signed black-and-white picture of surfing icon Kelly Slater.

"But…" The furrow between her brows deepened. "I thought you won two competitions."

"Did you see them?" Didn't deny it, but wanted to know how devoted she was to her cause.

"No, but—"

My stomach growled again. Matched my mood. "What do you want to eat?"

"What do you recommend?" She cut a glance toward the menu-board over the bar.

Rico slid two beers between us, then dropped an appraising look at her before arching a brow at me while he answered her question, "Fish tacos."

"Done." I gave a short nod. "Five. I'm starved."

She spread a paper napkin over her lap with an outward sweep of her hands. "Two, please."

Please. The proper way she said the word struck a chord. So did the poised manner in which she held herself and the way she'd schooled her expression after the phone call. Her overall demeanor, including how she controlled her breaths and her practiced smile, pinged an alert with me—an undercurrent rumbled beneath her carefully polished surface.

Impressed with the flair in which she hid her true nature, I crossed my arms and leaned back in my chair. I studied her with an unwavering stare.

"Why are you here?" Direct. I was all about getting to the bottom of her mission.

"Your sailboard."

I blinked. "My equipment brought you here?"

"And my brother." Almost imperceptibly, she let her perfect posture slump on a short sigh.

"Your brother." The word flattened with my growing confusion.

"Makani." She gave a nod, as if his name explained everything. After taking a healthy swallow of her beer, she stared at the amber bottle for several long seconds.

Then the most amazing thing happened: She smiled.

And the exotic girl who'd been merely pretty…became stunning.

I watched with fascination as a spark of wild defiance transformed her expression. Her honey-bronze skin flushed pink up her slender neck to her defined cheekbones. Long dark lashes blinked heavily an instant before greater amusement lit up her eyes.

And then it died. Gone in a flash.

Hmmm. "Gonna need more info."

"Those two competitions." She waved a hand toward the breaking waves outside the open window. "You won them on *his* sailboard. And *he* wants to sponsor you for windsurfing competitions."

Finally. The nuts and bolts of it. "Don't need a sponsor."

"He'll pay you well."

"So will all the others." Half a dozen big names so far. "Don't need money."

Without skipping a beat, her head tilted a fraction. "What *do* you need?"

Damn good question.

I stared long and hard at a girl vastly different than me… and yet entirely familiar.

She held herself with a certain grace I'd seen play out my whole life. You can't fake that. Refined. Well-mannered.

Yet I saw right through her mirror-calm surface no matter how expertly she masked it.

Because a similar rebellion railed deep within me.

"Not a damn thing." *Total truth.*

Because all anyone needed was food, water, shelter, and sex.

And…the size of my trust fund would cover that for small nations ten times over. But I'd abandoned civilized life to wander the world uncharted.

She frowned, and her lower lip pouted out into something almost as amazing as her smile.

"But there is something I want."

Her expression brightened. "What's that?"

"You live in Hawaii?" Educated guess with her name and accent, but had to be sure.

"Yeah, Maui."

"Perfect." *Actually,* fucking *perfect.* Windsurfing mecca. But I kept calm: the art of negotiation. Cade, my friend and former roommate, would be proud. "I need a place to live."

"To live?"

"Your place?"

"*Nooo.*" She crossed her arms, shaking her head. "Definitely not."

"Nearby, then. You'll hook me up with something."

The headshake thing happened again. Her lips parted, her hardening expression broadcasting loud and clear that a fierce protest was coming.

Unwilling to hear her argument on an empty stomach, I cut her off with a piercing look. Then I added to my list of demands, "Waves to windsurf."

Her features softened as she nodded. "All year round at Ho'okipa Beach."

An electric thrill charged through me as I pictured endless surfing—one thing I'd never gone after before.

"And a personal guide."

"Guide?"

"Assistant. PR rep. Whatever you want to call yourself."

"*Me?*"

"You."

"No way."

"*Only way* it's happening."

Her eyes narrowed, breaths shallowing as she struggled to maintain that cool composure. "Why?"

Yeah…why?

Pretty sure I hadn't knocked my head on coral in the surf today.

Damn sure wasn't looking for a relationship—just got out of one.

But when an adventure-bound guy, who could have anything, sits in front of a girl with enough fire in her to make every step of the journey ahead a glorious fight?

She becomes the only thing he wants.

Want a pre-order alert for *Rule Breaker*?
Keep informed of new releases by joining their Email Subscription list:
www.katbastion.com/email-subscription/
One lucky subscriber will win an eBook of their choice from the backlist AND a $10 gift card each time a preorder or new-release announcement is sent.

We promise to email only a handful of times a year to announce pre-orders and new releases.

ABOUT THE AUTHORS

Kat Bastion won several awards for her bestselling debut novel *Forged in Dreams and Magick.*

Kat and Stone Bastion's bestselling first novel *No Weddings* and the No Weddings series were named Best of 2014 by multiple romance review blogs.

When not defining love and redemption through scribed words, they enjoy spending their time mountain biking and hiking in the beautiful Sonoran Desert of Arizona.

Stay in touch with them on their social media pages:

@KatBastion
@StoneBastion
Kat & Stone Bastion
www.talktotheshoe.com
www.katbastion.com

Keep informed of new releases by joining their Email Subscription list:
www.katbastion.com/email-subscription/
One lucky subscriber will win an eBook of their choice from the backlist AND a $10 gift card each time a preorder or new-release announcement is sent.

We promise to email only a handful of times a year to announce pre-orders and new releases.

CHARITY SUPPORT AND AWARENESS

Your purchase of *Heartbreaker* helps the victims of human trafficking because a portion of the net proceeds of all Kat and Stone Bastion's books are donated to charities who support them. These charities are creating legislation and prosecuting criminals, rescuing and restoring victims, and raising awareness in the effort to eradicate the tragedy of human trafficking.

Please visit the Charity Support and Awareness page on their website www.katbastion.com and blog www.talktotheshoe.com to learn about some of the organizations they donate to and to find out how you can further support them.

"A single act of kindness is the foundation of many miracles."
~ Kat Bastion, *Utterly Loved.*